JON AND LINDA

HOPE YOU ENJOY MY 2ND NOVEL

NOGALES CROSSING

David R. Jones

1663 Liberty Drive, Suite 200
Bloomington, Indiana 47403
(800) 839-8640
www.AuthorHouse.com

This book is a work of fiction. People, places, events, and situations are the product of the author's imagination. Any resemblance to actual persons, living or dead, or historical events, is purely coincidental.

First published by AuthorHouse 03/30/05

ISBN: 1-4208-3253-0 (sc)

Library of Congress Control Number: 2005903007

Printed in the United States of America
Bloomington, Indiana

This book is printed on acid-free paper.

CHAPTER ONE

It was six in the morning and Detective Jeff Shackleford was irate, confused, and speechless. Worst of all, he was tired. With almost fifteen years of dedicated service to the Los Angeles Police Department, Shackleford was the consummate city employee. His chiseled features and positive outlook on life left everyone with a sense that he might be the perfect cop. Everyone, except perhaps the commander of Narcotics Division, Neaville Montgomery. Shackleford's boss decided that Internal Affairs should take over the shooting investigation, which involved the timely death of a pathetic, worthless drug peddler, at the hands of another detective. It now appeared that all of the conscientious effort put into the case by Shackleford was for naught.

"I'm leaving." Shackleford could not bring himself to discuss the matter, even with Gerry Duvane, his partner of just one night.

"Me too. There's no reason for either of us to stick around." Duvane was indignant with everyone, except his temporary partner who was assigned to assist him with the shooting investigation.

In spite of the anger festering inside him, Jeff steered the Mercury Cougar carefully onto the Hollywood Freeway, joining the sparse Sunday morning traffic. The car he was assigned for surveillance was little more than two years old, and with a dark blue paint job it was suited for its purpose. During a recent check-up he arranged to have the air conditioning serviced. With lengthy periods of sitting and watching major narcotic suspects, it paid to have good air in the stifling Los Angeles smog.

Heading north, he cranked up both the air and the radio in an effort to remain alert. Singing along to the upbeat tunes served the same purpose. This brought a few peculiar looks from other commuters, but soon he was a couple of miles out of town and the lone vehicle on the road.

Jeff was getting weary fast as he passed the Santa Monica Boulevard off-ramp. It was now twenty-four hours since he got out of bed and his eyelids were drooping. In his lane up ahead, where Sunset crossed over the freeway, he could see a woman standing, waving at him. At sixty miles an hour there was little time to react.

Instantly he broke into a cold sweat, as he realized he had already passed the point where she was standing. A fearful glimpse into the rear view mirror told him she never existed. The mind was playing alarming games with his senses. It was telling him to stop and get some rest. But he was confident that the memory of this scary apparition would keep him going until he was home.

However, it barely lasted another mile. After passing Hollywood Boulevard, he started the climb to Universal City, passing the Hollywood Bowl on his left. His car was now riding the striping that separated lanes and he felt he could get along fine if his tires would keep on this line.

Cresting the hill, he started to pick up speed on the descent towards the Ventura Freeway. At seventy he almost shot down the Vineland off-ramp, barely holding the left hand curve. There was another illusion passing on his left in the number one lane. A white Chevrolet Blazer was cruising around a hundred.

The apparition had its own obstruction ahead: a huge chunk of torn tire, probably from an eighteen-wheeler, judging by its size. Only yards to Jeff's left, the Blazer swerved violently, performing a miraculous maneuver to avoid the rubber impediment. Jeff lifted his right hand from the wheel and was about to give a congratulatory, clenched fist wave. However, the impetus of the direction change caused both left wheels of the Chevy to leave the road surface.

Jeff's phantom vehicle was now large as life. It flipped sideways across his path. Wildly out of control, it bounced from roof to wheels like a small toy. Another direction change took it rolling along his lane in front of him. He needed all of his weight standing on the brake pedal to stop, just feet from the distorted shell of a four-wheel drive.

Instinct and training took control of his fatigued body. On went the hazard warning flashers as he automatically keyed his radio mike. Broadcasting the disaster seemed futile, since the radio at his office was not manned on weekends. However, he hoped that Gerry Duvane, who had worked on the shooting investigation with him, would hear the message. Enough details were picked up by Duvane for him to pinpoint the crash, and he told Jeff he would use his cellular phone to call emergency services.

Jeff checked his mirror again and saw no mysterious woman in the road and no traffic approaching. He jumped to the rescue and made a quick inspection of the Blazer, which presented an unpleasant scene. He could see two young women inside the vehicle, seat-belted and upright as if they were crash test dummies in a television commercial.

It didn't surprise Jeff that both were unconscious, since the car had landed on its roof four or five times. The driver's door was facing south, towards his vehicle, with the Chevy broadside across the number three lane. He tugged fiercely on that door, but it was jammed by the crumpling effect of the impact. He had better luck with the passenger side and he instantly had the girl out of her belt and leaning onto his shoulder. An ominous smell of gasoline was present, together with an odd metallic whirring sound beneath the hood. Unwittingly, he took the girl out using a perfect fireman's lift, and with another look for approaching cars, he scampered to the shoulder. She moaned slightly with the bouncing motion of his step and he was heartened by the knowledge she was alive.

A disconcerting sound behind him was a familiar one. Whenever he pressed the ignite button on the propane barbeque at home, there was a *whoosh* as the fire started. This was the same, only louder, and he could feel this flame on his back from twenty feet away.

Jeff laid the passenger down gently and turned to face an inferno that engulfed half of the Blazer. Before he could move, his attention was momentarily drawn back to the girl he had saved. She was pretty and looked strangely familiar. He could not be sure if he had ever known her, or if this was a version of the sometimes disturbing *deja vu*. Not even a second passed, and this time he didn't even consider traffic, but instinctively ran towards the wreck. He could get no closer than six feet because of the intense heat. The gruesome sight of a young woman burning to death would live with him forever. The coroner would later tell Jeff that because there was smoke in her lungs, it was evident she was indeed alive while Jeff was forced to stand by helplessly.

Jeff's troubles weren't over, as his attention was suddenly drawn to the fierce squealing of brakes from beyond his own vehicle. There was no time to dash for safety. He could only hope that the buffer provided by two cars would save his life. A split second before the oncoming Ford Mustang struck Jeff's Mercury, the driver eased up on the brakes and the car twisted to the right. It barely clipped his back bumper and careened toward the shoulder. As with so many Mustangs, this one was fitted with low profile tires, producing a car that closely hugged the road surface.

The girl he had rescued seconds earlier was struck by the underside of the Ford as the reckless driver passed over her body. Momentarily, the muffler dragged her forward until her lifeless form was left some fifty feet from the original wreckage. Jeff Shackleford was devastated as he watched the red Ford quicken its pace. The homicidal driver, never to be identified, sickened the detective with the callousness of his actions. Another thought came to him, and then left, just as swiftly. The face of the girl he saved temporarily, now appeared before him and she was waving frantically. Could it be the same woman he thought he saw standing on the freeway? Like some kind of warning? Damn. It was just too weird.

When the first paramedics arrived they thought Jeff was also involved in the accident. His exhausted body had collapsed on the road, next to the Chevy. He had given his all trying to save the two young women, and would be haunted for years by the horrific sights of that early Sunday morning. However, his future would soon be threatened in a totally different manner by what might be considered an unfair dealing of the cards.

CHAPTER TWO

Less than twenty-four hours earlier, Special Agent William Martinet was insulting, taunting and ultimately intimidating his so-called witness. There is no greater affront to the hard working cop than being falsely accused of a crime. "You expect me to believe that you had no knowledge of dope planting in all of these cases? You were so closely involved with the task force, you had to know what was going on."

"Agent Martinet, you've done nothing but badger Detective Perez for more than two hours. He's co-operated fully with your demands and I think it's time we ended this interrogation." George Franklin was an outstanding defense representative who loathed the unseemly job of protecting dirty cops. Although he was a layman and not an attorney, he was convinced Franco Perez was innocent.

The Federal Bureau of Investigation had taken a front seat in the case against numerous narcotic officers, charged with a myriad of state and federal violations. William Martinet was single-minded about the whole affair. It was obvious to him that all of those accused were as guilty as sin; and their associates, who had yet to be indicted, were about to run out of luck. He would personally see to it that the evidence needed to put the likes of Perez away for a very long time, was disclosed in a timely manner.

As with so many of the Bureau's top investigators, Martinet had virtually no field experience. To his credit, he did have a reputation for relentlessly pursuing indictments against police officers with immense success. An impressive figure in the routine dark blue suit, matching tie and starched white shirt adorning his six-foot-two-inch frame, Martinet loomed over his quarry. At thirty-seven he was a year younger than Perez but the image portrayed was one of a seasoned, mature individual. The jet black hair was trimmed perfectly, his face was clean-shaven and one might suspect a manicurist had worked on his nails. Martinet exhibited no discernible flaws.

His closing comment came in the form of yet another threat. "The Government is far from finished with you, Perez, and I suspect your Department will not tolerate your actions." Martinet suggested that the Los Angeles Police Department would probably take an aggressive posture towards the detective. He could not have realized how prophetic this comment would prove to be.

Although Franklin advised against it, Perez insisted on his own parting shot. With the slightest shake of his head and a bewildered look in his eye, Perez was anything but sarcastic. "If it's called the Justice Department why do they employ people like you?" The remark stemmed from the entire format of the interview. He had been summoned to assist with the investigation and was told he was merely a witness. The Protective League, a kind of police officers' union, had assigned Franklin to attend the meeting with Perez to safeguard his rights. They were informed that Franklin could not tape record anything and that the FBI would also refrain from recording the interview. When Franklin interjected that he was concerned about his client subsequently having to sign a statement, without verifying the accuracy of its contents, he was unceremoniously shot down.

"Let's get this straight, Mr. Franklin, you are not an attorney and if we decide it is expedient to do so, we shall eject you from this and any future interviews." His hands were tied more firmly when Martinet and his assistant refused to let Perez view any of the arrest reports relating to the probe.

When the two detectives left the Federal Building they walked the single city block back to Parker Center, the Los Angeles Police headquarters, in silence. Franklin was frustrated with the treatment meted out by the FBI agents, particularly Martinet. Perez was simply disillusioned by the whole process. He was confused about why his fifteen years of diligent and sincere efforts in policing the city now counted for nothing.

Their cars were parked in the lot on the south side of the eight-story building. As Franco Perez unlocked his vehicle, Franklin realized he must counsel the young man to break the morbid trance that held him. "We're not letting these bastards get away with this! Keep your spirits up, Franco."

Franklin certainly accomplished his goal, primarily by the use of an expletive. Perez had known this defense rep personally for just a few hours but was convinced that his use of such words was uncommon. "Thanks. I guess what really bothers me is they may get some bizarre indictment when I haven't done anything wrong."

"The law is an ass!" Franklin waxed philosophical. It was a rare opportunity for him to comment on the imperfections of the judicial system.

"This won't stop me from doing the job I'm sworn to. It just leaves a bad taste in your mouth." It seemed that Franklin had lifted Perez to the level he was at before the interview. "We have a search warrant tonight on a rock house. That'll help me put this bullshit behind me."

Francisco Guttierez Perez celebrated his thirty-eighth birthday earlier in the month, on August second, 2002. The odds against him safely reaching his thirty-ninth grew longer as the days passed. He was to age a lifetime in less than a month and the signs would be clearly visible.

While growing up on the east side, it was a challenge to remain neutral with gang wars raging around his home. He buried himself in study and, much to the gratification of his parents, he was able to graduate from L.A. City College. His father pushed for further education with hopes that his son would become a lawyer. The fourth boy of five brothers had an idealistic outlook on life and immediately set out to join the then-renowned Los Angeles Police Department.

Perez senior was ecstatic when his prodigy faced severe obstacles during the police application process. Apparently the city was constrained by budgetary conditions and could recruit barely a handful of new officers. Because he was not female or black, he was well down the list, but at least he was in front of the larger proportion of candidates: white males. Fortunately, his scholastic abilities could not be overlooked for long. He was eventually admitted to the academy near downtown in the class of "8/87."

For years he had fought his friends' choice of Cisco as an unseemly epithet. He identified it as a lettuce-picking *bracero* (he refused to use the term wetback) who put nothing back into the system.

To him, the name Franco meant strength and leadership, signified by the Spanish dictator who ruled for almost as many years as Perez had lived. With a whole new set of colleagues in the police academy, he was able to start anew and apprise them of the name they should use.

Franco was proud of his Hispanic heritage and felt wounded when new acquaintances identified his as Italian. His skin color was light and the brown eyes were so dark, it was almost impossible to detect the difference between pupil and iris. His face presented a gaunt countenance with high cheekbones and recessed eyes sockets. Although Franco was serious much of the time, his smile had a warmth and openness that exposed a compassion for mankind.

That very smile was there as he gathered with his current comrades and discussed the potential excitement of the nights work ahead of them. He felt comfortable among his friends, most of who felt the same as he did about proactive police work. However, when a concerned detective asked how the interview with the Feds had gone, his disposition was turned upside-down.

"I can't believe we're on the same side. They treated me like I was on their top ten wanted list, or something." Franco's look turned somber in a second.

"Hey, Franco. That's just the way they play their little games. You know, bad guy, bad guy routine." Nina Kaplan put her arm around Franco's shoulders and tried to console him. She had been part of the team for almost four months and held the same affection for Perez, as did all of the guys. There was no suggestion of a sexual harassment claim due to her close contact with a male co-worker. In their labor active environment, only blatant, obnoxious and unwanted behavior was considered a violation of the overly activated legislation.

Nina Kaplan, nee Sanchez, was a breath of fresh air for policemen who saw most women on the job as fitting one of two categories. Firstly, and most predominant during the eighties, was the termagant who had to prove herself as good as, or better than, her male counterparts. Secondly, and one fast developing as the primary group, was the fragile and delicate lady, who knew she could earn as much as a man and do half the work. It was the latter assembly who were fastidious and made the phrase "sexual harassment" the most dreaded of the nineties. Nina, the only female in the South Bureau Narcotic Enforcement Team, was highly respected for falling into neither classification.

Nina had married a Jewish law school graduate while still in the academy herself. When their only son arrived, they named him Jeremy. Within a couple of years they both saw each other's ideals as vastly different, and quickly divorced without malice. Mr. Kaplan was now making a very prosperous livelihood out of suing police officers.

She chose not to revert to her maiden name of Sanchez after great deliberation. The decision was made easier when a female lieutenant strongly advised her to change back. The lieutenant told her it would prove doubly advantageous to be recognized as both female and Hispanic. It would increase her promotional opportunities. Nina desired only to advance as a result of her ability and application. So, Kaplan it remained.

"Nina, no matter what others might say about you, I think you're the greatest." Franco teased her incessantly.

"Oh! I'm the greatest, huh? Well, Franco Perez, if you keep up this moody attitude, I'll be your greatest nightmare." Nina wagged her slender index finger at him, pulling her eyebrows together showing mock intolerance.

When she marched away defiantly and sat at her desk, Franco admired the delicate curves of her trim figure. Nina appeared to immerse herself in the latest department special orders that had just been handed out. She had been a good friend over the past few months, but she had also been a good friend to most of the detectives they worked with. Franco was concerned that he felt a totally inappropriate yearning at this moment. Nina was not bound or constrained by the bonds of marriage, but he certainly was.

Nevertheless, he spoke his mind, but at a level difficult for anyone to hear. "I love you."

"What? What was that?" Nina could not be sure she had heard correctly.

"Just thinking out loud." Franco embarrassed himself and was fortunate that she had not caught his comment with any certainty.

Franco stared at Nina and began to appreciate the smooth, olive skin enhanced by the dark lines of her eyebrows. There was a roundness to her face, accentuated by her silken black hair pulled back into a tight bun. Thoughts he never expected to experience flooded his mind, and they were most agreeable.

A heavy hand was laid upon Franco's shoulder and a familiar voice brought him instantly to reality. "I trust I'm not witnessing any lascivious activity."

Nina had genuinely returned to the paperwork on her desk as their supervisor confronted Franco.

"I…..I…..I was just thinking about the rock house tonight, boss."

Jim Young, a much-respected senior detective, caught Franco in the act.

"Sure you were. And since you've been reflecting on that operation so diligently, I think it's proper that you should give the briefing." Young put Franco somewhat on the spot, but with a realization that his relatively seasoned subordinate was familiar with the pending case.

"Whatever you say, boss." Franco rummaged around among the papers on his own desk for a copy of the game plan. The rest of the team assembled close to their squad leader who continued to stand over the flustered Perez.

After what seemed an eternity to Franco, the ever gracious Nina leaned across his desk and handed him a photocopy of the document he was searching for. "Thanks, Kaplan." His cordial smile was evidence of his gratitude and a return of the status quo.

In less than five minutes Franco detailed the location, layout and method of attack upon the target. It was a first floor apartment on Manhattan Place, just north of Twenty Seventh Street. Another detective was responsible for the research leading to the warrant.

However, everyone present properly assumed that Young's choice of Perez for the briefing was intended to dispel his needless deliberation on the FBI inquiry.

Tactics were discussed in minute detail since Young was adamant that his squad should always maintain the upper hand. "We shall all return to our homes safely every night." That was his prime objective. Arrests and seizures of narcotics were of secondary importance. This philosophy served him well over the years, with not one single officer injured under his command; except for the occasional ineptitude of an overzealous cop. Perhaps an officer twisting his knee from kicking in a door, rather than waiting for the ram to arrive.

Once the discussions were over they set off for their quarry, anxious to continue their successful record. Young told Nina she should ride with him and promptly quizzed her on Franco's state of mind during the short drive.

"All I can say is that Franco is the best thing that happened to this city, this department, in the last fifteen years." Nina did not hold back in her defense. "He's really hurt by the way the City and the Feds are treating him. That stuff happened several years ago. If they don't have anything on him now, then they should stop their badgering. All they did in that interview was insinuate and threaten him. That's not right!" She was incensed by the travesty of justice.

Young digested her outburst for a moment. "I was thinking of suggesting to Franco that he take several days off. He's got plenty of overtime built up on the books and his fifteen-year reunion is next Friday. What do you think?" It only took a short time for him to regard her as a sound candidate for promotion, and gave her every opportunity to display her character.

"Great idea, boss. Just make sure it doesn't look like some kind of unofficial suspension." She was wise beyond her twenty-nine years.

Jim Young concentrated on the road as he followed the last of his detectives southbound on Manhattan Place from Adams Boulevard. He nodded his agreement with her evaluation, making a mental note to speak with Perez when they returned to the station. Unfortunately, the opportunity to do so would never present itself.

The lead car stopped just short of the intended apartment building and everyone slipped out of their vehicles silently. Doors were left slightly ajar to avoid the warning noises that could result from closing them. When all ten of the team members were pressed against the wall adjacent to the front entrance, Franco grasped the doorknob and gently pulled. Young's troops had reconnoitered the site well. During their surreptitious observations, they noted the lock on the security door was damaged in a manner that allowed visitors easy access. Peddling rock cocaine proved unprofitable if your customers couldn't get to your point of sale.

Gregory Rowland was being relieved at eight in the evening after a tiring twelve-hour shift. Saturday was always a fruitful day of the week for selling twenty-dollar rocks of cocaine. Rowland had migrated from Chicago some three weeks previous, and was convinced that LA was less violent. Perhaps it was as bad, but spread out over much larger neighborhoods.

As Franco stepped into the hallway, Rowland was about to close the apartment door leaving his relief inside the cramped, one room unit. The words were spoken softly to avoid alerting any occupants of the rock house. "Hands up. Do anything else and it'll be the last thing you do!" Franco was serious as the clichés instinctively rolled off his tongue.

His partners began to crowd into the tight quarters next to him, as Franco used his 9mm Beretta in a waving motion. He was trying hard to convince Gregory to raise his hands. The will to survive sent mixed signals to the infertile brain, as the small-time dope dealer ultimately turned and bolted up the stairs taking them three at a time.

Franco was dumbfounded, but reacted swiftly. The apartment was just ten feet from the main entrance, on the left hand side, and he moved automatically towards it to prevent the door from closing. After swinging it wide open, he pinned himself to the wall between the unit and the stairway. Several other officers positioned themselves on the opposite side of the door, and by now they were all inside the lobby.

Nina, having glimpsed enough of the episode to comprehend the ill fortune, took immediate and assertive action. "Joey, come to the back with me. We'll cut him off at the other stairs." She confidently directed another detective to assist her. Nina's only mistake was to pass along the hallway in front of the open apartment. Tactical awareness flew out the window as Jim Young could clearly see. This was unsafe since they had yet to secure the rock house, and firearms were common inside such places.

As soon as three of the officers had made entry into the tiny room, Franco felt he could turn his attention to the escapee. Since Nina was accompanied by a partner to the rear of the long, central hallway, he started up the stairs that Rowland had taken. His progress was painstakingly slow. He didn't rush to the top as a rookie might, but took one step at a time. With his weapon directed at the landing above him, Franco wisely anticipated a potential ambush.

As his colleagues screamed orders at the night shift dealer in the room below, Nina was starting to ascend the rear stairway, closely followed by Joey Naughton. He felt comfortable with her leading the way because of her greater experience in the narcotics unit.

Franco's view along the second floor hallway revealed a startling sight. Gregory Rowland was only twenty feet from the top of the stairs. He was now lying prone on the carpet, facing Franco, with his hands outstretched and palms face down next to each other. His eyes locked with the deep, brown, passionate pools of Franco Perez.

From the apartment there came the sound of chaos as the suspect resisted the attempts of three detectives to detain him. Nina was at the top of the rear stairs and even from that distance she could see Rowland's movements. "Franco, look out, he has a gun!" She shrieked the words franticly.

Just as they say, it appeared to happen in slow motion. Gregory Rowland scooped his hands together, lifting his small .380 semi-automatic from the stained and worn carpet. Not another muscle in his body seemed to move. The crook's right index finger twitched slightly and a slug was sent spiraling on its treacherous journey. Franco saw it coming. He could not fathom why a small pistol could discharge a projectile that appeared six inches in diameter.

Franco had never been shot before and he likened it to a red-hot poker being thrust into him. The bullet barely missed the barrel of his own weapon, then it forced apart the index finger and middle finger of his right hand. Taking an almost direct route, it raced eleven inches along the edge of his ulna, stopping just short of the elbow. He was aware of a new definition for the word excruciating. It took will power beyond his imagination to keep both hands on his gun.

His mind filled with the violent sounds that continued to emanate from the rock house. A beautiful vision at the far end of the building swept away those noises, as Nina lifted her hand to her mouth to suppress her screams of concern. Franco's eyelids drooped heavily and he felt a kind of drunken wooziness begin to overwhelm him. He searched the face of his nemesis for an understanding of the assault.

There was no remorse to be found anywhere in the depths of the crazed villain's soul. In fact, Franco detected the slightest movement of the trigger finger one more time. His own primeval instinct for survival kicked into gear as Franco realized his aim was directed at his adversary's forehead. One round, discharged from the Beretta, was enough to eradicate the world of Gregory Rowland for all time.

In real time, three seconds spanned the period from first eye contact to termination of the pathetic and basically worthless being sprawled on the floor. An instant after Franco sent his shot on its deadly journey, his right hand jerked away from the 9mm and fell to his side, bleeding profusely. He juggled momentarily to keep from dropping the weapon.

It has been said that there is a time and a place for everything. There would be grave concern by Franco Perez about the inevitability of the brief exchange of gunfire. However, the arrival of a first floor resident, Carlos Cordova, was to prove untimely indeed.

After working hard for ten hours on a nearby construction site, Cordova was seconds away from joining his wife and four children when he walked into the building. This was immediately following the commencement of the battle between three detectives and an unwilling dope dealer. His attention was naturally drawn to the commotion in the apartment situated just twenty feet from his home and family. Only after hearing the crack of the first round being fired did he look to the top of the stairs. What he subsequently saw and heard during the next two seconds would be interpreted in two distinctly different ways. As Franco leaned back heavily on the wall and began to pass out, there was really only one way: the way it truly occurred.

CHAPTER THREE

"It's been a long time, *pendejo.* Looks like you need somebody to take care of your *flaco* ass!" Kirk Driscoll never really learned Spanish but abused the language as often as possible.

The sight of an old classmate wearing the uniform blues seemed incongruous with Franco's situation. A persistent siren wailing its command got no closer or farther away. He closed his eyes again, hoping beyond hope that Driscoll, at least, was an apparition.

"Come on, *mi amigo*, don't leave me now. Shit, it's only a scratch." Driscoll even shook Franco as he lay on the gurney. It all fell into place at once. The siren belonged to his ambulance, which was taking him to hospital. But what the hell was Kirk Driscoll doing here?

"What the hell are you doing here?" It seemed a reasonable inquiry as Franco kept his eyes closed a while longer.

"Partner, I saved your butt out there, so be nice for once." Driscoll probably never saved anyone's butt in fifteen years on the streets.

"You weren't there when I….." Franco's mind drifted back to the horrendous showdown on the second floor.

"When you shot that nigger right between the eyes!" Driscoll smirked as he sadistically reminded Franco of his dirty deed. "Wish I'd been there. You nailed that sucker right where them Indian broads wear their precious gems. What a shot."

Franco contemplated the taking of someone's life and suddenly felt nauseous. There was never a doubt in his own mind that he had to shoot the black youth to save his own skin. However, the sanctity of the human soul was a precious commodity to the entire god-fearing

Perez family. He wondered what his father's reaction would be to his fatal act. "To protect and serve, son. That's what you swore to do." His father would be harder on him than even himself.

As Driscoll rambled on about the incident, he finally cleared up his earlier comment. "Yeah, I saved you from those leaches that call themselves the media. Jeez, they was crowding around you as they tried to put you in this ambulance. Asking why you murdered the nigger, and couldn't you have done something less lethal? How many of your sixteen rounds did you fire, officer?"

In recounting the pressure from the press, he puffed out his chest – this was difficult considering the enormity of his belly – and proudly described the defense of his academy classmate. "I kept them back and simply told them no comment."

"But Driscoll, I didn't murder him. It was self-defense." For the first time, Franco felt it necessary to justify his actions. He would explain a hundred times, what he believed was reasonable use of deadly force. A hundred times, there was to be some alternative interpretation of the facts.

"It don't matter what you say, partner. The headlines will be the same, no matter what: LAPD cop slays young black male." Driscoll was fatalistic but shockingly accurate. "What pisses me off more than anything is the reference to black when they describe the asshole. If he'd been white, there would be no mention that you wiped out some honkey mother. This shit is just perpetuated by the papers and the TV news. They're the real racists, not us."

Throughout Driscoll's tirade a male paramedic worked with meticulous care to monitor Franco's IV and constantly relayed his vital signs to the hospital. The patrolman finally addressed the medic, "Hey, nurse, you got a cup or something for my chew?"

There had been plenty that the medic wanted to say during the ride to LA County Hospital, but he held his tongue. Even with the objectionable attitude of the cop, he still said nothing as he handed over a Styrofoam cup.

Driscoll spat disgusting, brown saliva into the cup and continued chewing the wad of tobacco, as he berated the media a little longer.

As Franco was wheeled into the emergency room, Driscoll stuck to his side like a paid bodyguard. With one hand resting protectively on the gurney and the other holding his cup, Kirk Driscoll eyed the various sufferers in the waiting room with disdain. His bearing told onlookers to beware, should they entertain thoughts of intercepting his long-lost friend.

Even as doctors and nurses busied themselves with Franco's well being, the offensive officer refused to leave. Driscoll chewed and spat, cursed and gave opinions on all subjects. His forty inch belt was far too small to wrap around his waist, so it tried to hide beneath his stomach. If one looked up the word slob in a dictionary, Driscoll's picture would be alongside the definition.

"Not life threatening. Bullet wound. No obvious exit. Nurse, get him to x-ray. Right hand." The doctor in charge of ER snapped out his orders and moved to the next victim, barely breaking stride. "Better make that right arm, too."

"That's about as much attention we give to those damn family disputes, huh?" Driscoll compared the medical care with his own style of police work.

Within a couple of minutes, Franco was dispatched to x-ray. His colleague was intrigued by the speed of the hospital process, which had received, in his view, unjustified poor publicity.

An abrupt cessation of this prompt service soon returned Driscoll to his skeptical view of the medical profession. "Been waiting for x-rays for half an hour, and they haven't even looked at you yet." He was impatient but exaggerated the time frame.

"Driscoll, it seems there's always something eating you up inside. What is it with you? What turned you into…..well, whatever it is you are?" Franco saw a dispirited shell of a man that he remembered differently from their academy days.

"I could say the bullshit that happened in Foothill Division years ago was the end for me. With how they treated our guys for trying to arrest some jerk who wouldn't go quietly. I could say that, but it's not the truth." Driscoll began to open up to Franco. "Fact is, I saw it all going downhill since day one. You get no thanks for doing the job. There's always someone who will second-guess you; someone who will find a department manual section that you violated. Big fucking deal!"

"It's not like that all the time." Franco pled the case for a positive viewpoint.

"If you're talking about commendations, shit like that, well try and spend them when you're on suspension." Fifteen years of contempt for the system was now manifesting itself. "I took five days off back in 1995 for hitting some fool once too often. If that happened now, they'd give me five years in Federal lock-up."

There was no stopping Driscoll as he mounted his soap box. "Liberal do-gooders have problems facing the facts. There is no nice way to arrest a potentially dangerous, combative suspect. We're the bodyguards for society; the hired guns, hired fists and hired batons.

"They pay us to do the dirty work of protecting them. The work they're too afraid, too unskilled or too civilized to do themselves. They expect us to keep the bad guys out of their businesses, cars, homes and out of their face. They want us to take care of the problem. They just don't want to see how it's done.

"I blame groups like the NAACP. It doesn't help blacks, it only hurts the rest of us. As for the ACLU, all I can say is that I finally found out what it stands for: Allow Criminals Leniency Unlimited." Kirk Driscoll was red in the face at this point and stopped to avoid a coronary.

They were quiet, reflective for several minutes, as Franco absorbed everything he had heard. Driscoll felt he had said enough, particularly considering he was lecturing to a fellow peace officer.

An x-ray technician broke the silence as she stole Perez from the philosophical grasp of Driscoll. He could not follow, even though he made a move suggesting such an attempt. Nobody was allowed into her x-ray room except the patient. She was adamant, and so it had to be.

During the process of having numerous x-rays taken, Franco lay on the table thinking of the points Driscoll made. With his own positive outlook somewhat in opposition to that of his friend, there was a mental tennis match taking place. The more he faced the shots, the more difficult it became to return the ball to Driscoll's court.

For fear of developing a perspective similar to his dissentious friend, Franco tried to think pleasant thoughts. Nina's face swirled about his mind but soon brought about a cold sweat. Her features were tormented and pained, just as they had been the last time he saw her. She was crying out to warn him of the danger.

There was terror and there was love in her eyes at the same instant. Or was it his own desires, his own anxiety, that he saw reflected in her beautiful, sympathetic eyes. He knew what he wanted to believe, but suspected that reality might prove to be disappointing.

CHAPTER FOUR

In the comfort of his living room, Jeff Shackleford read Golf Illustrated, absorbing the facts and fancy of golf like a sponge. The ten o'clock news was just about to start but he was more interested in eagles on the course, than spotted owls in the Pacific Northwest. It had become an obsession for him, playing, collecting, reading, anything about golf. He worked so that he could live for the game.

With the volume down low, he was hardly aware of the breaking story. In less than two hours since the shooting, all of the major networks and local stations were carrying an account of the Manhattan Place incident. "…..earlier this evening. Twenty year old Gregory Rowland was gunned down on the second floor of the apartment building where he had lived for….."

This was not news to Shackleford, as with most of the residents in Los Angeles County, he had become immune to the mayhem, the day-to-day wanton violence. He concentrated on the article proclaiming the endurance of a man of Trevino's age, who could still shoot under par rounds consistently.

"…..appeared to shoot the black youth first, according to eyewitness, Carlos Cordova. A police spokesperson tells us that the officer, Detective Francisco Perez, a fifteen year veteran of the LAPD….." Suddenly the mention of a familiar name jolted Shackleford from his preoccupation and he tried in vain to learn the thrust of the news item. "…..currently in stable condition at the county hospital. In sports, we'll tell you all about an unusual episode today at Dodger stadium….."

He sat frozen, with the remote in his hand until his beautiful, blonde wife Jessica bounced onto the couch next to him. "Honey, what's up? Why are you watching the TV with no sound?"

The remote control had not worked quickly enough when he attempted to increase the volume. As the newscaster moved on to another story, Shackleford depressed the mute button and he stared straight ahead thinking about an old acquaintance.

"It was a shooting, babe. I think Franco Perez was involved and he may have been shot." That was all he had assimilated from the sparse facts he heard.

"Who is Franco Perez? Do you work with him?" Although she was genuinely concerned, Jessica Shackleford would not show it in her face. As a model in her youth and now the owner of an upscale beauty salon, she strived daily to abolish the mere hint of a line that dared spoil her perfect complexion.

"We were classmates in the academy. I've seen him a few times over the years, but not for some while now. I'm pretty sure he works street dope." Shackleford formed a mental picture of Perez, recalling a man of character whose worst trait was being devoted, unconditionally to the job.

Jeff Shackleford had his own high moral and ethical standards when performing his duties as a detective II. He lived by them at all times, but his job was simply that: a job. Working for the city was a means to an end.

Six years earlier, he met and instantly fell deeply in love with the stunning Jessica, who was considerably younger. Now that he was nearing forty, he wallowed in riches of every nature. A gorgeous wife, a thriving retail business they bought together and a comfortable job with week-ends off for golf. How could he ask for more?

"Did they say if he's badly hurt?" She slipped her hand into his and squeezed gently.

"Stable condition. Whatever that means. At least it doesn't sound too bad." Jeff turned to admire her soft, blue eyes for a moment, then recollected the first words he paid attention to on the news. "I don't like the tone of the broadcast. I've got an eerie feeling about this."

"Don't fret about it, honey. There's nothing you can do."

Jeff wished he could heed her words, but felt compelled to find out more. "I have to call, at least to find out how he's doing."

His own assignment was in narcotics but he left street enforcement many years ago. Major violators section was his haven now, and he intended to stay. Their responsibility was to develop and cultivate information on the big time narcotic traffickers. These investigations took weeks, sometimes months. A squad of about eight detectives would conduct a surveillance of a suspect, until such time they had enough evidence for a warrant.

There was a number he was about to call, where a skeleton crew monitored the off-hours operation of the police department, even on week-ends. His intent was to inquire about the condition of Franco Perez.

As he reached for the telephone, it burst into action, ringing louder, it seemed, than ever before. Startled by the timing of the call, Jeff was paralyzed with his left hand hovering over the instrument. Three rings had passed before Jessica's voice broke his trance. "You okay, honey?"

"Sure. I just…..let me get this, babe." He was visibly shaken as a dark foreboding overwhelmed him.

"Is this Detective Shackleford?" It was a formal inquiry.

"Yes. Who is this?" Jeff was taken off guard. He would normally not respond in the affirmative until he had queried the caller as to their identity.

"Robinson, detective headquarters. You're on the list for call out in the event of a narco OIS." This was a reference to officer-involved shootings. "We couldn't contact at least a half dozen who were scheduled above you on the list. You're to report to the command post at Twenty-seventh Street and Western."

"I see. Do I report to anyone in particular?" He was still somewhat dazed.

"Commander Montgomery. He should be there by the time you arrive." Robinson had called the commander of narcotics prior to any other notifications.

"Thanks. I'm on my way. Bye." Jeff's initial fears were bubbling to the surface. He stood with the telephone handset still in his grip, staring out of the window, looking at nothing in particular.

"You're beginning to scare me. I don't like what this news has done to you." Jessica was a confident businesswoman but the oddly distant behavior of her husband was disconcerting.

"I'm fine." He lied. "I have to go on an investigation. I was put on this call-out list a couple of months ago. One of the obligations of promotion to a detective two position."

"Will it take long? It's awfully late."

"It'll be eleven when I get there. Could be an all night job." This time he was more truthful. "Do me a favor and call Pete. Tell him I won't make our eight o'clock tee time tomorrow."

It was a ritual. Jeff and a close friend played eighteen holes every Sunday morning, somewhere, anywhere.

Jessica worried more about what Jeff was driving to, rather than being left alone on a Saturday night. Jeff set off steadily until out of sight, and then accelerated dramatically, speeding southbound in the darkness, from their suburban dream home in Valencia. His abstract fears for Franco's situation would soon take a more tangible and troublesome form.

CHAPTER FIVE

Several hundred people thronged the command post and the crime scene, which were a short city block apart. Activists of all walks seemed to have flocked to the area and a disconcerting chant was gaining momentum. "We don't want you, we don't need you, killer cops keep out."

At eleven in the evening on a Saturday, one might expect a few folks on their porches in most neighborhoods. However, this was south central and following years of being downtrodden, discriminated against and persecuted by the white man, locals demanded to be heard. Lawyers and other self-proclaimed representatives of the community, most of them having their own secret agenda, constantly stirred up emotions. They cared little for the impact on the real people, as they claimed the drug problem was brought on by the CIA, DEA, or any other target worthy of adverse publicity. As a result, there was cynicism and distrust towards the thin blue line that fought daily to protect those same citizens.

"I can hardly understand you, commander." Detective Gerrard Duvane was given scant information when he was called at home. Now he had to listen to the inane remarks of his commanding officer.

Neaville Montgomery, Commander of Narcotics Group, which was comprised of some four hundred sworn personnel, cupped his hands in front of his mouth to direct his instructions to Duvane. "Let's get this one right, Gerry. If one of our cops stepped over the line, then I want him nailed firmly to the cross."

"Aren't we being a little premature?" Duvane wished his boss would go home and wait for developments over the phone. He spoke in a calm manner, which caused the commander difficulty hearing him over the bedlam. "Perhaps we should conduct the investigation thoroughly before reaching conclusions."

"Don't get me wrong, Gerry, my boy. I'm a fair man." This was stretching the definition of the word. "But IA have already spoken with the only civilian eyewitness, and it seems clear to them."

Montgomery made passing reference to the department's Internal Affairs Division. Generally, it was the responsibility of narcotic's own detectives to inquire into a shooting, where one of their fold discharged his weapon. IAD got involved only if a criminal deed was perceived.

"What the hell are they doing here already? And speaking with a witness, I don't like it, commander" Duvane was incensed.

"Watch your mouth, Gerry! They're here, so live with it." There was an earnest attempt by the commander to put Duvane in his proper place.

Gerrard Duvane was about to say something he would probably regret, when he felt a tap on his shoulder. It was Jeff Shackleford, reporting to the command post as directed. Jeff had seen that Duvane was speaking with their boss and knew that the much-respected senior detective was on the call-out list. There were obvious signs of conflict between the two and he felt it was prudent to interrupt.

"Hi, Jeff. Boy they must have gone way down the list to call you on this one." Duvane shook Jeff Shackleford's hand vigorously, with more than a little relief that a serious confrontation had been forestalled.

"I take it that isn't a compliment." Jeff was glad to have broken up the feud in time.

"You know what I mean. Good to have you on board." Duvane then addressed Montgomery. "Commander, this is Shackleford. We'll be teamed up for the investigation."

Only a grave nod of the head acknowledged Shackleford's presence. The chief of narcotics never proffered his hand but left them both in no doubt about his attitude. "Get on with it! There's going to be a lot of questions asked from above. And I want answers."

He turned to his driver and directed him to "get me the hell out of this god-forsaken place."

Duvane and Shackleford watched solemnly as the Ford Crown Victoria nudged its way through the ever increasing, angry crowd.

"Whatever happened, this is not going to be a pleasant task." Duvane spoke to Jeff Shackleford without taking his eyes off the commander's car.

"Where do we start?" It was Shackleford's first OIS.

"Jeff, I guess we try and pry the civilian witness from the greasy paws of IA."

"How come they're here before us?" Jeff knew enough to expect narcotics to do the initial work up.

"Good question. Something stinks. I just hope it isn't Perez that's giving off the odor." The lead investigator was as optimistic as possible, given the circumstances.

With distant French ancestry, Duvane was basically Caucasian and Shackleford was a California born, beach bum, as blond as his wife. Forcing their way to the crime scene caused an uproar among the congregation of black and Hispanic faces. It took them fully five minutes to cover the two hundred yards to the fateful apartment building.

Shackleford wondered where the uniform officers were. There was usually a plentiful supply of cops at any homicide, and this one warranted extra coverage. He almost forgot the persistence of the City Council, over the years, to cut back on the number of officers in order to balance their suspiciously fat budget.

Unharmed but shaken from the spirited jostling, they arrived in the hallway where the evening's tragic events began. Unknown to them, they stood on the exact spot from where Carlos Cordova had surveyed the split-second performance of Franco Perez.

Duvane and Shackleford peered into the rock house for a while. Then they moved on cautiously to the door, pointed out to them by the patrolman guarding the front of the building. It was the only door to the Cordova residence: a two room, roach infested apartment. The living room also served as kitchen and bedroom to the two oldest Cordova children. A minute bedroom housed Carlos, wife Marta and the year old twins.

Somebody was asking questions belligerently in Spanish, while most of the kids screamed or whined incessantly. Marta pleaded in both of her languages for them to be left alone.

As the narcotics pair filled the doorway with their tall frames, what they saw infuriated them. Carlos was sitting on the couch, helping his wife comfort their distraught offspring. His conduct was one of a criminal caught in the act; of a deer blinded by approaching headlights. The two sergeants from IA towered over him, the Hispanic one was assailing Cordova with question after question.

"Looks like these folks have had enough of this kind of treatment!" Duvane raised his voice above his normally calm tone.

Both sergeants spun around, displaying somewhat guilty expressions for a moment. Cordova and his wife exhibited a pitiful, imploring demeanor, seeking deliverance from their tormentors.

"Well, well, well. If it isn't Gerry Duvane." Sergeant Russ Keach relaxed more than a fraction. "You still got a two spot in dope?" Keach referred to the rank of detective II.

"Yeah, still in dope, Keach, but I'm a D-three now." Duvane recalled past confrontations with Keach as he endeavored to regain his composure.

"Ooooo.....D-three. You're not going to pull rank on me, are you Gerry?" Keach's sarcasm betrayed a deep-seated hatred for the detective.

"We need to speak, Keach. Why don't we step down the hallway?"

"Whatever you say, Gerry." Keach then turned to his partner. "Stick with the questions, Hugo."

As Russ Keach slipped into the hall, Duvane nodded towards the Cordova family and spoke with Shackleford. "Keep an eye on what happens, Jeff."

Shackleford stepped in the room as Keach also gave his directions. "Yeah, Jeff, keep a close eye. Hope you can speak fluent Spanish." The IA investigator re-directed his contempt toward the junior detective, whom he had never met.

Once they were some thirty feet away from the apartment, Duvane and Keach faced each other and the confrontational sergeant spoke first. "Well, Gerry, what could I possibly do for you?"

"Keach, what is it with interrogating our witness this way, and before we have a chance to talk with him?" Duvane was straining to be as cordial as possible.

"Gerry, we don't care much for each other, and we never have. So let's cut the crap here and get down to what's bugging you." Keach almost spat the words out as he recalled the tumultuous working conditions years ago when they were teamed together. They had a totally different philosophy as to how they should handle people, and it appeared that nothing had changed.

"As you wish." Gerry Duvane took a deep breath to clear his head before the battle commenced. "This is a narcotics OIS and I don't need you two head-hunters getting in my way."

"You don't need us yet." Keach was too smug, considering what Duvane knew so far. "Look, Gerry, I can save you a lot of time. RHD are upstairs doing their thing with the crime scene and we are obviously going to be involved too."

He made reference to Robbery Homicide Division, who would have the overall investigative responsibility, since Gregory Rowland was dead.

"I think you might be jumping the gun on this one." It was a faltering optimism on Duvane's part.

"Let's put our differences aside for a moment." Russ Keach said this with an absence of sincerity and Duvane could not believe one word of it. "Your boy, Perez, goes after the victim who is seen leaving the rock house. We'll admit to the place being a dope pad, since there was a bundle of cash inside, together with several ounces of rock.

"However, this youngster could have simply been a customer just leaving. May not have had anything to do with the actual selling. But Perez shoots him as soon as he reaches the top of the stairs.

"A second shot hits your cop in the right hand and the impact dislodges his hand from the weapon. Seems to me that Perez is the one that jumped the gun, not me." It was inadequate information from which to draw any fair conclusions but Keach was resolute.

"If the punk was a customer, did he have any dope on him? A rock or two that he just bought, maybe?" Duvane saw flaws with every stage of the one sided summation.

"Nope. But from the account given by other members of the team, the victim, Rowland was his name, was standing at the door. They probably interrupted the buy."

"So where did the gun come from?" The detective could not believe that such a serious incident warranted little more than a cursory explanation.

"Hey, even users carry a piece to protect themselves sometimes." It was not the answer that Duvane wanted from a question he meant to ask in a different manner.

"But this hood, Rowland, had a gun, right?" Gerry Duvane rationalized the action of Franco Perez. "And he shot our officer."

"The problem is, that a genuinely decent citizen saw Perez just shoot first, without any apparent attempt to avoid killing the victim." It was all quite simple in Keach's mind.

With a shake of his head, Duvane tore into the sergeant's reasoning and character. "So, what I saw was the way you treat genuine, decent citizens, huh? If the shots were that close together, then this Rowland idiot had his gun in his hand already."

"You're missing the point, Gerry. Your boy went up the stairs very slowly, very cautiously. He had time to take other action, but all he did when he saw Rowland was…..bang!" He raised his own voice to emphasize the shot.

"I'm not satisfied." Gerry searched for anything that might overcome this steamroller approach." Any other witnesses?"

"A couple of other cops rushed to the back stairs, but only one was at the top in time. Some broad named Kaplan. Too excitable to be any use." Keach dismissed her with derision.

"What exactly did she see, Keach?"

"From the other end of the hallway, she couldn't see nothing. Besides, she's real pally with Perez." The headhunting instinct revealed itself in all its glory. "In my estimation, she's too emotional to be of help to your boy. In fact, too emotional to be on the job."

"Better watch who you share those opinions with. She might take you for all you're worth with a sexual harassment suit."

"Gerry, I could give a damn. All I know is, this cop is in deep shit, and there ain't no way he's coming up smelling like a rose."

Without further comment, the discussion was clearly over. Duvane returned to the Cordova residence. He signaled to Jeff Shackleford to follow him and proceeded to leave.

"It's a dirty job but somebody has to do it." Keach could not let the encounter terminate without a sneer.

Duvane stopped at the front entrance and held the door for his partner. He slowly shook his head and expressed his view of Keach succinctly and to his face. "If somebody has to do it, they couldn't have picked a bigger asshole."

When the pair of narcotic investigators were on the sidewalk, Jeff made a comment that Duvane fully expected. "That's a little strong, isn't it? Talking to a sergeant from IA, I mean."

"Probably so, but Keach and I go way back and none of it has been pleasant."

Jeff felt it was not his place to inquire further into the relationship. He did surprise Duvane with a revelation about the statements of Carlos Cordova. "Promise you won't tell anyone, but I got every word of the interview between the Mexican IA sergeant and Cordova."

"You speak Spanish!?"

"I speak it pretty well, but I understand it perfectly. Want to know the scoop?" Jeff was proud of both his ability to interpret, as well as his restraint when the sergeant known as Hugo rebuked Cordova several times. When the answers were not to the liking of the investigator, he would tell Cordova that he was going to ask the question again. On at least one occasion there were veiled threats about calling immigration. The implication was that Cordova should modify his statement, or suffer some potentially unpleasant treatment by INS.

What Shackleford recounted actually substantiated the events as divulged by Keach. Carlos Cordova told of a fight in the apartment and then the first shot above him. When he looked up, Carlos saw detective Perez with his weapon pointed straight ahead. A split second later, the witness heard another shot and saw the right hand of Perez fall away from the gun, as if it had been shot.

"Okay, let's speak with Kaplan. She may be able to throw more light onto the whole damn mess." Duvane looked around for a friendly face. He spotted Jim Young, who he knew was the same rank as himself, guessing correctly that he was in charge of the South Bureau squad. “Hey, Jim, how are you?” They shook hands as old friends happy to see each other under strained circumstances.

“I don’t know why they bothered calling you guys out. It looks like IA are taking over.” Jim Young held back at first but then let his real feelings show unabated. “Those two goons are pissing off all my people. Seems as if they have it in for Franco, and I don’t know why.”

“I guess they already got to Kaplan. How’d she hold up?”

“Gerry, she’s a class act, but they went through her like a laxative.” Jim Young pointed to his car at the end of the line of undercover police vehicles; the same position where he stopped at eight o’clock. “She’s in my car. I know she’s all broke up, especially about Perez, but she won’t cry – not with us around, anyway.”

Duvane directed Shackleford to interview Nina, while he spoke with all of the other squad members. It was close to a tearful session but Nina struggled to maintain her dignity. As soon as she realized Shackleford was seeking only the truth, she opened up swiftly. He learned of the position that Rowland had taken on the floor; he heard of Nina’s chronology of the events that lasted a couple of seconds. There was no doubt in his mind that she believed in what she was telling.

There was nothing significant to report from the rest of the team and Duvane was anxious to discover what the girl had seen. Jeff relayed her version, which clearly asserted that Rowland shot first. She recalled the muzzle flash from the floor, before the one almost directed at her from Franco’s gun.

“What do you make of it?” Jeff had his own point of view but needed to hear the voice of experience.

“If she is adamant about her observations, I believe her.” There was a frown on the face of the senior detective. “What causes me problems is the shot that knocked his hand from the gun. From Cordova’s angle, he had the better view and he was much closer. I can’t see why he would lie and he’s so certain of what he saw and heard.”

"It's a tough call. Let's go see Perez before they get to him." Jeff was as determined as his partner to seek out the truth, but it would prove more formidable than he could imagine.

CHAPTER SIX

With x-rays perched precariously on the gurney, it was back to the emergency room. Driscoll could not fathom the system of backtracking from one department to another place already visited. "Like a fucking maze. We'll probably never get outta this place." Franco remained silent. The pain in his hand and arm was now worse than listening to the patrolman bemoan each hospital procedure. He was kind of anaesthetized against the onslaught of Kirk Driscoll.

The ER doctor had little difficulty diagnosing the impediment. Some tendons were severed in the hand and surgery was also required to remove the foreign object from Franco's arm. Once more they were on the move and Driscoll cursed the surgeon general, medical insurers, nurses and doctors everywhere. Deep down he was pleased to see his old friend about to have the bullet removed. He also worried about the outcome. It was not major surgery, but it was surgery, nonetheless.

While the cutting, probing and fixing was going along splendidly, Shackleford and Duvane joined Driscoll in the waiting room. The street-wise cop could not bring himself to trust anyone who had the responsibility of investigating other officers. Even though one of the narcotics OIS team was a classmate, he avoided answering their questions directly.

"What did detective Perez say about the suspect and the shooting?" Duvane made an effort to glean what clues Driscoll might be privy to.

"He was kind of delirious from the pain, or maybe from what they gave him for the pain." Driscoll was diplomatic but unhelpful. Several questions and non-answers later, Driscoll excused himself. He told the detectives he needed to check in with his watch commander. Once out of view, he informed a nurse he would make a call in a couple of hours to check on Perez. One minute later he was in the parking lot, scrounging a lift back to his division from some paramedics. He would have tried to get a black and white to pick him up, except that it was about midnight on a typically busy Saturday; as they say, you can never find a cop when you need one.

Meanwhile, Shackleford and Duvane stubbornly waited for the patient to be sent to post-op. They were determined that the IA pair would not get to twist anything Perez had to say; at least, not before they spoke with him themselves.

Just minutes after Driscoll's departure, Teresa Perez arrived with her thirteen-year-old boys, Anthony and Daniel. She was distraught, knowing little about the shooting, or her husband's condition.

Jim Young was occupied with coordinating additional officers to protect the scene, which kept him busy for a couple of hours following the incident. When he realized that nobody at the station had made contact with Franco's wife, he was seething. To add to the predicament, two sergeants from IA apparently took over the investigation. They overruled his decision to send one of his squad to pick her up since they were all potential witnesses. This caused him to spend even more time on a phone with the watch commander.

It was change of watch by the time he procured a patrol car to expedite the notification. The officers assigned the task were ill informed and knew little of their colleague's condition. However, it must have seemed serious to them, as they headed out to the bedroom community of Diamond Bar at a high rate of speed. They returned to Los Angeles almost as rapidly with the worried Perez family aboard.

With a delicate, four feet ten inch frame, Teresa Perez was already dwarfed by the twins, seated protectively either side of her. Having such diminutive stature, one might incorrectly expect Mrs. Perez to be the weaker of the boys' parents. Nothing could be further from the truth. She was the stalwart member of the family during times of crisis, and she would need to summon all of her strength to face the impending turbulence that was to turn their lives upside down.

Franco's compassionate heart and easy-going approach to his duties made Teresa seem thick-skinned in comparison. When a minor emergency reared its head, she would be the one to stand up to the world, all one hundred and two pounds of her. Franco would take a back seat, exhibiting a quixotic attitude. In truth, his confidence derived from her strength.

An alarm was sounding deep inside of Teresa, spurred on by the banal comments of the uniform officers in front of her. They told her that Franco was going to be okay, and that there was nothing to be upset about. When questioned about his exact injuries, they could say nothing she really wanted to know. Her resolve was being severely put to the test recently, with the FBI investigation seemingly never ending. It had taken its toll on her health, but she refused to trouble Franco at home, while he had to face the frustrating situation at work.

"So! Do you two know any more about Franco than the characters that brought me here?" She was polite but her aggravation was evident.

"Mrs. Perez, I'm Jeff Shackleford. Franco and I went through the academy together. They tell us that a bullet went into his hand and up his arm a little. Even though they are operating, there really is no cause for alarm. He's going to be just fine."

"Thanks for that at least." She was genuinely grateful and immensely relieved. As tears welled, she hugged her sons, hiding her face from the detectives. Both boys comforted their mother but said nothing. She was raising them in a strict, respectful atmosphere and they knew it was not their place to comment. Several awkward minutes passed before Teresa was sufficiently composed to continue a conversation with Shackleford. They discussed every detail of her husband's evening except for the inconsistencies in the statements of Cordova and Kaplan. Jeff tried not to draw any conclusions, even when Teresa pressed for his opinion of the shooting.

"Well, it sounds like it's in policy, doesn't it?" It was a rhetorical question. She knew about Police Department standards when it came to officers discharging their weapons. Franco was involved in two previous shootings, both of which were judged to comply with the department policy.

"I can't comment on that until all the particulars are documented." He tried a diplomatic response, when he should have changed the subject.

"What particulars do you mean?" Teresa was stunned by the remark. "From what you told me, it sounds cut and dried. Franco was defending himself."

"Routine stuff, you must know by now." Jeff was stumbling and Duvane had no way of helping him out of the hole he was digging.

A nurse saved the day as she entered and proclaimed, "Francisco Perez. He's doing just fine. Everything went well with his surgery."

Both Duvane and Shackleford approached as if to pass the nurse and enter the postoperative room. To dispel any doubts as to who ran the hospital, she held up her hand barring their way. "Are you family?"

"I'm his wife." Teresa jumped in assertively.

Quickly summing up the situation, the nurse set the ground rules. "He can see three at a time." As she declared this, the nurse gathered the boys together and ushered them towards their father.

As an afterthought she asked, "Unless he's a suspect, is he?"

With this question in the air, Teresa stared fiercely at Shackleford, daring him to respond incorrectly. Jeff attempted a smile and told Teresa to go ahead and see her husband. If it were not for the legal requirement to appear impartial, he would have told her Franco was far from a suspect in his eyes.

At Franco's bedside, Anthony and Daniel showed their devotion to a loving father, as they hung on every word he spoke. They were created in his image and they longed to be like him more as each day passed.

Teresa listened intently. She sought any trivial detail that deviated from the account learned from Shackleford. There was none. Franco did the right thing, for the right reasons. Why then, was the detective so cautious? The husband; the father; the good cop; Franco was not proud of what he did, but he did it to protect himself. He did it to save his own life. He did what he was trained to do.

"Franco, be careful when they talk to you about tonight. I don't trust them."

"What's not to trust? I just tell them what happened. It was all I could do, Baby."

"Yeah, Mama, he had to shoot that bad man." Daniel could hold his tongue no longer.

"Hush, *mijo*, don't talk like that." Teresa did not want her children talking so freely about killing.

It was Anthony's turn next. "Papa did it 'cause he had to. Didn't you Papa?" Franco's boys wanted more than anything to believe their father killed another person because he had no choice.

"There was nothing else I could do." He almost pleaded with them to accept it as the truth, placing a palm on the cheek of each boy.

There were tears in everyone's eyes.

* * *

Throughout the night, Shackleford and Duvane were able to spend periods of time with Franco Perez. They listened intently for inconsistencies, but were ultimately convinced Franco was telling what he believed was the truth. The interview was protracted because nurses would frequently ask them to leave while medical attention took priority. Several hours were then spent at the command post recording the details of their investigation. This was followed abruptly by the revelation that the commander was passing the matter into the hands of IA. Sergeant Russ Keach and his partner were ecstatic, while Shackleford left for that fateful journey home on the freeway.

CHAPTER SEVEN

"C'mon, Alice, gimme a couple more beers over here!" Kirk Driscoll's idea of holding his beer was not using the bathroom for hours, so he could keep his place at the bar.

"I don't think her name is really Alice." Franco Perez was still doing too much thinking, considering the number of beers he had downed.

"Who gives a fuck what her name is, as long as she keeps serving us." Driscoll smiled as the woman behind the bar delivered two more icy cold bottles. Amy, which was her given name, could care less what they called her, as long as they tipped well. The quicker she serves, the quicker they get drunk and push good tips across the bar. There were few regulars at the police academy lounge that could say they had been drinking there longer than Amy had been working as the barmaid.

"How's that wing of yours, Franco?" Driscoll banged his beer against Franco's glass, tipped it sharply and drank half the contents before his friend could answer.

The choice of the academy lounge for the fifteen-year reunion had its pros and cons. It was adequate for the numbers involved and the food served was okay. A rowdy element, however, preferred to have some place away from the police environment. Although, if somebody was too drunk to drive home it was relatively safe to sleep in the academy parking lot.

Franco hoisted his bandaged right arm off the bar and proclaimed, "Good as new in a few weeks. It's tough learning to drink with my left hand though."

"I bet that's not the only thing you had to learn to do with your other hand. Know what I mean, huh?" He nudged Franco on his left side and winked suggestively.

"I'm married, remember. So I don't have to do that, like you single guys." Franco was tuned into the innuendo.

"Yeah, right! I've been married twice and I can do without a permanent woman in my life."

"Driscoll, they say the third time's a charm."

"Ain't nothing charming about being married." Kirk Driscoll caught Amy's eye and placed his next order visually.

Franco pondered that last remark and thought the two ex-wives would certainly agree with the big fellow.

After the dinner and a few speeches, most of those present retired to the bar and dance floor. Almost thirty of the class from August 1987 had survived thus far. Twenty-six showed up for the party, many with wives and girlfriends. They were not necessarily their own wives and girlfriends! Both Driscoll and Franco came alone. Kirk had nobody to bring and Teresa was at home with the boys. Franco had a momentary thought to ask Nina Kaplan to join him, but realized that could lead to trouble.

"Tell me, Driscoll, how is southwest division treating you?"

"Patrol sucks! Like I told you last week at the hospital, ever since the Foothill Division caper nobody wants to work, and you can't blame them. For throwing some sleazebag in jail, you can lose everything. So why bother?" Driscoll did not appear to be drunk but he was loosening up with each bottle. "Got me a nice business on the side as a firearms agent. Buy a few guns here; sell a few there. Whatever people need."

"Are you talking illegal weapons?" Franco was uneasy about the possible answer to his question.

"You kidding? Naw, it's all above board, license and all. But you'd be amazed how many folks want them. They figure we can't protect them, so they get their own piece to blow away that burglar, or whatever. Besides, it pays so well I ain't staying one day past twenty years. I'd pull the pin now but those leaches at City Hall are gonna give me every dime of my pension."

"Is it all about money?" Franco was not sure where the inquiry was leading, but he asked it anyway.

"For me it is. A million bucks in my hand right now and I'd give up what the City owes me. It'd be tough but I'd make do somehow." Driscoll had his price, although he selected it without serious thought to the amount or circumstances. "What about you, Franco, my boy? What's your figure?"

"I can't think of anything like that right now. There's this FBI business dragging on and now IA are giving me shit about my shooting on Manhattan Place."

"Sounds like they have your number. Once they get their claws in, they won't stop 'till they tear you to shreds." Driscoll was finally slowing down with the cold ones, but his scathing remarks about authority were becoming sharper.

"That's very promising. Any other words of reassurance?" Franco was catching up with the pace of drinking.

Before Driscoll could respond, Jeff Shackleford slipped into the first empty seat to become available for some time. It was on Franco's other side; his injured side.

"Can I buy you guys a drink?" Jeff waved to Amy.

"I shouldn't drink with someone in your line of work. Might give me a bad rep." Driscoll was suddenly as cold as the beers he was consuming.

"Driscoll, you probably already have a bad rep." The newcomer to the conversation was thrown on the defensive.

"C'mon you two. We're celebrating fifteen great years here tonight." Franco tried to mediate. "Besides, Driscoll, I should tell you that Jeff did interview me at the hospital, but the whole thing was taken from him and given to IA."

"That's right." Jeff confirmed his defense, and then went on to explain the particulars of the how and why he was relieved of the investigation.

"Okay, Jeff, if you got all sides, tell me your honest opinion of the shooting." Driscoll was more restrained.

"Well, obviously I believe Franco, but you have to consider the statement of an eyewitness which contradicts him somewhat."

"This eyewitness, would it happen to be a nigger?" Driscoll pulled no punches.

"Mexican, actually, and a decent type from what I saw." Jeff tried to remain impartial.

"That's something in his favor, I guess." Driscoll had more to say on the subject but was distracted by something across the room. "Did you come with a good-looking blonde tonight?"

This was obviously directed to Shackleford, who responded in the affirmative, adding that it was his wife.

"Well, Jeff, there's some horny slimeball hitting on your wife as we speak."

Just for the amusement factor, Jeff checked out Jessica's would-be suitor. "Nothing to worry about. Anyway, I trust her implicitly."

With the booze flowing freely, war stories abounded and the noise level gradually grew. Driscoll suggested they should go outside to the rock garden, a cascading yard of several levels behind the lounge.

"Of course, it depends on how implicit that trust is." Driscoll taunted Shackleford who was too mellow to take the bait.

"Noooo problem. Let's go."

They took an extra round of beer that Franco ordered and slipped into the slightly cooler night air. Three tiers up from the back door of the bar, the threesome settled on some large boulders. They could not agree whether the rock garden construction was real or imitation. Driscoll's negative outlook was naturally the one that declared them to be fake, like so many things in life.

"One thing that is real, I can assure you, and that's the computer the department uses to track troublesome cops." He lectured Jeff and Franco, wagging his finger, as if informing them of this fact for the first time.

"So, what's your point?" Jeff had been aware of the system for the ten years it had been operating. In a desperate attempt to protect themselves from civil litigation, the Los Angeles city council and police department management developed a tracking system for recalcitrant police officers. They considered a pattern of shootings or incidents involving use of force to be evidence of a propensity for trouble. Even though most of these violent contacts with suspects were deemed to be legitimate and proper, the officers were tainted by their inclusion in the lopsided computer program.

"My point is this: Franco surely has his own niche on the computer's hard drive."

Franco was stunned by this revelation. "Wait a minute! I don't have one personnel complaint, not one suspended day, and you're telling me I'm on their bad boys index. That doesn't make sense."

Driscoll put the matter into its proper, yet distorted perspective. "Face it, Franco. With your two previous shootings and the FBI chasing your ass, this latest killing has put you on their hit list."

"That can't be true. Both shootings were justified.....and so was this one. As for the FBI, they just need more scapegoats. It's no more than a fishing expedition."

Jeff rested a consoling hand on Franco's shoulder and confirmed Driscoll's assertion. "He's probably right. It's cruel and unreasonable, but it's also a fact of life."

"And you think I'm in trouble with last week's caper, don't you?" Franco seemed to be asking too many questions lately, when he really did not want to hear the response.

"I'll be honest, Franco, it seems to me they have a hard-on for you. Those two from IA are convinced you shot that Rowland guy the moment you set eyes on him. Didn't even give him a chance. That's what they think." Jeff knew this would hurt Franco, but he felt a forewarning was appropriate.

"I suppose a dead guy shot me in the hand, huh?"

Jeff Shackleford felt Franco's inner pain, but was powerless to provide further solace. Both he and Kirk Driscoll stared across the roof of the police academy, toward the skyline scattered with palm trees. All three drank in silence for a while, as their emotions were tossed around like small boats in a storm.

Driscoll inspected the narrow opening of his empty beer bottle for a moment before sending the trio in another direction. "Funny, isn't it? Franco tries hard to do his job as best he can, but some chief can get away with swindling the whole fucking department!"

This got their attention, as Jeff and Franco looked at him with incredulity. Neither wanted to ask the obvious, since they were not sure of his sincerity. They should have realized by now that despite his insufferable, fatalistic character, Driscoll was not one for glib remarks. Because no comments were forthcoming, he assumed they both had knowledge of this inside information. He stood and started down one level of steps to the bar. "Another round, gentlemen?"

"Driscoll, get your fat butt back here now. We want to hear about this…..corruption." Jeff spoke for both of them.

"No need to get personal, Jeffy baby. All you had to do was ask." The lowly patrol officer actually felt a surge of self-importance, knowing he was in possession of such a sensitive scoop. As he sat between Jeff and Franco, Driscoll pointed a finger outward at each of them. "To be precise, it's your boss."

Jeff frowned and asked whom exactly he meant.

"Does the name Neaville Montgomery mean anything?" Driscoll was avoiding the smug approach, but could not resist giving tidbits to his captive audience.

It was Franco's turn to jump in. "Commander Montgomery! You mean the commander of narcotics?"

Driscoll affirmed his pronouncement. He went on to tell the others all he knew. A close friend, now working the asset forfeiture section of narcotics, had sworn him to secrecy when he was given the account of Montgomery's misdeed. Over the last few years tens of millions of dollars had been seized either by the police department or with the cooperation of other law enforcement agencies. These sums were held, pending the outcome of court actions designed to permanently deprive the major drug dealers of the cash. Upon successful completion, the cash was divided between the authorities involved with the seizures, to be spent as they saw fit. None of the money was misspent and it was all finally used in some way to fight the war on drugs. The misappropriation transpired when Montgomery declared exclusive responsibility for the cash during its latent period. His brother owned a small banking corporation for years and between them they conspired to deposit the monies in a non-interest bearing account.

"So you see, for every million there should be, let's say, fifty-thousand interest a year. Over the time frame we are talking about, my friend estimates a conservative figure of more than two mil in the brother's pocket." He rounded figures that he had previously heard, for simplicity purposes.

"That's an amazing tale, Driscoll, but why haven't Montgomery and his brother been brought to justice?" Franco was lightheaded from the thought of such vast sums.

"Franco, my boy, will I ever relieve you of your idealism? There's one justice for you and me, then another justice for those that have influence and power."

Jeff finally gathered himself enough to ask, "If it's common knowledge, then there would have to be some inquiry at least."

"Therein lies the all-important factor, my friends." Driscoll added this with a flourish. "As far as I am aware, we three and my confidant are the only ones who know. He stumbled upon the info and followed up through various banking sources. This triggered a red flag at the brother's bank and within hours there was a call from the commander himself. A brief discussion followed and my friend was left in no doubt about the consequences of his disclosing what he had unearthed."

"You mean he was threatened?" Jeff had genuine difficulty with the latest bombshell.

"Call it what you will. Just use your imagination."

It was the turn of Jeff and Franco to stare off into the distance. They missed the beauty of the night sky and the silhouettes thrown by the surrounding Elysian Park. Their minds raced with the burden of this news, as Driscoll slipped away to buy another round.

When he returned, they discussed the revelation and its connotation. The sharing of his secret relieved Driscoll, but Jeff and Franco were vexed by the added burden.

"Makes me want to throw up." Franco was getting close to the alcohol level that would produce such a result.

"How about getting even." Driscoll contemplated an evil course of action. "You know, getting our share for a change."

"I can't imagine what you have in mind, but I don't like it already." It was a predictable remark from Shackleford.

"You guys are both in dope. One of your snitches could direct us to some stash pad where they have a lot of bucks. We have the firepower.....and whamo! We're rich." The fat guy was in his cups by now.

"You're crazy." Jeff dismissed the suggestion.

"No. He's just drunk." Franco was closer to the mark.

Driscoll's words were definitely slurred now. "Why am I even considering your contacts?" He jabbed a finger into Franco's chest. "Anybody you deal with would lead us to a couple of balloons of heroin or a single rock of coke. Jeff, baby, you're the one who could find the big shit!"

He was swaying from side to side, waving his bottle and spilling more than he was drinking. Jeff whispered to Franco that they should carry him to his car and hide his keys. It was painful for the injured Franco, but they managed to get the big fellow standing with an arm over each of their shoulders. After just a few steps, Jeff looked down in the direction of the back door and exclaimed, "Oh, oh, we're in trouble now."

Jessica had eventually brushed off the advances of another fifteen-year veteran cop. She was standing at the lower level of the rock garden, hands on hips.

CHAPTER EIGHT

The early morning sun was unmerciful. His shirt was completely soaked with perspiration and his right cheek felt glued to the vinyl covering of the passenger seat. Driscoll exerted what little energy he could muster, lifting himself into an upright position. With all of the windows in his Ford LTD tightly closed, there was no air available to breathe. A sadistic demon was hammering on both temples from inside his head. He was sure that at no time in his life had he ever wished he were dead with such sincerity.

When the window was wound down, the heat outside was just as unpleasant. If he turned on the engine, he could achieve some relief from the air conditioner. Alas, the keys were nowhere to be found; not in the ignition; not in his pocket; not on the floor. It was a miserable and pitiful sight as his chin sank and he watched his chest heaving in an attempt to inhale precious oxygen. On reflection, it looked more like his distended stomach was convulsing. What had he done to himself? Never again! Not until the next time!

As his eyes focused, he finally realized where he was parked. It was a gas station on the corner of Exposition Boulevard and Figueroa Street, just off the Harbor Freeway. Saturday morning traffic was moderate and there were a few students on the sidewalk. Directly across Figueroa was the campus of the famed University of Southern California. People were going about their business as he was dying. He could not fathom why he was in southwest division, which was the area where he worked. If he remembered correctly, the previous night had been spent carousing at the academy bar. There was a vague image of two buddies struggling to drag his overweight form though the parking lot.

If he had subsequently driven away, why head south? His home was in Van Nuys, in a somewhat northerly direction the last time he checked. The only answer could be that his subconscious propelled him towards his workplace. With three o'clock roll call this afternoon, it seemed that his involuntary actions were the smartest.

In acquiring his bearings he also glanced in the rear view mirror. A perplexing white object was blocking his vision. Only a meager quantity of gray cells was operational, but he instantly deduced that since his car was white, then his trunk must be open. A cold sweat immediately replaced the hot one as Driscoll scrambled from the vehicle. What he saw at the rear of his car brought him great dismay. Only the spare wheel remained in the trunk while his precious and very valuable cargo was missing.

Driscoll cursed the fiendish crooks that stole his property; he cursed himself for his stupidity; he cursed Alice for serving him so promptly last night. Now he was mad. If somebody he could suspect came close to him at this moment, he would choke them until they admitted the larceny. Then he would continue until there was not a breath left. Yes, he was mad.

If he had his keys he would drive to his station some two miles away and make out the report himself. However, all he could do was call for a patrol car just like the average victim. Now he began to realize what those citizens felt like, with a lengthy wait for a black-and-white, and no way to vent their frustration. At least forty-five minutes elapsed before anyone rolled up. It was ten in the morning, during a weekend, and he could not fathom why they were so busy.

"Driscoll!? The call didn't say it was a cop who'd been ripped off." Officer Mike Anderson was actually mildly amused. "Why didn't you tell communications when you called? You know we'd have been here sooner."

"I didn't want everyone to know, okay! Let's cut the crap and get this show on the road." He was tired, hung over, disheveled, thirsty, hungry, irate, and now he was also broke.

"Alright, sir, can I see your ID?" Anderson proceeded with the routine approach.

"Shit! You don't need no ID, just ask me the fucking questions, asshole."

Anderson feigned indignation. "Please, sir, I have procedures to follow. A formality, you understand?"

Driscoll had known the day watch officer for several years and eventually got him to lighten up. As the initial investigation showed, there appeared to be no forced entry into the trunk. However, an assortment of firearms, amounting to many thousands of dollars, had been taken. Driscoll had various customers, all of them awaiting imminent delivery of the guns. It was the only cash his ex-wives didn't take from him in alimony. Perhaps because they knew nothing about it.

"Damn niggers!" Kirk Driscoll cursed under his breath.

The very white Anderson heard the remark and asked, "So you got a look at them? Can you give any kind of description?"

"I was asleep, dammit. Who else would it be around here?"

"Hmmm.....suspects unknown." Anderson recited, as he completed the crime report. "Method of entry.....unknown."

Just as he stated this last point, his partner called him over to the trash dumpster behind the gas station. Driscoll's keys had been tossed in with the garbage, after the crooks used them to unlock the trunk, revealing a precious loot.

"So they must have opened my door and taken the keys from the ignition, all while I was asleep." Driscoll shuddered as his imagination ran wild. "Man, I'm amazed they didn't take the wheels."

Anderson was more pragmatic. "Just be grateful you have your life and....." As he continued he eyed the Ford dubiously. ".....your car too, I suppose."

"Yeah, yeah, yeah. Without my guns, life ain't shit. Got a lot invested in that particular load. I'll probably have to work 'till twenty-five now." Driscoll made reference to serving a longer period of time on the force than he originally planned.

"Pity the poor public." His colleague had sympathy only for the people Driscoll was supposed to serve.

"Sure. Thanks for everything." Kirk Driscoll was about to drive to southwest station for a shower and a few hours rest in the cot room.

In a rare yet significant display of gratitude, he turned to Anderson's partner. "I appreciate you finding my keys, buddy."

When Driscoll sped westbound on Exposition, Anderson shook his head in dismay. "Partner, it's a pity we didn't get that parting remark on video. We could have blackmailed his fat ass for years to come."

* * *

Before roll call started, Officer Kirk Driscoll begged the watch commander to let him work the desk. He felt that it might be more dangerous if he fell asleep in a patrol car, than if he faded from consciousness in the station lobby. Lieutenant Havighurst could not decide which was worse: Driscoll in the field, being obnoxious to the people on his radio calls; or Driscoll at the desk, being obnoxious to visitors and callers. It was likely to be a wrong choice either way, but the fifteen-year veteran certainly looked a little rougher around the edges than usual.

"Roll call." Havighurst shouted above the pandemonium of twenty-five officers to secure their attention. "There's one change from the scheduled line-up today. Branson, you'll have to put some bullets in your gun. You're going out as 3A63. Driscoll will work the desk."

An officer with many more years on the job than Driscoll was first to comment. "Oh, no! Better lock the front door to the station. Lieutenant, what's the public done to deserve this?"

Their watch commander came back in a timely fashion. "Blame the staff at the academy for not implementing euthanasia while he was in training."

Driscoll was used to the sick humor. In fact, he gave at least as much as he received. However, with the distress he had been exposed to recently, his attention was elsewhere and no rebuttal was forthcoming.

By the time he handled several reports that were *kissed off* to him by the day watch desk personnel, it was five thirty. Driscoll sipped on an ice cold soda from the machine situated in the station lobby, wondering to himself if things could get worse. The lack of a decent night's sleep was rapidly taking its toll on his exhausted mass. With one of the lobby doors propped open, a warm, smoggy breeze was wafting his way. It was a comforting sensation that engulfed him, as troublesome thoughts receded to a far-off haze. A solitary sound in the distance was similar to an angel in heaven, softly calling his name.

"Driscoll." It called to him again. "Driscoll, wake up and grab line two. It's for you!" A female officer was filling the other post at the desk.

He awoke with a sudden jolt and sweat streaming down his cheeks. This was becoming an all too common event. After gathering his faculties, he punched line two and grabbed the handset. "Good afternoon. How may I help you?" It was textbook phone etiquette.

"Driscoll?" The caller seemed confused.

"This is Officer Driscoll. Who, may I ask, is calling?"

"It's Franco. Man, what have they done to you? They brainwash you, or something?"

"Hi, Franco, old buddy. Listen, don't worry about that crap. I'm just trying to show the lieutenant I can handle this desk bullshit. After all, he did me a favor letting me work inside. You know last night, after I got to my car, I must have driven….."

"Driscoll! Shut up, will ya?" Franco interrupted the officer's digression. "I had to call somebody. Those goons from IA were just at my house, and they were with this Martinet feller from the FBI."

"Aw, shit. What they want?"

Franco went on to tell Driscoll that the two sergeants delivered some papers to him and told him he was suspended. When he inquired what the reason was, they told him it was in connection with the shooting on Manhattan Place. There was an attempt to interview him, but he sensibly refused until he could speak with a defense representative. Martinet stood in the background and never uttered a word. He watched the proceedings intently, with a hideous smirk on his face.

"They can't suspend me when I'm IOD, can they?" Franco made reference to his status of being off work due to an injury on duty, as distinct from simply being sick.

“Those bastards can probably do whatever they want.” Driscoll’s remarks were heated now, as he felt the same outrage that engulfed Franco. His female counterpart at the desk scowled at his use of strong language. “Look, Franco, you should be calling your defense rep right now, instead of pouring your heart out to me.” Strangely, for Driscoll, his comment was as sincere as the words sounded.

“I tried already. He’s out for the evening. They told me he would call me back tomorrow.” Franco then lowered his voice, as if he expected the girl next to Driscoll to be listening at the other end of the line. “I’ve had enough, Driscoll. I’m interested in that business you were talking about last night.”

With his hand cupped over the mouthpiece, Driscoll whispered as quietly as possible. “I was drunk, buddy, and probably not making any sense. Besides, those idiots may have your phone bugged. Especially if the Feds are involved.”

“You made a lot of sense last night, but you’re also right about the phone.” Franco was suddenly more cautious. “When can we meet?”

“When I’m done tonight, I’m gonna need about twenty-four hours sleep or I may never make it to Monday. Why don’t you wait ‘till your rep calls and see what he has to say. It might not be as bad as you think.”

“Okay, but I’m working on some ideas about that job.”

“That’s my boy, Mr. Big Shot. You got all the connections, huh? I hope you sleep tight tonight. I know I will.” When Driscoll hung up, he stared at the phone, trying to make sense of his conversation with Franco.

CHAPTER NINE

"This is the big one, my friend!" Cornejo spoke in his native Spanish, having lived most of his twenty-six years in Michoacan, Mexico. He had not bothered to learn any English, particularly since he found out even the Department of Motor Vehicles did not require it.

Jeff Shackleford had used the services of Cornejo Ballesteros Ramos for nearly two years to their mutual benefit. Cornejo had raked in somewhere close to eighty thousand tax-free dollars, while Shackleford had promoted in the detective ranks. This was all thanks to numerous outstanding cases stemming from the snitch's ability to infiltrate the most elite drug operations. "I've heard this many times before, but not from you, Cornejo. So let's go over it again." He spoke slowly to make sure his Spanish was understandable. His doubts stemmed from years of handling other informants, all of them convinced they were tipping him off to the *big one*. To Cornejo's credit, he had always delivered what he had promised and made a comfortable living for himself. There was an arrangement whereby Cornejo worked occasionally with the DEA, but only when Jeff agreed to the case being given to the Feds. This was usually because Shackleford's squad was busy on another investigation. However, his squad leader, Ricardo Montoya, was always keen to follow up on Cornejo's terrific leads. Because the informant was so dependable, this was often done at the expense of an ongoing operation.

Shackleford was conducting the meeting alone in the small interview room at the downtown office. It was generally the practice to have two detectives in these situations to avoid claims of misconduct, but Montoya and the rest of the crew were on a surveillance. Jeff had decided to take the initial information and call someone else in, should he feel it necessary. With painstaking attention to detail, he made copious notes of the tale that Cornejo unfolded enthusiastically. It centered around a distant cousin who was the real inside man this time. The cousin, whom he wanted to refer to only as Juan, worked for a connection believed to be a key man with the Medellin Cartel. This was reputed to be the most powerful and feared drug smuggling organization in the Americas.

As with many crooks-turned-informant, Juan had been wronged by the organization he worked for. A mix up in the intelligence he was supposed to pass on caused a near disaster. He gave the all clear to a shipment of cocaine to be flown over the border, which, in actuality, was minutes from being intercepted by Customs. Good fortune and incompetence on the part of the Border Patrol allowed the plane to land safely on US soil, going completely undetected. Juan fully expected a reduction in remuneration for his blunder but the reaction by his employer was more drastic. A close relative of Juan's suddenly disappeared without a trace and it was the last straw for him. On the surface he displayed an appropriately obedient attitude, while biding his time until retribution was within his grasp.

Cornejo was able to recite sufficient details, including technical data, that Shackleford could not ignore the potential for a major bust. His thoughts manifested themselves in a quiet exclamation, "A ton of coke. Man that would sure make me look good." Almost every word was lost on Cornejo since the cop was speaking in English.

"What? I don't understand." It was the first time during the discussion that the informant was unable to follow Jeff Shackleford.

"I was just wondering how much we would pay you if this works out." Jeff translated the words to suit himself.

"The usual would be nice, my friend." Cornejo was optimistic.

"If we did that, you could retire, but the city would be broke." Shackleford contemplated the price paid by the police department, which was substantial but always negotiable.

"Whatever is fair. It's okay by me." The informant was also a realist and an amiable one at that.

They said their goodbyes and Shackleford promised to get back to him real soon. For most of the day, the detective spent his time working up the case. He reviewed mileage charts, weight limits on a certain plane, extended fuel tanks, radar capabilities, and all of the technical aspects. He also made the usual checks to insure that there was no other agency working the same deal. This was somewhat inexact in this instance, since he had no names, addresses or vehicle licenses. All he could verify was that the general location did not currently have an active major investigation. Although much of Cornejo's material could not be verified without a long trip and possibly some surveillance time, it was looking good on paper. Shackleford was excited about the prospect of bringing in the biggest haul of cocaine for 2002 so far. He worked late into the evening with maps and gathered phone numbers of other police agencies he would need for support.

The rest of his squad called it a day around nine o'clock but Montoya had paperwork of his own to take care of at the office. As he entered the sprawling room that housed six major narcotics squads, the twenty-four year veteran detective was surprised to see Shackleford still working. "What the hell you doin' still here? I hope you don't expect me to sign your overtime slip." It was a poor attempt at sarcasm. Montoya would sign for whatever Jeff put in for. He had no doubt that the most conscientious detective he had the pleasure of supervising was working late with good cause.

"Hi, boss. You guys do okay out there today?"

"We sat for nine hours and drove like maniacs for two. Nothing unusual, I suppose." Montoya described a typical day on surveillance, although it could easily have been nine driving and two sitting. As both men busied themselves with their chores, Montoya went through his mail and tossed an envelope along the squad table. "This has your name on it, Jeff. Looks official. From the City Attorney, I think."

"City Attorney, huh? That's all I need, another lawsuit!" The comment was made jokingly and because the only correspondence they normally received from the CA was, in fact, notifications of pending civil litigation. Jeff slipped a pencil into the top of the envelope and tore it open. As he scanned the contents, blood drained from his features and he turned deathly white.

Montoya glanced up momentarily and noticed an anguished look coupled with the ghostly pallor. "Hey, *amigo*, you okay?" His concern was that of a close friend, not just a supervisor.

Jeff did not answer. He simply shook his head slowly in disbelief. After what seemed like an eternity in the quiet, deserted office, he folded the legal documents and slid them back down the long table. His boss inspected the front sheet as the despondent detective stared at the paperwork he had so diligently worked on all day.

"Aw, shit! It is a lawsuit." Ricardo Montoya had seen his share of them during twenty-four years of throwing people in jail. Even though none of them had been worth the paper they were written on, the city had settled several. Twenty thousand here, fifty thousand there; maybe there was some logic in handing over a small fortune to an undeserving scumbag, but it continued to escape Montoya's way of thinking. "What's to worry about, buddy? If you done nothing wrong, the City Attorney's gonna have to defend this bullshit. And I know you done nothing but good while you been working for me."

Slowly, deliberately and with a tormented countenance shrouding his furrowed brow, Jeff lifted his head and gazed into the distance. He did not look at Montoya when he spoke. He did not look at anything in particular as he addressed the subject that now pained him so deeply. "The name on the lawsuit. It's the woman I saved from the wreck last week. Her family is suing because she was killed after I put her down on the shoulder of the freeway."

The color was gradually returning to Jeff's face as anger replaced the dismay. His boss struggled to come up with words of encouragement, but he realized it was more than the thought of a successful suit against him that gnawed at Shackleford's insides. He imagined himself in the same position, having risked his own life to save another, only to see that same life instantly wiped out. Then to add to the heartache, he was now basically being blamed for her death. Montoya approached Jeff and placed an understanding hand on his shoulder as he carefully laid down the offending papers. "It's times like this you want to come up with just the right thing to say. But I don't know what it is, Jeff. I just don't know what to say."

"There's nothing to say, boss." The spirit was gone from his voice as he flipped the legal documents into his open briefcase. He picked up the work he had spent so much time on and held it in front of him, looking right through the *big one*. The last thing his supervisor was about to do was ask about the case. There would be another day more appropriate for such discussion.

Fifteen years of exceptional police work were behind him. The crimes solved, lives protected, even lives saved, they merged into an unrecognizable blur. Jeff Shackleford's mind was racing in several different directions. He would soon make a calculated decision to turn a corner, leaving himself no chance of ever going back.

CHAPTER TEN

About the time Shackleford was completing his interview with Cornejo, Franco Perez was waiting to meet with George Franklin again. This time it was a preparatory discussion, together with an attorney, to review the impending criminal charges related to the Manhattan Place shooting.

"Detective Perez, they're ready to see you now." The sweetness of the receptionist's voice was lost on Franco, as he stood up automatically and walked to the conference room.

"Franco, glad we could all get together so quickly." George Franklin pulled a huge leather seat away from the equally impressive table and nodded for Franco to join them. "This is Loren Kaminsky. He's as good as they come. Loren, this is Francisco Perez. He likes to be called Franco."

Although Franco believed he was as good as they come, the private attorney looked a little too greasy to be employed by the Police Protective League.

"My pleasure, Franco." Kaminsky held out a huge hand that completely engulfed Franco's.

The detective was still not fully appreciative of the situation he was in, but attempted to keep pace with events. "What do we have to do first?" It was a feeble bid on his part to kick things off.

"Seems to me they are determined to go after a filing of some serious charge through the DA's office." Kaminsky was clearly taking charge and pulled no punches with his opening remark.

"What specific charge do you expect?" The defense representative showed himself to be a willing participant in the conference.

"Too early to say." It was a predictably cautious approach from an attorney. "With what they have, I think we are in deep trouble with holding onto the job. Our main concern should be keeping Franco out of the joint."

"You think they want to see me behind bars? All I did was defend myself, for Christ's sake!" Franco was appalled at the line taken by Kaminsky. There was his job out the window and they were now fighting for his freedom.

"All I can go on right now are the reports that IA have made available." His attorney quickly reviewed some papers. "It looks like they have some basis for going with a manslaughter. I'm not pre-judging, you understand."

Franco's usually gaunt look now presented a vision of a man at least twenty years older. His shoulders drooped in resignation while his dark brown eyes held an expression of hopelessness.

"Franco, we're going to do all we can." Franklin was as propitious as possible. "We all know they are hunting for a scapegoat. Lord knows they've had enough of them in the last couple of years. It's not going to be easy, but we'll fight this with every last breath."

"Yeah. It'd be my last breath, if that Martinet guy had anything to do with it."

Franklin spoke of the FBI agent with a rare contempt. "I feel sure that misguided fool is in the thick of things. You said he was at your house when IA gave you the suspension notice?"

"He sure was. I don't think it was my imagination either, but he looked like he was enjoying the whole thing."

"Gentlemen, I think we must get to the matter at hand." Kaminsky's booming voice silenced the others, both of them meekly awaiting his guidance. "Now, Franco, there is some discrepancy between your version of the events at the shooting, compared to this witness, Carlos Cordova. Do you think there is a likelihood that this Hispanic witness would have a connection to the rock house?"

"From what Detective Shackleford told me, Cordova is a pretty genuine guy. All I can say is that he must have been mistaken." Franco accepted Jeff Shackleford's opinion of the eyewitness.

"But looking at his statement I see no cracks that we might use to our advantage." It was an admission that Franco did not want to hear from the attorney. The proceedings were interrupted by a phone call for Franklin, which he took in another office.

Alone with his attorney, Franco Perez became earnest as he pled his case. "Look, Mr. Kaminsky, I saw that dope fiend with a gun. He pointed it at me and fired. When I returned fire, I got him between the eyes. It was then that I felt the pain in my hand and I guess I couldn't hold onto the gun any longer. That's the way it happened. The dead guy knows it and I know it.....hey, and Detective Kaplan said she saw the flash from the asshole's gun first, then mine."

"Ah, yes, Kaplan. It would appear that the investigators don't put much credence into her observations."

"Of course not. Why should they believe anyone who can prove they are setting me up?" Franco was trying to conceal his frustration for the attitude of the man appointed to defend him.

"Well, I think setting you up is a little strong. It's really a matter of interpretation....."

With this last remark, Kaminsky showed Franco his true colors and was about to get a piece of the detective's mind. However, it was probably fortuitous that George Franklin returned to the room, forestalling a total breakdown in relations.

"Bad news, Franco. That was the DA's office. They want you to voluntarily appear on Wednesday to be formally charged."

"Wednesday. That's two days. Just two days of freedom." Franco was crushed. He could not bring himself to think of asking about the charge. All that swam before his eyes was the image of his boys, Anthony and Daniel, crying because they could not understand why their daddy was being locked up.

"It is bad, I'll admit. But they told me there would be no need even for bail. The DA will allow you to remain free on your own recognizance." Franklin stood behind Franco Perez and placed a comforting hand on his shoulder. The detective could not continue with the conference, as tears welled rapidly, filling his once hopeful eyes.

* * *

Facing light midday traffic, Franco reached his home thirty miles east of downtown in less than forty-five minutes. Diamond Bar was a distinct step up for the Perez family, after surviving many years in the gang-infested neighborhood of East LA.

Teresa was at her part-time job as a teacher's aide and the boys were diligently completing their homework at a friend's house. The two-story, three-bedroom townhouse was too quiet for him to be alone. The investigators looking into the shooting had taken his 9mm for testing purposes and seized his original department issue revolver when they suspended him. However, he still had a two-inch Smith and Wesson with five shots, sitting in a bedside drawer. His original idea was to have it available for Teresa to protect herself when he was working. She detested having the weapon in the house, but he insisted.

With the press blasting him nightly over the shooting, the Feds clearly out for his hide and now the department pushing for formal charges, all seemed lost. An empty feeling engulfed him from within and his heart was so heavy that it seemed to sink into this newly available space. Sitting on the edge of the bed, Franco weakly pulled open the nightstand drawer and stared at the stainless steel that shone too brightly to be a lethal weapon. It felt smooth and comfortable in his left hand. The right hand still ached from the surgery, and he knew it would be difficult to move the trigger finger. As he looked into the short barrel, he wondered if he would see the bullet just like he had nine days earlier on Manhattan Place.

Then, without wanting to think of anything else, the sight of his boys appeared before his misting eyes one more time. They were comforting their petite mother whose body heaved with huge sobs. Anthony and Daniel had no grief or despair in their eyes, only anger. Their faces told Franco that they could never forgive him for giving up. They would not mourn the passing of a cowardly father. With a greater determination than before, he replaced the gun, closed the drawer and sighed heavily. He was not sure if he could fight the battle that confronted him, but he was certain he would never take that way out.

In very little time he was wearing a sweatshirt and shorts, setting off on a break-neck run through his relatively affluent surroundings. He ran faster and further than ever before. The poisonous thoughts he had just experienced were flushed from his mind. After several miles of pushing his body to its limit, he felt he could go on this way forever. Nothing could touch him if he could only keep on running. The Feds, the city, the department, they could all go to hell as he ran from them all. Yes, even the people he had sworn to protect, to hell with them all. They didn't care about him, and after all he had done to protect and to serve them. Go to hell! Everyone.

His sweatshirt was totally soaked and he felt pounds lighter. Before showering he made several attempts to contact Kirk Driscoll. The only answer at his home was a machine, which Franco used to leave a brief message. At southwest station they told him Driscoll was scheduled to work but it was still an hour or so before his watch started. Franco deduced that his classmate was somewhere between Van Nuys and South Central.

It was imperative that he speak with someone who had at least a remote understanding of how it felt to be persecuted. He called Jeff Shackleford's home, confident that this other classmate was aware of the facts surrounding his shooting. Jessica was at home, since she took Sunday and Monday as her weekend off from the beauty salon.

"He's at work right now, Franco. Can I give him a message?" She was polite and quite pleasant.

"Please ask him to call me. I'll give you my number." Franco recited his telephone number and added, "It doesn't matter what time he gets in. Just have him call."

"I'll do that." As she heard the phone being hung up, Jessica Shackleford wanted to ask Franco if he was doing okay. However, he seemed a little too businesslike and was anxious to speak specifically to her husband. She was feeling a sorrow for Franco that would soon be needed for her own loved one.

CHAPTER ELEVEN

Here lies Kirk Driscoll. He worked hard, drank hard and didn't give a damn what anyone thought of him. Oh, Yeah, and he always paid his alimony on time – to both ex-wives. It would be a fitting epitaph should he die today. Unfortunately, it would be all they could say about him. There was nothing extraordinary about his achievements neither on nor off the job. Of course, there had been the occasional incident where he had saved a life or two. Problem was he never made the front page of the paper or the eleven o'clock news. There was always something or somebody stealing the limelight. Once in a while there would come along a benign sergeant who wrote commendations every time an officer did good police work. Driscoll wondered, in his own derisive manner, if it was a self-serving effort. Make it look like your cops are the best and you will look good for supervising them.

However, he did relish some of the old time antics that you could not get away with today. As he cruised south on the Hollywood Freeway to another eight hours of tedium, a memory of one spectacular prank came to mind. It was early 1990 when a fellow officer was gaining a reputation for handling more radio calls than anyone else. He would *buy* the calls from communications even when they were dispatched to another black and white. There could be no doubt about his exuberant work ethic, but it was beginning to make the rest of the watch look bad.

Driscoll and his partner were determined to resolve this imbalance by sending a clear message to the rouge cop. At three in the morning, when they knew he was safely engrossed in a call that required him to take a report, they executed their dirty deed. They were armed with all of the tools necessary to complete the work rapidly, including a spare set of keys to his parked patrol car. All four wheels were removed from the '88 Chevy Caprice Classic and placed in the trunk. The vehicle's jack was taken for good measure and the antagonists retreated to a safe location nearby.

A graveyard radio operator who was in on the prank, broadcast several fake but urgent sounding calls to the division. With predictable reactions the officer intercepted two of the calls and came running out to his car with his trainee officer in tow. He obviously did not believe his eyes, since he walked around the vehicle three times to verify that all of the wheels were gone. Shoulders were shrugged, foreheads were slapped and eventually hands were rested on hips. To his credit, the officer popped the trunk and discovered the missing items and momentarily regained his composure. With the trunk emptied of its contents, the officer was unable to locate the jack but did find a note. It read: "You've been burning too much rubber.....these wheels are 'tired' and need a rest." He shook his head in silent resignation, and then radioed for the police garage tow truck to respond. After a few minutes of hysterical laughter from the two mechanics that answered his call, they had him mobile in short order.

If the message was not clear enough, it was punctuated during a ceremony after work at the local watering hole. Every member of the graveyard shift attended a viewing of the videotape that Driscoll had filmed of the event. The officer in question knew better than to turn down the emphatic invitation and even began to laugh at the third showing of the tape. The good old days. Driscoll savored the thoughts with a sentiment that had been absent from his life for longer than he could recall. His recollection was that the officer in question even modified the speed of his activities to accommodate those less fervent on his shift.

Arriving at the station with twenty minutes to go before roll call, Driscoll had more than enough time to carelessly throw on his uniform. He was indeed the ultimate slob. Sergeant Brannigan stood in as watch commander on this Monday afternoon. When it came to the assignments, Driscoll was to work a radio car with the same female who was on the desk with him on Saturday. He took it philosophically but the girl complained that two days out of three with Driscoll was too much punishment for anyone.

"Bitch, bitch, bitch! Some people just complain about everything." Driscoll threw his hands in the air.

A voice from the back row retorted, "That's a twist, Driscoll complaining about somebody complaining."

Meanwhile, the female officer stared daggers at the pig she was partnered with. There would be more than those looks she would direct at him. Later, as Driscoll stood in line for radios and car keys, he was summoned into the watch commander's office. Brannigan closed the door and abruptly told the officer to sit.

"Hell, it must be important. A closed door session." Kirk Driscoll was short on respect. "If I had a dollar for every one of these talks, I'd be able to retire today."

"After today, I hope you can afford to retire sometime before you grow old."

"Whadda ya mean, sarge?" The gravity of the situation filtered through his beleaguered brain.

"I'll tell you what I mean. That officer you were supposed to ride with today came to me right after roll call. She wants to make a sexual harassment complaint."

"You've got to be kidding. Hey, I might tell the odd blue joke around here, but I ain't never sexually harassed no woman." Driscoll's reaction was predictable and essentially accurate.

"The word bitch, Driscoll, that's the problem."

"Wait a minute! I didn't call her a bitch. That's not how I meant it. You know that as well as I do." He beseeched his supervisor.

"It's all in how the victim perceives the harassment." His sergeant was sympathetic but unable to divert from department policy.

"Victim! I'm the damn victim here. This is bullshit! Everything is getting turned upside down just because we're scared to say boo to some cunt." Blood was rising rapidly to all areas of his face.

"Look, Driscoll, I'll ignore that comment since it's just you and me. But you have to control yourself."

"You'd better give me a special before I control the flow of air to that bimbo's lungs." Driscoll was asking for a special day off, using overtime hours he had stored up.

"That's probably a good idea. Just make sure you come in tomorrow so we can go over this together in a less hostile frame of mind."

"And what makes you think twenty-four hours will calm my hostility?" Kirk Driscoll did not expect to receive an answer, and all he got was a wave of Brannigan's hand in dismissal.

He wanted to go directly to the police academy bar, but suspected it was too early to get drunk. For reasons that were logical, his subconscious drove him to a bar much closer to home. There he remained for the same period he was supposed to have worked, sinking one beer after another. His tolerance level was higher due to his rage. As with many such previous acts of debauchery, he was unaware of his later maneuvers. He did, however, manage to direct his Ford home, where he collapsed on the bed without seeing the blinking light on his answering machine.

CHAPTER TWELVE

It was almost midnight when Jeff quietly slipped between the sheets and snuggled up next to his wife. He needed the comfort of her smooth and presently very warm body. She purred contentedly as he wrapped an arm over her and gently pulled her close.

"Rough day at the office, honey?" She whispered.

"You could say that." Jeff was swiftly brought down to earth, after temporarily dismissing the lawsuit from his mind.

Jessica almost forgot the message as she floated dreamily in that serene space just before falling asleep. "Call Franco." She managed to tell him softly.

Jeff digested these two words for a moment before responding. ""I'll call him in the morning. It's late."

"*It doesn't matter what time he gets in. Just have him call.*" The words forced themselves into her consciousness and an urgency about them awoke her fully. "Jeff, honey, you must call him. He sounded.....desperate, maybe."

"If that's what you think, I guess I should call." Reluctantly, he left that exquisite body to make the call. He used the bedside phone, hoping that he could return to the reverie in a couple of minutes.

Teresa Perez answered the phone and it was evident she was upset by the lateness of the call. "Franco's sleeping. I'm not going to disturb him at this hour. Haven't you people done enough to try and destroy him?" She would defend her man to the ends of the Earth.

"Mrs. Perez, this is Jeff Shackleford. We met at the hospital. I'm a classmate of Franco's."

"I know who you are. You were involved in the investigation, and now Franco might go to jail. Do I thank you now or later?" Anger was building gradually but inevitably.

"Jail? I didn't know anything about that. Please trust me, I believed Franco that night. That's why I was taken off the case. Let me speak with him. He called my home earlier today and said he wanted to talk." Jeff pleaded with her.

There was silence on the line for what seemed an eternity to Jeff. Then Teresa Perez sighed almost imperceptibly and said she would get Franco.

"Jeff, thanks for calling, buddy." Franco Perez sounded agitated and relieved at the same time. "Man, do you work some late hours?"

"It's easy to make a big case out of all our work." He made an attempt at dismissing the importance of the *big one.*

Franco lowered his voice as if they were discussing a secret. "The DA is filing charges. They want me to turn myself in on Wednesday. Huh, I guess that's tomorrow, now." He glanced at the clock and noticed it was after midnight.

"I can't believe they're doing that to you." Jeff sympathized.

"Maybe I should abscond. You know, just split."

Jeff was astounded even more by this suggestion. "That's a little drastic, Franco. I wouldn't recommend it."

"Don't fret, buddy, I just said that because I figure they have the line tapped. You know these Feds." Franco's spirit lightened as he made the cynical observation.

"But it's not a Federal indictment if the DA is handling it." Jeff was somewhat confused.

"Oh, there's this Martinet guy – hey dickhead I hope you can hear me. Testing, testing." Franco was speaking to some unseen eavesdropper. " He's been after me for the crooked things some guys did when I was on a task force years ago. He doesn't have anything because I did nothing wrong then either."

It was the kind of vendetta that Jeff might expect of the FBI. They did good work much of the time but frequently sought indictments using unfair means. He told Franco of this conclusion and asked if they could perhaps continue the conversation after some sleep. That was agreeable to Franco, considering his doubts about the security of his phone line. They arranged to meet at a coffee shop just north of downtown around ten o'clock the next morning.

When Jeff Shackleford hung up the phone, he sat for some time on the edge of the bed. With his face buried in his palms, he murmured softly to himself. "Oh, God, this isn't fair. It just isn't fair for either of us."

The frown that formed between the beautiful eyes of Jessica was uncharacteristic. She peered through the darkness, trying to determine her husband's frame of mind. "What do you mean by either of you?"

He was unaware that his conversation with Franco had kept Jessica awake. There was a heavy burden on his shoulders from his colleague's ordeal, but circumstances of the lawsuit were also devastating in their own right. "I wasn't going to trouble you with this until morning, but since you heard me say that, we may as well talk now."

Jeff recounted the sorrowful discovery that the freeway victim's family was suing him. He did not have to tell her that it hurt so much more because of his fifteen years of dedication to the job. The few years they had been together were sufficient for her to know him well enough. There was anguish in his voice and in his eyes as he shared the crisis with her.

"Although it seems vindictive, I'm sure they don't wish you any harm." Jessica tried her best to console the troubled detective.

"I don't know about that. It has to be tough to lose a loved one, and they have to punish someone. The driver of the Mustang will probably never be found and I'm an easy target for their outrage." As Jeff shook his head slowly, his wife slid closer to his side. She wrapped both arms around him from behind and rested her left cheek on his shoulder. As Jessica whispered her most heartfelt love for him, the tears fell slowly but steadily in an unashamed demonstration of his own feelings.

"Jeff, I know that what you do is always for the right reasons. There is no way you would deliberately hurt anyone. Whatever you do, I'll always believe in you; I'll always love you."

"No matter what I do?"

"One hundred percent. That's how much of me is behind you."

"Jessica, I hope nothing I ever do will change that."

As she put her lips closer to his ear, she purred once again, content that her man was attuned to her feelings. The warmth of her breath melted him, almost dismissing his fear that he was headed on a course that she would not approve.

CHAPTER THIRTEEN

Nick's Café was very much a throwback to the old style diner, with a counter surrounding the waitress on three sides. It was not pretty, it was not even very comfortable. However, if you were hungry for good food, it was a place to bring a healthy appetite. Sitting just north of Chinatown, it nestled among the factories and warehouses that shared the area with the railroad. From five in the morning business was brisk until around nine. After that it could be sporadic, depending on the whims of distant office workers and the inevitable share of cops, mostly in business suits or plain clothes. Huge slices of tasty ham were dished up constantly. This was more than a meal to many but it came with eggs, hash browns and toast too. A plentiful serving of welcoming cheer made Nick's a genuinely pleasant culinary retreat.

Because he now had no work schedule to adhere to, Franco arrived twenty-five minutes early and was on his third cup of coffee when Jeff walked in, carrying his briefcase. Their handshake was firm and warm as if they were long lost friends who had not met for some considerable time. Franco was clearly pleased to have Jeff's company and was openly grateful that he had agreed to the meeting.

"I'm famished. I worked late last night and only grabbed a snack around seven." Jeff scanned the simple but ample menu.

"This is the right place then. I worked my share of Central Division and came here for breakfast most days. You'll never leave here hungry." Franco recalled the day watch hours of years ago.

Although there were so many people crowding into the downtown area for work, there was always plenty of time for patrol officers to fill up with a good breakfast.

"I only came here once or twice but I remember it having a good rep." Their respective memories would not be disappointed by the current fare.

As they ate heartily, there was reminiscing back to the days in the academy. There were times when both of them had thought it was too tough, and quitting seemed the easiest route. Somehow, the prospect of serving as one of L.A.'s finest proved such a compelling influence, they stuck it out.

"Any regrets?" Franco inquired tentatively.

"Tough to answer that, Franco. If you asked *would I do it again?* I guess the response would be.....probably."

"Yeah. I reckon my answer has changed over the last few weeks." Franco was getting his response from the last drops of coffee as he stared into his cup. "There were times as a kid that I would dream of being a good cop. You know, doing all the things that people admire you for. All of a sudden, I'm out of the academy and finding out that there's a lot of folks that don't have the respect for us that I anticipated. But I worked hard and think I made a decent cop for most of our fifteen years."

"What I know about you, it's been a full fifteen years of being a good cop." Jeff Shackleford was sincere in his praise.

"Well how come they want my hide so badly? This damn federal investigation that can't go anywhere unless they fabricate some shit about me. And now IA wants to drag my ass through the courts when all I did was defend myself." Franco's voice carried across the diner, causing a small group of DWP workers to stop their own conversation.

Jeff was slightly embarrassed by the attention they were receiving, but Franco was oblivious to the discomfort he was bringing to the other customers and his friend. When Jeff suggested being more discreet, Franco responded positively and simulated a secret discussion. He continued with a quieter diatribe, denouncing the city council, police commission, internal affairs and the FBI.

At the conclusion of the tirade of condemnation, Jeff interjected with his depressing revelation and the possibility of losing all he had worked for. Franco was empathetic and their mutual tribulations brought them closer together. Eventually the depressing nature of the dialogue halted them both. The two of them now stared into their coffee and remained hushed for a while. It was Jeff Shackleford that finally broke the uncommon silence with a probing question.

"This bullshit isn't why we're meeting, is it?"

"I guess not. It's just difficult to ignore what has been going on." Franco almost came to the point himself but still steered away from the subject.

"Franco, we both know that what has happened is unfair, but we can't do a thing to change what others are doing to us."

"So what's the bottom line, Jeff? Where do we go from here?"

Jeff Shackleford cleared the counter space and carefully placed his briefcase in front of him. With a thumb on each of the catches he looked Franco square in the eyes, searching for some sign of affirmation. He needed a solemn declaration from his classmate that they were on the same wavelength.

"Go ahead, Jeff, you know I'm committed. I just don't know what it is I'm committed to yet."

When Jeff popped open the lid, he reached inside furtively and handed Franco the bundle of documents he had worked on so diligently. Nothing was said for nearly twenty minutes, while Franco studied every item of information that had been prepared neatly the previous day. After he was satisfied he understood the case package, he nodded his head slowly, still thinking of the implications. "A thousand pounds of cocaine and around twelve million in cash." He nodded some more. Then he tilted his head to the side and frowned. "At fifteen thousand a kilo that seems a little out of balance."

"A lot out of balance. They fly the dope in once a week but they only take the cash out every other week."

Franco started with the knowing nod once again. "That's more like it."

He was treating it too casually for Shackleford's liking and he was not sure the gravity of it had sunk in.

“”Franco, although it’s not written down, do you realize what we are considering here?”

A sinister smile grew on Franco’s face as he responded. “Yeah, I figure we are going to rip off this drug cartel and end up with as much as twelve million dollars in US currency.”

“Maybe end up dead. Probably end up wanted felons.” It was as simple and as serious as that to Jeff.

“I take it you have thought out a game plan.” Franco was anxious to learn more about what Shackleford had not written down.

Jeff had indeed thought out what he anticipated would be a great game plan of attack. Most of this was formulated in his head while driving downtown to meet Franco. It incorporated the use of three vehicles, special weapons, hotel accommodations and the addition of a third team member.

“Someone else!?” Franco was not so keen on the idea.

“Necessary, I’m afraid. And it has to be Driscoll.”

”Driscoll!” Franco’s voice squeaked as it raised an octave.

Jeff explained that he was a logical choice for several reasons. At least one more was needed, to help persuade the four crooks they expected to encounter to turn over the money. Driscoll had access to superior firepower and they had already discussed a possible operation with him at the reunion.

“He was drunk at the time. I doubt he would remember that.”

“Don’t be so sure, Franco. We were all drunk and you remember the crazy talk we had. I think we need him, anyway.”

It was easy to agree on the Driscoll issue, but how to get him in on the deal was a problem they discussed at length. Jeff finally stated that he had to check in with his supervisor to find out the status of his squad. He would also obtain Driscoll’s home number.

While Jeff used the payphone outside to make his calls, Franco combed the paperwork for any points that his cohort in crime might not have covered. The waitress was getting a little unfriendly, not knowing if the two customers were about to skip without paying. So he ordered a couple of pieces of pie and more coffee. This seemed to appease her, temporarily at least.

Jeff returned with an abundance of results. He made contact with his boss via the cellular phone in Montoya’s car. The squad was once again sitting on the same suspect's house, without any movement to that point. They agreed that Jeff could continue working on the case he started the previous day.

"What if he wants to see the results some time soon?" It was a reasonable concern by Franco.

Shackleford planned to tell Montoya that the case was already being worked by the DEA, if it came to that. Getting Driscoll's number proved much easier than getting the cop himself to meet them both. However, after much persuasion and little discussion about the reason for the meet, Kirk Driscoll gave an estimate of two hours to the diner.

"Shit. That means maybe another two or three hours at this place. She ain't gonna be happy with that." Franco pointed a thumb at the waitress as Jeff attacked his slice of peach pie.

With his mouth full, he suggested to Franco that they make themselves scarce until one o'clock. Jeff would attempt to hook up with Cornejo while Franco intended to have a light workout at the academy weight room, just a mile away.

Upon their almost simultaneous return, they found Kirk Driscoll in an all to familiar pose. His Ford LTD was parked in the lot and Driscoll was parked in the driver's seat, sound asleep.

"I swear he must spend half his life getting drunk and the other half recovering from the booze." Franco Perez spoke loudly as he stood next to the open window, hoping it would waken the occupant.

"It's gonna take more than that." Shackleford had a sure fire way of solving the problem. He reached into the car and sounded the horn for a couple of seconds.

Perspiration was already trickling down his cheeks from the heat and smoggy weather. The deafening din from his horn all but made Driscoll jump out of his skin. His pulse rate was doubled and no machine could measure his blood pressure.

"What the fuck?" Everything was hilarious except that Driscoll had fallen asleep with his right hand under his thigh, gripping his 9mm. When the weapon appeared and leveled off at the two assailants, things were less funny.

Driscoll's eyes focused, slowly and unwillingly. "You two schmucks would be dead now if you'd been robbing my ass."

Jeff's composure returned first. "If we'd been robbing your ass, we would have shot you first and you'd have woken up dead."

"With friends like you, who needs enemies?" Driscoll stuck the weapon in his waistband and pulled part of the shirt out to hide it. When he stepped from the car, Franco was reminded what a slob this cop was. The third member of the trio marched directly inside Nick's and perched on one of the precarious barstools. He needed no menu, only service. As the waitress watched the other two sit either side of Driscoll, she gave them a look that said, "you've been here long enough for one day."

Nevertheless, she asked them what they wanted. Coffee was all they needed. The peach pie was still sitting heavy with both of them. Driscoll asked for a double hamburger with all the fixings.

"We're about to close." She responded, more brusquely than she had for many weeks.

"What time do you close?" Franco saw no times on the door or window.

Looking him right in the eye, she sneered, "When there's no customers left."

Jeff and Franco glanced at each other and back to the waitress.

"Then I guess we'll both have the same as him." Jeff figured this would keep the place open long enough.

Without another word she wrote the checks and gave the orders to the cook. In fact, she did not say another word to the threesome. This was not the atmosphere that brought customers in by the droves.

"So, this better be good. Oh, and I expect you guys to be buying my lunch." Driscoll dried off by wiping his face with half a dozen napkins.

The original two conspirators again faced off and Franco was the first to suggest a course of action. "It sounds better coming from you. Besides, he'll probably listen to you more than he will to me."

"Damn right! So let's get down to business, Jeffy baby."

In an unhurried and logical manner, Jeff laid out the entire plan as it existed so far. From the meeting with Cornejo the previous day, to the best estimate of the cash they might expect to see, he divulged every detail except the location of the border crossing.

Driscoll stared pokerfaced, digesting the whole account, waiting until Jeff had obviously finished. There was a moments pause before he reacted to the proposal.

"Did this Mexican put you up to this?" He nodded towards Franco, who was quicker to respond himself.

"Hey, why do you say that, fat boy?" Strangely enough, Franco Perez was hurt by this suggestion.

"Only 'cause of the call I got from you on Saturday. Remember when you begged me to join you in some such hair-brained scheme as this?"

"Listen, Driscoll, I would never beg you for anything, even to save my life."

"Children, children, let's not fight among ourselves. To succeed with what we are thinking of doing will take a team effort." Jeff tried to maintain what little adhesive they had to keep them together.

Driscoll concluded the temporary conflict. "This whole affair sounds absolutely crazy….." The other two unwittingly held their breath as the street cop paused. "But don't let it be said that Kirk Driscoll turned down such a crazy offer. You guys got yourselves an artilleryman." He held out an upturned palm to each of them and both responded by giving him five. All three laughed, more from relief than humor, until Driscoll became solemn once more. "Is this business down south of San Diego somewhere?" He inquired over the one piece of the puzzle that was missing.

"Nogales." Jeff said plainly.

"Nogales. Where the fuck is Nogales?" Driscoll's timing could not have been worse. His profanity shocked the waitress as she was about to deliver the food. He was lucky not to be wearing his burger as she tossed his plate down in front of him. Skillful use of the hands stopped it from sliding onto his lap.

"Sorry, dear. These guys got me all excited. Please accept my apologies." He was sincere but wondered if that would have been the case if he had not caught his plate in time. There was no visible calming effect, as she also slammed the other two meals on the counter. French fries flew in different directions and they knew better than to ask for drink refills.

While Driscoll inhaled his own food and most of the other two portions of fries, Shackleford elaborated on some of the finer details of the operation, including the fact that Nogales was due south of Tucson at the Arizona border. He had managed to reach Cornejo by phone during their midday recess, learning some valuable information. The next day was to see a load of cocaine incoming, but the next exportation of cash was a week away.

With Franco's mandatory attendance at the DA's office the next morning, they agreed to gather again in twenty-four hours. Nick's diner would most likely be closing at that time, so they picked a restaurant in nearby Glendale. It was a unanimous opinion that they should continue their conspiracy while outside the City of Los Angeles.

Accordingly, the rebellion was under way.

CHAPTER FOURTEEN

"Three rental vehicles! Shit, why so many? And what the hell we gonna do with the car we drive there, anyway?" Driscoll could not fathom the reasoning behind this requirement.

Jeff calmed him down and explained his logic. "I can't quite figure how much space we'll need for all the cash. It depends on the ratio of smaller bills to twenties and hundreds." He scribbled some quick calculations on the notepad he was using for the game plan.

After the street cop had waited long enough, he had to speak again. "So, Einstein, what does the math say?"

"Tough to be sure, really. But I think if we all approach in a vehicle it might give the appearance of a greater presence of officers." Jeff Shackleford attempted to rationalize his conclusion.

"What happened to the old adage of divide and conquer?" It was a profound question for Driscoll. "We divide and they conquer. End of story."

Franco was merely an onlooker at this point. His appointment with the district attorney had been humiliating, to say the least. After being advised of his rights, they told him he was under arrest for the unlawful killing of Gregory Rowland. Did he have anything to say, they asked.

At first he thought the presence of the attorney, Loren Kaminsky, was purely symbolic. However, at this particular juncture Franco was about to say something he would have regretted forever. Kaminsky, realizing Franco's intention, took a firm hold of his arm and addressed the deputy district attorney. "You gave my client his rights and perhaps you assumed his silence was tantamount to waiving those rights. Well, I'm advising my client not to answer any questions until we have had time to discuss the matter." He was taking charge, alright. Maybe he was *as good as they come.*

The next stage was to transport Franco to Parker Center, Police Headquarters, and formally book him. This involved taking his fingerprints and photograph. He wondered to himself why they didn't use the prints they took when he joined the department. Obviously his appearance had changed in fifteen years, but he was sure his prints were still identical.

Before the trio had begun their deliberations over the trip to Arizona, Franco related the events of the morning to a somber audience.

"At least they kept their promise about an O.R." Driscoll alluded to the fact that Franco Perez was allowed to remain free on his own recognizance.

As the debate continued over the rentals, Jeff put his foot down firmly. "Since me and Franco are footing the bill, I think we should go with the three four-wheel drive vehicles."

"Don't forget I'm providing the weaponry." Driscoll defended his status. "Actually, as you both know, I pay so much in alimony, that's probably more than I can afford to contribute." He was now genuinely hurt by the comments of Shackleford.

"Hey, Kirk, don't feel bad. I didn't mean to put you down or anything." Jeff felt a sincere affinity for the fat guy and the mutual risk he was undertaking.

Franco and Jeff had consented to relieve Driscoll of a heavy financial burden. They would fund the operation completely, with the patrol cop supplying some very sophisticated firearms.

As if awakened from a deep sleep, Franco suddenly interjected with a comment. "I was wondering what changed your mind about doing something illegal."

"I take it that's a question I have to answer." Driscoll was blunt but not indignant. "Well, I don't see it as illegal. I figure we're more like modern day Robin Hoods. We take from the bad guys and give to the poor; that's us."

Franco Perez looked dubious, as he examined Driscoll's motives from across the booth in the moderately priced restaurant. It was as if he was actually suspicious of the man's involvement.

"I can see I might as well put my cards on the table. Since you both have told your tales of woe, here's mine." Driscoll went on to describe the events of the Monday afternoon roll call and the subsequent *one-twenty-eight.* This number derived from the form used for a personnel complaint against an officer.

"So, let me get this straight." Franco wanted it clear in his own mind. "Just because you used the word bitch, this female officer has a legitimate complaint?"

"I never said it was legitimate. Only that the department brass is so spineless, it has to cower whenever some civil libertarian says jump. Besides, I think I used the word three times…..in a row."

"In other words, you're going to get shafted by the department and this broad." Franco felt Driscoll's frustration. "Funny isn't it? Women want to be treated equal when it comes to the job. Then when the language they hear offends their delicate sensitivities, they want to be treated sooooo differently. Go figure."

In the silence that followed, it was as if a final bonding took place. Franco felt empathy for Driscoll and his situation, in spite of the overwhelming problems in his own life. As Jeff tried hard to concentrate on the game plan, he saw the cloud of injustice hanging over each of them. In light of what faced them in California, the business in Arizona seemed more like an exciting adventure.

"I reckon we should travel on Sunday and be in the area a couple of days ahead of time. Gives us room to do some final preparations. Plus, if they bring the stuff in a day early, we're ready." Jeff gave them both food for thought with this time frame.

"No problem for me. I got a bunch of overtime to take off. And nobody will miss my butt while I'm gone." This was obviously Driscoll's summation of his state of affairs.

"I'm not working anyway. So my only obstacle is convincing Teresa I have to go away for a few days." Franco saw the break as a positive event for him, given the pressure around him. "She'll say it's best if she's with me, but I'll convince her I have to be alone with my thoughts; for a while at least."

"What about you, Jeffy baby?"

Jeff would take vacation days and had decided to almost tell Jessica the truth. He would say it was a big case in Arizona, with several days of surveillance. A big case that could make his career. Or end it! Or even end his life! *'Whatever you do, I'll always believe in you.'*

He dismissed the shaft of guilt that attempted to penetrate his heart and went on with the plans. "I'll drive to Van Nuys and leave my car at your place." He was talking to Driscoll. "Do you have a carport at your apartment?"

"That's about all I got. One bed, one bath, one kitchen and a carport."

"Fine. Then we take your car out on the Pomona Freeway to Diamond Bar. Franco, you have to let us know where to pick you up. Somewhere your car won't seem suspicious being left for a few days."

"I'll think of a place."

Jeff went on. "The Sixty east to the Ten, and the interstate all the way to Tucson. Take us maybe seven or eight hours, unless we push the speed. Since we'll have some heavy duty guns on board, I'd rather we didn't attract the Chippies."

"If the Highway Patrol are the Chippies in California, what the hell do we call them in Arizona?" Driscoll wondered out loud.

"How about, sir." Jeff almost made them laugh, but things were headed in a serious direction. "About twenty miles south of Tucson there's a place called Green Valley. It's still forty miles or so from Nogales, but I like that distance. A kind of comfort zone. Anyway, we stay at the only hotel I can find listed. It's a Best Western and rated pretty good by the Auto Club."

"How many rooms?" Franco contemplated the cost.

"Three to a room would be a little cramped. It's not their high season right now, so I think we should get one each." More calculations on Jeff's pad.

There would be a multitude of other details to consider when they got to Green Valley. Jeff was to instruct Cornejo to be in Nogales by Sunday evening, and expect to be contacted at the phone number he gave for Juan's residence. It was to appear as if the operation was an official police incursion.

"We all have a list of necessities. Driscoll, just be sure to have the weapons in your trunk, ready to go."

"Roger. I'll also have enough ammo for a small war."

"Let's hope we don't need it."

CHAPTER FIFTEEN

Franco should never have mentioned to Teresa that he intended going away somewhere on his own. It should have appeared an impulsive move on his part. Instead of a relatively simple but tearful farewell, she pestered him for three solid days. It was an unwanted, additional burden on his already overtaxed mind and body. To her credit, she kept the persistent badgering out of the view of the boys. Anthony and Daniel were told only on Sunday morning that their father had some soul-searching to take care of; that he would be back in a couple of days, and things should be better then.

It was made all the worse following a phone call on Thursday evening. Teresa answered the phone, as she had since the shooting took place. With so many official calls making Franco's time at home downright miserable, she felt it only fair that she should run interference on his behalf.

"Hi. Is Franco there?" A sweet voice indeed, thought Teresa.

"Who is this?"

"Detective Kaplan. I work with Franco in narcotics. I hope this isn't a bad time."

Teresa figured the call was harmless enough, but she sure sounded a little too cute for a detective. "Just a minute, I'll get him."

When Franco took the call, he displayed perhaps more delight than his wife thought appropriate. "Hey, Nina, how ya doing? I'm really glad you called. I miss all you guys."

At least he said guys. Teresa listened to one end of the conversation, feeling guilty for doing so. It was an exchange she knew she would deny hearing, but wanted so badly to question Franco about.

"I hope it isn't a problem, me calling you at home."

"Not at all. It's good to hear from you. With me off work right now, you can call any time you want." Franco expected the next few days to drive him insane, waiting for the big adventure.

"I got the news today. About you being charged by the DA. That's bull, and we both know it." Nina so desperately wanted to encourage Franco to keep his chin up. Unfortunately, her understandable anger erupted.

"Don't worry about it. They're trying to railroad me. You're all I need to see me through this, Nina."

Franco alluded to her witnessing the two gunshots. However, from Teresa's point of view, it sounded somewhat more sinister.

Numerous other comments were also taken out of context by Teresa Perez as the dialogue continued. Since Franco never told this Kaplan girl about being out of town for a while, she concluded that Kaplan was probably aware of that fact. A sobering thought, given the pressures her husband was experiencing lately.

"Okay. See you soon, I hope." These were Franco's closing words before hanging up the receiver. Of course, he used the collective *you.*

"Known her long?" This was all Teresa could manage after several minutes of deliberation, following what she had overheard.

It had been an innocent discussion as far as Franco was concerned. His response was equally ingenuous. "Just a few months. She's turning out to be a good dope cop."

"Pretty, too?"

"What kind of question is that?" Franco's defense mechanism kicked into gear as he suspected an ulterior motive behind his wife's cross-examination.

"It doesn't matter. Forget I even mentioned it." But to Teresa it did matter, and she could not forget it.

It was a routine case. That is what Jessica Shackleford was told by her husband. A lengthy surveillance was required to outsmart this particular organization and it would all be in Arizona. He had been away from home periodically, but never for more than forty-eight hours. Jeff expected to be home by Friday, at the latest.

"I'll call you every evening, so there's no need to bother them at the office. If it's an emergency, they won't be able to get a hold of me until we check in at the end of the day. So be patient and don't worry. This is as safe as any other case I've worked."

Jessica heeded his words and believed most of them. However, there was always the ultimate takedown, when even major drug peddlers had to be arrested. Few, if any, were ever unarmed. Dutifully, she wished him well. It was seven o'clock, on a beautifully clear September morning. Not a cloud was in sight and it promised to be a warm and only slightly smoggy day. She kissed him passionately, reluctant to set him free from her enveloping arms.

"Remember, I'll call you, so don't fret." Jeff Shackleford loathed deceiving his wife, and hoped he had not overdone the business of preventing her from calling the office.

"Jeff, be careful, honey. I love you."

"Love you too." He held her squarely by the shoulders and gazed into her soft, azure eyes that put the sky to shame. "I'll miss you, Jessica."

He was gone, quickly and without turning back. His feelings came close to changing his mind, but he knew he must see the conspiracy to fruition.

Long before eight, he was on Sylmar Avenue not far from the Van Nuys division police station. He rang Driscoll's doorbell and almost jumped out of his skin when the door flew open instantly.

"Been waiting for you, Jeffy baby. Couldn't sleep a wink, just thinking about the caper. 'Course, I didn't touch a drop either. That's really why I didn't sleep." Driscoll was excited, to say the least, talking a mile a minute.

"Got everything?"

"You betcha! Had the car loaded yesterday morning. Even went to work with all my shit packed in the trunk. Amazing, huh?"

"You said it, buddy. Let's get my car in your space and hit the road."

Before long they were headed east on the Ventura Freeway, then south on the 101, through the heart of downtown Los Angeles. Conversation was a one-way road at first, with Driscoll's nervous energy sending him in various directions. He prattled on about ex-wives and the burden of alimony, and then how thankful he was to have no kids. Jeff listened politely but little of his companion's monologue registered with the gray matter.

After covering almost thirty miles of the Pomona Freeway, they took the Brea Canyon off-ramp to meet up with Franco. He told them he would be in the lot on the southwest corner, right ahead of them as they left the freeway. It had a supermarket that was open twenty-four hours and the rationale was that his car would not seem suspicious, even left for several days.

Franco was anxiously waiting with suitcase in hand, standing at the entrance he calculated they would use. The trunk of the Ford was now full with equipment and belongings of the other two, but Franco did not even consider putting his case there. He simply slid into the spacious back seat, nodding a silent acknowledgment to the front seat occupants.

Silence ruled for an hour before anyone spoke. The Pomona Freeway had given way to the Moreno Valley Freeway. Driscoll was now steering his heavy tank through its final winding stages before it meets Interstate 10.

"If someone don't speak soon, I'm gonna drive this wagon right off the road; just so you guys have something to discuss."

Franco burst out laughing. "You crazy son of a bitch! I'm glad you're along."

The ice was undoubtedly broken. Jeff turned around and high-fived with Franco, smiling himself for the first time.

"Why don't we go over a few ground rules while we're in such good humor." Jeff was not asking the others for their approval. They had come to accept his experience as a shining light for them to follow.

He proceeded to tell them about the meetings they might expect with Cornejo Ramos. To continue the pretense of an official police investigation, he would meet Cornejo and cousin Juan with Franco present. It was customary for all rendezvous with informants in the field to have two detectives attend. There would be nothing unusual if they were to see Driscoll covering the meeting from close by. Franco should not be surprised if Jeff tentatively agreed to a large sum of money for the information. He would tell them it was subject to approval and it would be paid as soon after the caper as possible. His intentions were to give Cornejo and his cousin some cash from the seizure. Having them both sign department vouchers for the money would eliminate the chance of them contacting someone else from narcotics.

"You got this whole thing figured out, huh?" Driscoll complimented Jeff.

"There's a whole lot of unknown factors to compute into the equation yet. I have to speak with this Juan character before I know it will all work out."

"You mean this might all be for naught?" Driscoll was negotiating the merging of the freeways and decided to contest the right to a particular lane with a truck. His concentration was broken by the thought that some wetback could decide their fate. The truck won the battle, but the Ford remained unscathed.

"Let's look on the bright side." Jeff released his death grip on the edge of his seat as Driscoll eased in behind the eighteen-wheeler. "Both of these guys want cash more desperately than we do. So they are going to do what it takes to make it work."

There was more contemplation for a few minutes until Driscoll pushed in a cassette. Predictably, they were bombarded with Country and Western music.

"How long you say it'll take to get there, Jeff?" Franco was covering his ears and screwing up his eyes.

"I know just what you're thinking." Jeff was on the same wavelength. "Driscoll, this is a democracy, and we vote two to one for a radio station of our choice."

"Man, you guys wouldn't know good music if it jumped up and bit you."

Jeff's response to Driscoll was no surprise. "You're tape just jumped up and bit us. Now we're going to put it out of its misery; ours too." The cassette was unceremoniously popped out, tossed back to Franco, then flipped onto the rear window shelf.

Driscoll protested, "That's not fair, guys."

"Keep your eyes on the road, and be thankful it didn't get eighty-sixed completely." Franco playfully ruffled the driver's thinning hair.

Jeff played with the tuning knob and found a station that identified itself as K-DES, 104.7. The music was golden oldies and soon all three of them were singing along to recordings they each claimed were "before their time."

When they were too far past the Palm Springs area to receive the station, Jeff took over the driving and Driscoll immediately began snoring as his face pressed against the window.

"I'm glad we have separate rooms. I couldn't stand this racket." Franco knew he would not sleep on the trip, and would be quite capable of taking the final phase of driving.

When they reached Blythe, near the California border, Jeff pulled off for a pit stop and gassed up the car. Franco and Jeff visited the restroom but Driscoll never woke up.

"Should we wake the baby?" Franco was tempted, but Jeff informed him that the big guy had not slept the previous night. They agreed to let him be. A few miles down the road they crossed into Arizona and Driscoll came alive.

"Man, I gotta pee! Where the hell are we?"

"Just another hundred and fifty to Phoenix." Jeff informed him hopefully.

"Can't wait that long. There will be a serious accident right here in the back seat. Gotta stop soon, Jeffy baby."

Jeff Shackleford relented and pulled the car off the freeway in the middle of nowhere. Quartzsite, to be precise.

Franco offered to take the wheel but Jeff suggested they switch when they got to Phoenix. That was the next stop and it was three o'clock by then. Later than Jeff had expected but not too soon for them all to eat.

Driscoll was rightly astounded by the appetites of his compadres. He struggled to keep pace with their gorging, worrying when they even eyed what he had left on his plate, not realizing they were fooling with him.

Between Phoenix and Tucson all they found was a radio station that played hits from the forties and fifties. Not once did any of them guess the artist or title. This convinced them that the whole area must be inhabited by very old folk.

For the first time in hundreds of miles, they made a transition from Interstate 10, as it continued east through Tucson. They were now southbound on I19, about seventy miles from Mexico. Franco pointed out the striking vision of the San Xavier Mission on their right, just outside the city limits. The poignant beauty of the well-preserved structure profoundly moved him. If he had been alone, the Ford would be off the freeway and headed for the solace he believed it would present him.

"Hey, Franco, this is the turnoff. You dreamin' or what?" Driscoll shouted out loud as he critically scolded the driver.

For twenty miles, Franco had indeed been daydreaming. He pictured himself inside the mission praying for the soul of Gregory Rowland and forgiving the cruel wretches who sought to wreak havoc on his own life. They were doing a fine job of it!

With seconds to spare, Franco negotiated the Ford off the freeway and onto Esperanza Boulevard. One more southbound turn at the signal and they were at the Best Western Hotel.

"Looks like a place I could retire to." Jeff admired the cleanliness and charm of Green Valley, Arizona.

CHAPTER SIXTEEN

"Fifty-five bucks a night each! And we're in the middle of nowhere. Sounds a little steep to me." Driscoll complained bitterly and he was not even footing the bill.

"That's a discount rate and it's actually quite reasonable. Besides, the best I can figure, there's just a couple of places in town to stay." Jeff appealed the case for the Best Western Hotel.

Franco had just unlocked his room and pushed the door open. "Looks real nice to me. Driscoll, you're probably used to paying for your motel rooms by the hour."

"Very funny.....but actually pretty close to the truth." Driscoll went along with the crude remark that alluded to his superficial love life.

Before they all entered their rooms, Jeff suggested an arrangement for the evening. "Let's get unpacked and clean up. I have to make a couple of calls. Then we could maybe go check with the front desk for a decent place to get dinner."

"If there's only a couple of hotels, perhaps there's only a McDonald's for food." It was supposed to be a derogatory remark from Driscoll, but in actuality he hardly cared where he obtained his sustenance.

"Let's hope there's more. Anyway, how does seven-thirty sound, in the lobby?" Jeff fixed the time and they all retired to the very comfortable rooms that would be their home for the next few days and nights.

Following his shower, Jeff called Jessica, as promised, and spoke the soothing words she had waited for all day. Next, he made contact with Cornejo who had made it to Nogales in record time. All was well with him and cousin Juan. Both were anxious to meet the cops and talk business. Jeff advised his extraordinary informant that a meet would take place the following afternoon. It would be at a place and time to be communicated to Cornejo as soon as Jeff found an appropriate location. He could have simply asked the snitch to name it, but the more tactically sound method was to control everything about the encounter himself. Any deviation from the routine handling of an informant might give rise to suspicion that the department was not involved. After he verified that cousin Juan would be available, Jeff gave a few words of encouragement to Cornejo, showing his anticipation for a positive outcome.

In the lobby, Franco and Driscoll were already waiting for Jeff. They had spoken to the clerk at the reception desk and discovered that Green Valley was resplendent with fine eating establishments. However, they were also informed that it was a little late to be going out to eat at this time on a Sunday. When Driscoll asked what was considered a suitable hour to be eating dinner, the clerk answered in a manner that explained everything. “You have to realize that Green Valley is a retirement community. The average age is probably around seventy.”

“That explains the music on the radio.” The pieces of the puzzle fell into place for the hungry cop.

It was suggested that they try a Mexican restaurant just around the corner. “It has a bar and might be open later than most places.” The clerk tried hard to sound optimistic but failed to instill Franco and Driscoll with confidence.

“We’ve got nothing to lose. Let’s try that place, then.” Jeff agreed with the inevitable majority ruling.

They walked the short distance along La Canada Drive before turning onto Esperanza again, heading back toward the freeway. A late summer breeze warmed their faces as they sought out the Mexican bar in the distance. They joked about being carefree in spite of what was haunting each of them back home; in spite of the outrageous proposition that had brought them so far from Los Angeles.

It sounded like juke box music, filtering out of the doorway. With the sun gone, there was a comforting orange glow from the porch area of the restaurant. The Pied Piper himself could not have woven a stronger spell to lure these three visitors inside. With not more than five strides to go before wallowing in the welcoming atmosphere, a loud bang startled them. It was close behind them and so much like gunfire it caused them to react instinctively. Each of them ducked and searched for cover until Franco eased their concern. "Damn! It's only a backfire."

Driscoll cursed profusely, castigating even Chevrolet, for that was the make of vehicle that passed them, headed east. An old and dilapidated Chevy Caprice, whose brakes squealed as the driver slowed enough to turn into a gas station equipped with a mini-mart. The place was no more than a hundred yards away and typically well illuminated. As if the job and all of the outside influences were not enough stress-causing events, they certainly did not need such a shock at this point in their lives.

The clunker did not pull in at the pumps. Instead, it lurched to a stop directly in front of the store. When the driver slipped out of the car, three hearts simultaneously skipped a beat. He carried a weapon in his right hand and from their position each thought it looked like a revolver.

There was no question in their minds about his intentions and Franco spoke for the trio. "Two-eleven in progress, guys." He made reference to the California penal code section, two-eleven, that defined robbery.

"Maybe it's not two-eleven in Arizona." Driscoll's caustic wit brought a look of incredulity to the faces of Franco and Jeff. He continued, as if explanation was necessary. "You know, perhaps it's another number, or something."

"Perhaps that's how you order a six pack and bag of chips, with a gun!" Sarcasm shot to the surface as Franco responded.

"Gentlemen, we gonna do something here, or just joke around all night?" Jeff put matters in perspective.

"Let's go get him, boys." Driscoll pulled a two-inch Smith and Wesson from his pants pocket and asked, "Anyone got a real gun? All I have is this peashooter."

Franco lifted up his loose fitting shirt and displayed an identical firearm. "Same here." They both looked to Jeff Shackleford with anticipation.

"I got my nine mil, but Franco, you're not supposed to be carrying." Jeff's concern was for having the authorities discover that Franco was currently on suspension.

"How much worse can things get for me?" Franco was resigned to his fateful status back in Los Angeles. "Besides, we gonna let this punk do the dirty deed right under our noses?"

"He's got a point, Jeffy baby. You could say it's a great chance for some training before the big caper."

"I have a feeling I'll regret this." Jeff immediately led the way to the gas station, where they set up at the corner of the storefront window.

There were two females face down on the floor inside, and the crook was at the cash register removing its contents. The clerk was also face down but out of their view, behind the counter. As Driscoll watched the action, Jeff gave directions to Franco and sent him quickly on his way.

Only one additional car was in the station and they concluded it must belong to the two female customers. Jeff took up a position utilizing this second vehicle as cover. Judging by his frail frame and extremely nervous mannerisms, Driscoll assumed the thief to be a basehead: a smoker of rock cocaine. He wondered how many hits from the pipe the crook hoped to achieve through this serious crime. As the miscreant made his way around the counter, he fired one round into the ceiling, probably to impress the store clerk and customers as to the danger they were in.

It most certainly impressed the three California cops, particularly Franco who was unable to see the events from his position. Driscoll took aim at the door with his trusty two-inch revolver from his corner spot, a mere thirty feet away. In reality, he had as much chance of hitting the robber if he closed his eyes.

Franco's temples were pounding as he anticipated his course of action. Jeff worried about the task he had set for his partner, but realized it was too late to change the plan. The shabbily dressed suspect pushed open the glass door by backing through it, and shouted some obscenities to the occupants for good measure.

For an instant, Driscoll thought the crook was going to look in his direction. He squeezed ever so slightly on the trigger, then released this pressure as the driver's door opened and the chance to blind side him was gone.

Jeff had a good line of sight from behind the customer's car, and from fifteen feet figured he had an outstanding shot with his 9mm Beretta. However, he knew he had to wait. It seemed to take too long but then, finally, Jeff saw another person in the Chevy.

Benny Faxton was a loser. He had spent most of his adult life in prison and cared not one iota for other people or their possessions. Manslaughter, armed robbery, rape and various drug convictions; these were the fabric of Faxton's history.

He had stolen the Chevy in Tucson earlier that day and committed two other armed robberies, before heading south out of the city. The communities further south were even less populated and so posed less of a threat of capture; or so he thought.

Cold, hard steel pressed firmly into the back of Faxton's neck. "Don't move, asshole. A thirty-eight caliber round in the back of your neck might not kill you, but it sure will spoil your day." From Franco's position in the back seat, he literally had the drop on Benny Faxton. There was never a hint that Franco might actually shoot him. However, his mind was set to do the job if the crook went for his gun.

Jeff moved the moment he saw Franco. The driver's door flew open one more time and Jeff demanded to know where the weapon was. Faxton wisely kept his hands raised, where they had first moved when Franco admonished him.

While the two of them took care of their end of the business, Driscoll entered the mini-mart. Both customers were motionless but the clerk was peeking over the counter. When he saw Driscoll walk in, there was an obvious connection between the two men; both had guns in their hands.

Driscoll recognized the need for explanation without delay. "You just got robbed, but there's no cause for alarm. We have the….." His voice trailed off as he stared down the barrel of a twelve-gauge shotgun.

"Damn right there's no cause for alarm. Except for you buster." The clerk sought vengeance for the frightening actions of Benny Faxton.

"You got this all wrong, my friend. I'm one of the good guys."

Before Driscoll could continue, the clerk gave directions. "Shut the fuck up! Hey ladies, one of you call nine-one-one."

Both women remained frozen with fear.

"You forgot something." Driscoll wanted to gain the clerk's confidence. "I still have my gun and before you say anything else, I'm putting it on the floor." He did so.

"All that means is I ain't gonna be able to blow your brains out now."

Driscoll was relieved at this remark, but began to sweat profusely. "I'm a good guy. Why else would I come into your store after that other feller robbed you?"

It was a point that was being considered when Jeff walked in. He instantly summed up the situation and spoke before Driscoll could blow it. "You need help?" He asked the clerk

"Yep. Call nine-one-one, why don't you?" He obviously believed Jeff to be a customer.

When Jeff got behind the counter he simulated calling in the emergency then hung up. With total faith in Jeff, the clerk handed him the shotgun and told him to cover Driscoll while he could pick up the handgun. Naturally, long before the clerk could get to the weapon, Driscoll had it in his hand.

"Shoot the bastard!"

Both females screamed at this demand from the clerk. The thought that someone might be killed in front of them was terribly frightening.

"Look." Jeff unloaded the shotgun. "We're good guys. We caught the robber outside in his car. This guy is with me."

Jeff was convincing enough, especially when he handed over the shotgun and the single round of ammunition.

The clerk turned to Driscoll and demanded an explanation. "Why the Hell didn't you say you weren't with the robber?"

"Good question. Just give me some heavy duty tape, if you have any." The street cop was too frustrated and relieved to argue.

There was a roll of strapping tape handy and Driscoll took it to the crook's car where Franco still held him at gunpoint. After an excessive amount of tape was used, the culprit was firmly attached to his own steering wheel. Weapon and car keys sat prominently on the front passenger seat, unquestionably out of reach.

Jeff consoled the two women, who found him quite charming, and handed over the wad of currency from the heist to the clerk.

"One last thing. You might want to call the cops again. My call never got through."

With that, Jeff left and all three of them disappeared into the night. To the south, they found a maze of an open-air shopping mall where they hoped they would not be found.

"Gosh, just like the Lone Ranger." One of the women stated whimsically.

"Except that I think there were three of them, lady." The clerk brought her down to Earth as he made the emergency call.

A somewhat remote Chinese restaurant was still open for service at the furthest area of the mall from the gas station. Their hunger for action had heightened their hunger for food, and so they agreed to try it out.

When the waitress took their order, Jeff was first to comment on the escapade. "I'm not saying I regret what we did, but if I had the choice I don't think I'd do it again."

"Nearly made that asshole shit his pants." Franco was still on a high from his part in the affair.

"It wasn't no fun, looking at the business end of a shotgun." Predictably, Driscoll was unhappy and still visibly shaken.

"Might be lots of that when we get to Nogales." Franco gave them all food for thought, as they waited for their meals.

CHAPTER SEVENTEEN

With some reluctance, Jeff was persuaded by the others to rent only two vehicles. Even in Tucson they had difficulty finding the specific models to fit their needs: a Jeep Cherokee from one place and a Toyota 4-Runner from another. With this arrangement Driscoll was happy not to have to leave his own car in the city.

After the short trip south to Green Valley they dropped off the Ford, and Franco joined Jeff in the Toyota so they could discuss the impending meet. Driscoll followed in the Jeep as they headed towards the border. He found it confusing how they switched the freeway signs from miles to kilometers. At one stage he was convinced the distance to Mexico was further than it had been twenty minutes earlier.

They took the freeway to the very end, where it dumps out into downtown Nogales. The road splits and the right fork goes directly to the border crossing. They kept straight and at the corner of Sonoita Avenue they pulled into a Burger King, tucking themselves way in the back of the lot. It needed only a brief discussion before they settled on the fast food restaurant for both lunch and the subsequent conference with the informants. When they sat down inside with their food orders, Driscoll eyed many of the Hispanics who filled the place.

"Hell of a lot of Mexicans here. Glad I brought my own nine millimeter along today."

"Driscoll, this is directly across the road from the Mexican border. Who do you expect to see here?" Franco endeavored to defend his race. "Anyway, they're not like many of the Hispanics you have to deal with in Southwest division. These are primarily hard working people. They crowd around both sides of the border because of the *Maquiladores*."

"I'm sure if I asked, you would explain that term." Driscoll expected an explanation even if he did not ask.

Franco went to some length expounding on the cooperation between Arizona and Sonora that brought employment to vast numbers in the area. The program involved shipping parts into Mexico necessary for a finished product to be sold in the USA. Assembly would be completed by Mexican labor at their standard wage and the completed item was returned to the originator of the project. *Maquiladora* loosely translated as twin plant or border industrialization.

The success of these agreements was demonstrated by the number of plants, exceeding sixty-five, and the three hundred thousand or so people living in Nogales, Sonora.

"That explains the huge number of trucks we saw on I19." Jeff had wondered about those trucks.

"That's mildly interesting, Franco. But the bottom line is: there's far fewer assholes here that are likely to rip us off." Driscoll pulled no punches with his summation.

Franco laughed out loud, almost spitting some of his hamburger across the table, unable to speak.

"I say something funny? What?" Driscoll implored Jeff to divulge what knowledge he had on the subject. All Jeff could do was shrug his shoulders.

Franco took a long drink of coke, cleared his throat and clarified his amusement. "That's sweet, Driscoll. You're concerned about some two-bit crooks hanging around and here we are, preparing perhaps the largest heist in Arizona history."

It was Driscoll's turn to shrug in silent resignation, with a lopsided grin across his chubby cheeks.

"I'm done. While you two finish, I'll call Cornejo." Jeff took his tray to the nearby trash container and dumped the remarkable amount of waste associated with fast food.

There were payphones on the north wall of the building but Jeff had to hang around a few minutes before one was available. Cornejo was clearly waiting for the call, judging by the speed with which he answered the ringing. Even with such a friendly informant, Jeff made it his business to regulate every minute detail of the relationship. He verified how long it would take for the cousins to reach the Burger King and what type of vehicle they would be driving. They were also told exactly where to park in the lot. It was imperative they thought this was still a legitimate police operation.

"Fifteen minutes, guys." Jeff recounted the telephone conversation for his fellow officers. He rightly assumed that Juan's house was in Nogales itself, given the short estimate for arrival.

Franco was to position the Toyota away from the Jeep and sit in the back seat, somewhat hidden from view, until both informants were inside the building with Jeff. Driscoll could stay inside the restaurant several booths away, since he was to remain the unknown quantity. Both of the vehicles would, therefore, not be seen until perhaps a later time. Jeff stepped outside pretending to be waiting in line for the phone again, and Franco moved the 4-Runner to a position of advantage.

Right on cue, according to Jeff's watch, a large and very dilapidated, blue Chevy pickup truck rumbled into the lot with two occupants. As the diminutive driver steered the truck into the prescribed location, Jeff began to approach. He recognized the passenger, although he had never seen Cornejo wearing a cowboy hat before.

The salutations were friendly and cheerful as Cornejo and his cousin gathered around the passenger side, shaking Jeff's hand with fervor. The cousin was a slightly built man of forty years, barely five feet tall. He also wore a cowboy hat that seemed a couple of sizes too large. Since the few words of English that Cornejo knew were a few more than his cousin, the entire discussion was in Spanish.

Jeff steered them both into the Burger King and Franco quickly joined them surreptitiously, making sure he did not startle either of them when he sat at the same table. The less they knew about Franco, the better. So, he was introduced by his first name only.

Cornejo stated that his cousin felt better about telling who he was, now that they had all met in person.

Juan Villenuevos Maldonaldo set off immediately with infinite detail about the cartel's smuggling operation. His confidence in the cops was built partly on Cornejo's endorsement. Additionally, he was greatly impressed by the distance they had traveled to meet with him. He secretly wondered how many cops had been brought to see this through.

Jeff was amazed at the mental agility of Juan Maldonado who recited the particulars of the business from memory. He stopped only briefly to sip on the cup of coffee he picked up before they all sat. The other three each had a large soda, expecting the exchange to be lengthy.

There was a third associate who would never come into contact with the cops. Jeff suspected this silent partner was unaware of the law enforcement involvement. Juan stated that his connection worked at Davis Monthan Air Force Base, a little east of Tucson. His invaluable participation included passing on scheduling of flight plans for the Citation plane, used to detect aircraft crossing the international border. The duration of these regular flights was normally seven to eight hours.

It was Juan's job to take into consideration the weather in the area surrounding Nogales. This determined if the Aerostats, or tethered balloons, were up. They served a similar purpose as the planes, but from a static location; Fort Huachuca being the nearest. If wind conditions were bad then they would not be up.

Juan added that now they were into September, it was hurricane season off the west coast of Mexico. This provided a tail wind for the smugglers' plane and frequently caused the Aerostats to be grounded. Naturally, they got better distance on a flight with a full load when these winds from the southwest helped them. With stronger winds prevailing, senior members of the cartel tended to add dangerously to the shipment.

As the story unfolded, Driscoll sat nearby but unnoticed, without understanding a word. Inevitably he could not sit in a fast food establishment for long without ordering again. He was eager to begin some serious action and hopefully keep his calorie intake at a modest level.

Juan's narrative extended to the transportation that was utilized. A considerable amount of cash had been invested in a Piper Chieftain with extended fuel tanks. This gave them a flying time of five hours, or around a thousand miles. Flying out of Guadalajara with the cocaine meant they were generally pushing the limit, with a thousand pounds on board. The reckless pilots that were employed landed several flights in the US with only fumes remaining in the tanks. Juan was also responsible for bringing in a small refueling truck, providing just enough to get them south to Hermosillo and friendly faces.

A landing strip had been hacked out of the rough terrain just west of Nogales. It was barely suitable to put down any craft but they had found a mesa with sufficient flat space. The unladen plane could take off within fifteen hundred to two thousand feet. This was all that was available on the largest area they could locate.

When the shipment was ready in the heart of central Mexico, all of the calculations were taken into consideration and a time of departure was set. The factor most influential in this reckoning was always the time that the Citation began its flight from Davis Monthan. At least three hours would be allowed before their own plane would take off, ensuring an undetected crossing when it reached Nogales.

This was the point where Juan had earlier fallen foul of misinformation. His contact at the air base misled him, unintentionally, causing the incoming load to be observed and almost intercepted. It was another cousin of Juan's who helped him with the fuel truck. This was the man who disappeared without a trace, sending a clear message to Juan Maldonado: they don't tolerate screw-ups lightly.

"So let me ask one thing. It's almost always on a Wednesday, is that right?" Jeff had continued his extensive notes that started during his initial meeting with Cornejo.

"That is correct. Maybe once or twice in six months it has been put off, but only until the next day." Juan had difficulty understanding Jeff's Spanish until he asked him to speak slowly.

"How many people should we expect to encounter?"

"When there is only cocaine coming in, two workers with a large van, the pilot, and I would normally be there with my cousin. Since he has been gone I do the refueling on my own." Juan conjured up a mental picture to insure he gave Jeff only the facts.

"Two more men come when it is time for the money to be flown out." Juan spoke gravely as he added this. He advised Jeff that all persons were armed. "But the men who bring the money have automatic rifles. You must be very careful. They will not give up easily. These men are ruthless and would rather die than have to answer to their bosses." Even though he was directly involved with the importation of tons of cocaine, Juan was a family man and feared for the lives of the police that were doing this work.

"I'd like you not to show up. You tell us exactly when this will actually happen and we'll do the rest." Jeff could think of nothing worse than this little man with a big heart getting killed.

"That will not work, detective. If I do not show, they might suspect something and perhaps the plane will turn around. Perhaps."

Jeff shook his head, thinking of the logistical nightmare this posed.

Juan saw the dilemma in his own mind and tried to ease Jeff's confusion. "You must arrest me too. I go to jail for a short time and no case goes against me. Cornejo has told me of these things." The little man put a hand on the shoulder of his cousin and gently shook Cornejo, displaying an admiring smile.

"I'll think about that." Jeff Shackleford was not convinced. However, he knew something about the operation that Juan did not, and never wanted him to know.

"One last thing, detective. My family and friends, they do not know about me working in this cocaine business. I don't want them to know about me working with the police either." Juan perhaps feared for his family's safety, perhaps for their mental well-being. Either way, he considered himself an honorable man.

Some final details were discussed about the location of the airfield and how to find it. A map was drawn showing the Mariposa off-ramp from the interstate and a side road just before the border crossing for commercial vehicles. This was the roughly hewn track that led over the hilly territory to the landing strip.

Everything was set, and Jeff instructed them to stay near the phone. He would call every four hours on Tuesday, then every two hours on Wednesday. Farewells were exchanged and handshakes crisscrossed the small table.

As the old Chevy truck pulled out of the lot, Driscoll joined the other two. "Man, you guys been at it for a while."

"Sorry you have to be out of these meetings. I think we have to keep as much from these guys as possible." Jeff had his mind on many things at once.

"No problemo, Jeffy baby. Just as long as you fill me in later."

"Why not sooner? Let's all go in the Jeep and check out the landing strip." Jeff stood and gave the keys to Franco, indicating he should drive while the story was relayed to Driscoll.

The side road was less than a half mile from the commercial border crossing and they just about missed it. Once on the road, which was more like a goat trail, Franco barely got above five miles an hour.

"Lucky we got the right type of trucks." Driscoll spluttered as he was tossed around in the back seat.

"I'll take that as a compliment." Jeff also found it difficult to speak during the rough ride and remained silent until they came to a stop.

Brush and small trees abounded, with large and small chunks of rock scattered everywhere. Nobody could imagine a plane coming down intentionally in that unfriendly territory. In spite of their anticipation, it came as a total surprise to the trio. Cresting a steep incline, Franco slammed his foot on the brake pedal. Billowing clouds of dust surrounded the Jeep as the heavy-duty tires fought with the loose gravel and sand.

Their breath was taken away by the sheer ingenuity of the men who had prepared the land before them. As the dust settled they could not mistake the view as anything but a landing strip. Although it was certainly crude, it was cleared for one apparent purpose only. Barely a mile from the main road, it was out of earshot and view of civilization.

"Man, whoever has to land a plane here must be crazy." Driscoll stated the obvious, admiring the guts it must take to perform such an exploit.

"I bet you'd be crazy enough to do it for the right price." Franco felt he knew Driscoll well enough.

"Not for a million bucks." This was his immediate response.

Following a few seconds of silence, with all three staring at the jagged terrain, they looked at each other and literally burst into uncontrollable laughter.

Jeff Shackleford had momentarily forgotten the consequences of having Juan Maldonado in the danger zone; forgotten about the prospect of losing his own home to an unfair lawsuit; forgotten about all of the injustices that were being imposed upon his two classmates, who were now very close friends.

Franco Perez had struggled with the thought of spending time in jail, not seeing his family for days, even weeks, at a time, and not being a cop for the next fifteen or twenty years. All that was far away at this instant. Far away from the potential battleground that stretched out before him, making him laugh until he cried.

Kirk Driscoll had given up hope on society. He was convinced that Los Angeles was indeed the armpit of the Earth. If he had to die, what more beautiful place than here in the Arizona desert. This was what he lived for now. Lead, follow or get the Hell out of the way! When he thought of the firepower at their disposal, he laughed even louder.

As they headed north to Green Valley, it was five miles before they realized they had left the Toyota at the Burger King. This caused another raucous round of laughter as Franco swerved down the Rio Rico off-ramp, then headed back to Nogales.

CHAPTER EIGHTEEN

It was an uneventful trip back to the Best Western where Driscoll stated he needed a nap. Franco thought that an hour or so by the pool, soaking up the late afternoon sun, would be a pleasant diversion. Jeff also retired to his room, but his intention was to study the notes he had taken and chart out the plan of action.

"Well, wake me if you need me, Jeffy baby."

"Driscoll, if I get stumped over something, I'll be sure to call your number." It was rare that Jeff Shackleford made a facetious remark but he found the street cop's presence inspiring.

Within ten minutes, Driscoll was cutting some serious zees, having given Jeff's parting shot no regard whatsoever.

In the quiet of his room, Jeff hashed over the strategy that he felt would best serve them on Wednesday. He knew he could simply tell Cornejo not to show up at the landing site. In fact, the informant probably considered his part of the bargain already complete.

Of great concern to Jeff was the danger that Juan Maldonado was likely to face. Even if he stayed away at the last moment, the loss of such a vast sum of cash would likely arouse suspicion within the cartel. Retribution would be swift and final. It was a no-win situation for Juan, of which he was blindly unaware.

Forty-five minutes was all he could take before he felt a headache coming on. A long, soothing, hot shower solved his physical needs and helped a little with the mental impediment. When he dried off, Jeff called home but got only the answering machine. It was Monday, so Jessica would not be working at the salon. Perhaps she is out shopping, he thought. Go ahead, honey, shop 'till you drop. It might help take her mind off the fictitious surveillance for a while. He made a mental note to try again before dinner.

Meanwhile, Franco stretched out on a poolside lounger wearing a pair of running shorts. The last thing he had expected to need on this trip was a swimsuit. The hotel boasted an exceedingly attractive interior courtyard area with palms, a spa and a small but very inviting pool. With all four sides protected by the hotel itself, the pool deck was warm and without the slightest breeze. Franco's crisis back home drifted slowly, yet deliberately, into the distant horizon. All was well with the world and nobody was out to get his body behind bars. With a thick, soft blanket gently falling upon him from above, he let himself dissolve beneath it until there was nothing but a feeling of absolute serenity.

There came a voice from so far away, it was mystifying how one could even hear it. But there it was, without a doubt, a voice he recognized. He strove to ignore it but its persistence was compelling.

"Franco. Franco." His own name. He knew that much. "Wake up, dammit!"

Was he dreaming? Was it important to at least find out why someone was calling his name? Without wanting the warm glow to disperse, Franco reluctantly lifted his eyelids, focusing his eyes with extreme difficulty. In the distance, across the pool, stood Jeff Shackleford. It was his close friend that caused him to break from the luxurious reverie. Perhaps a matter of some importance.

"Franco, get dressed. Things have been moved up. We gotta go now."

Why now? Life showed more promise while he was asleep.

He set off for his room, surprised to see Driscoll ready to go; his hair was disheveled, but he was ready to go. In fewer minutes than he imagined possible, he was ready and willing to do battle himself. As Driscoll started to climb into the Jeep, he noticed a flat tire, probably caused by the off-roading earlier in the day. To expedite matters, all three rode in the Toyota.

Jeff impressed upon Franco how much behind schedule they were and so he floored the accelerator until the Mariposa off-ramp came into sight. Veering in and out of traffic, he made it to the next turn in short order. Negotiating the rough track at twice the recommended speed was hair-raising for his two passengers. On the other hand, Franco was oblivious to the dangers that lurked within feet of each side of the 4-Runner. One last ascent and they would arrive at the landing strip.

At the last second before reaching the summit, they saw a figure off to their right. They had not arrived first, as planned. And now a guard was pointing his automatic weapon at them, leaving little prospect of defending themselves.

Simultaneously, with the first burst of gunfire, Franco viciously yanked the steering wheel to the left. There were sudden gasps of pain from Driscoll and Jeff. This conveyed to Franco that many of the rounds had ripped through the thin, pressed steel doors and buried themselves into the bodies of his comrades.

He seemed unscathed himself, but his actions sent the Toyota rolling sideways off the edge of the mesa. Time after time the bouncing, rolling motion threw the now lifeless bodies around the inside of the vehicle. With every panel severely crushed by contact with sizeable rocks and boulders, the rental came to rest right side up.

Franco had hit his head on the doorjamb numerous times and was barely conscious. He struggled with a futile attempt to come to his senses. There was an obvious and immediate danger from the gunman, but he felt almost comfortable with his situation. It was one of those moments in life when fate must be allowed its course. Franco waited for the inevitable.

A soft voice spoke to him through the haze. It was a woman's voice. "Are you okay?" She repeated it slowly, over and over.

He sat bolt upright, sweat running through his hair and down his cheeks. The sun was still warm and the pool was glistening. Two ladies had joined him at the pool and one was standing close, with a disconcerted look about her.

"Are you okay?" She asked it again and Franco felt foolish and relieved all at once.

"Yes....at least I think so. Bad dream, I guess. I hope I didn't disturb you." Franco wiped away the embarrassing perspiration with a towel from his room.

She was quite attractive, with a round face and petite features. Her nose was cute, to say the least, and she wore her black hair in a pageboy style that complimented the pretty face. Thirty-two years had been very kind to her.

"Well, I'm glad I was able to disturb **you**, if the dream was that bad." Delicate lashes fluttered as her eyes flirted unashamedly with a slightly more composed Franco.

"The pleasure's all mine." She brought out the perfect gentleman in him. "Friends call me Franco."

"Then I would be honored to be considered a friend and call you Franco. I'm Jeanette and this is April." She introduced herself and the girl sitting a polite distance away.

April nodded in their direction. She was the same age as Jeanette but not nearly as trim, carrying a few too many pounds.

Franco engaged the girls with small talk that seemed superfluous to the overriding effort by Jeanette to become quite familiar. He kept things as conservative as possible but she would stall these attempts every so often. She pointed out how fit he looked or that his legs were strong and muscular. Franco brushed aside such comments by describing his extensive running program.

Time spent with these two pleasant women sped by and he eventually excused himself, stating he had to shower before dinner. Jeanette intended asking him to join them but he was gone too quickly. She gazed at the view from behind as Franco padded off to his room.

"Must be in heat!" Franco bounced down on the bed in Jeff's room.

"Must be desperate!" Driscoll's attention was on the television as he tried to get some local LA news, but he maintained his ability to put Franco in his place.

"Pity there are only two of them." Jeff pitched in with his own comment.

This got Driscoll's interest. "Jeffy, baby, you really surprise me. You're the last person I'd expect to hear that from."

"Just thinking out loud, buddy. Maybe I should keep my thoughts to myself."

"Not if this is the real you." Driscoll tossed the remote onto the bed and folded his arms across his chest. He raised his eyebrows in mock judgment and waited for the detective to plead his case.

"How about trying the hotel restaurant tonight? Maybe we won't get into trouble this time." Jeff changed directions abruptly.

"I think it's time for you to call home, lover boy." Driscoll was not going to let him off the hook easily.

"Took care of that just before you guys came in here. Oh, and I contacted our man in Nogales for good measure. Things are still on track for Wednesday. He's received no directions either way yet."

Neither of them were paying heed, as Franco dreamily thought how flattering it was to be admired by such an engaging young woman; Driscoll was back to the news.

"Glad we got that settled." It was another statement from Jeff that escaped their notice.

Five minutes later the threesome stood at the entrance to the hotel restaurant, which was tastefully appointed, yet distinctly informal. As the hostess led them to their table, Franco was looking around. He half expected to see Jeanette and April, and he was not disappointed.

Franco was last in line as they weaved between tables, and he started to wave in the girls' direction. He felt it would be rude to pass so close and not stop to greet them. While his compatriots were being seated he suddenly found himself with a broad smile as he approached.

"My, you look handsome. A lot different with your clothes on." Jeanette continued where she had left off. April tried in vain to hide her giggle with a hand.

Even with his light brown complexion, a slight reddening showed through. After he mumbled a vague greeting, Jeanette said they would be happy to have Franco and his friends join them. Strangely enough, this sounded most agreeable and he managed to catch the hostess on the way back. He asked if she could make the table up for five and it posed no problem at all.

"I'll go get them." He took his temporary leave.

"Hurry back, Franco." Jeanette implored him.

There was no choice to make when Franco told his partners about the arrangements. The table was already being adjusted and they could find no logical grounds for turning down the offer. On the way over Jeff whispered to Franco that he would come up with an answer to their occupation if the subject were raised. Unfortunately, Driscoll was not privy to this aside, since he was making haste to get the seat of his choice. He parked himself next to April and started with the introductions before the other two arrived.

Jeff sat across from the girls, allowing Franco to be next to Jeanette. It was at this moment that Jeff Shackleford felt sure he knew these girls from the past. The names rang no bell, but the faces certainly stimulated some memory cells. But only a few of them.

"Oh my God! I don't believe it!" Jeanette put her hands on her cheeks and gaped, open-mouthed, at Jeff.

"What's wrong?" Franco toyed with the idea that she might be transferring her affections to his fellow detective. However, there seemed a little stress in her exclamation.

"You're the one. You saved us in the gas station last night." Jeanette had looked up for a second while Jeff was behind the counter, pacifying the attendant. She had seen only the back of Driscoll but was now thrilled to recollect Jeff's face.

After recounting these facts she added a point that they had dreaded hearing. "The police want to see you. They said it was crucial that they find you."

"That's not possible…." Jeff's mind was racing, as he was about to create an acceptable explanation.

"Why not? The Sheriff's station is just two blocks away. We passed it this morning when we took a drive around town." Her reasoning was sound.

With a lowered voice, Driscoll interjected with a sinister tone. "You see, we can't meet with the authorities because we're spies."

As the girls' eyes opened wide, Jeff and Franco looked at each other and rolled theirs as pained expressions developed.

"No kidding?" April actually placed her hand on top of Driscoll's, as if to confirm a bond of secrecy that his admission had clearly demanded.

Before things went too far, Jeff used the idea to their advantage in an attempt to avoid declaring too much, either true or false. "He likes to use the word spy, but he's always been the melodramatic one. Our mission is of grave national importance and secrecy is our greatest ally."

"Oh, Jeffy baby. You say so much and tell so little. I'm convinced these delightful girls can be trusted with at least what we have already said." Driscoll now had April's hand in his and squeezed it gently. She giggled, nudged Jeanette and swore herself to confidentiality. Both of them did so as Jeanette looked at Franco with greater admiration than before.

During the meal they all relaxed and enjoyed the playful banter that Driscoll put forth. He was in his element after the first large glass of wine. Stories flourished that clearly came from the streets of south central Los Angeles. With a masterful, spontaneous embellishment he was capable of adding an international flavor to the events.

Franco endeavored to keep Jeanette at arms length but she persevered with her affable comments. Driscoll was less inhibited with his attention to April. At times they spoke softly to each other, then erupted in fits of laughter. Towards the end of the meal, Driscoll wrote something on his napkin and April grinned foolishly as she tucked it in her purse.

For more than an hour after finishing their food they sat at the table enjoying each other's company. Jeff felt far from the odd man out because of Franco's straitlaced demeanor. Indeed, at one point it seemed as though Jeanette had, in fact, redirected her efforts towards Jeff. Both of them later surmised it was a bid to make Franco jealous.

When the restaurant staff had dropped enough hints, they all realized that their table was the only one keeping the help from going home. As they headed towards their rooms, there was a split in the hallway and the girls had to take a different route. Courteous farewells were passed around and all retired to their rooms in excellent spirits.

The following morning found the three revelers basking in the sun, poolside. Even Driscoll wore shorts and showed off his portly torso.

"Just as well the girls aren't here. They might use hairpins and harpoon you, mistaking you for a whale." Franco was ready for a little friendly, verbal jousting.

"Say what you like, but April didn't complain last night." Driscoll wore a smug and very contented grin.

"What are you trying to say, big boy?" Franco was intrigued.

"I got laid last night. That's what I'm saying. That April screwed like a fox." He needed to say no more.

"Lucky you, Driscoll." Jeff was delighted for him. "Perhaps you want to keep it down a little. They might be close by."

"No way. They had an eight-thirty tee-time at some local golf course. That's why we didn't see them for breakfast. Of course, Franco just about strained his neck looking for them."

"Thanks for telling me sooner." Franco was a little peeved.

"Don't take that attitude. You know you could have had all that Jeanette was willing to give, but you played hard to get. I have to say she must have wanted it bad. April spent the first ten minutes after she got to my room simply pleading me to tell which room was yours. Jeanette wanted her to ask."

Franco was depressed but rationalized the issue. "I'm happily married. I don't need to fool around."

"Good for you, Franco." Moral support was forthcoming as Jeff gave him a thumbs up gesture.

"I wouldn't call what I did, fooling around. We got serious, that's for sure. 'Specially when I told her that you were a Cuban and about to defect, and that it was against international code to screw an American before you been accepted. This seemed to get her going again on the spy business. Man, it made her wild!"

"I'm happy for you, too, Driscoll. But I think that's all the information we can handle." Jeff wanted nothing more than to keep his band of men content.

The day passed slowly with the regular calls to Nogales bringing no news. Franco remained dream free but Driscoll lounged somewhat fitfully as if dreaming himself. If he did so, it must have been pleasant since his grin never left his chubby face.

Juan simply informed Jeff of the status quo during the calls at seven, eleven and then at three in the afternoon. It was a different story as Jeff made a call just before they went to dinner. Juan Maldonado had received instructions to be prepared for the next day. He expected the usual call around mid-morning when they would ask about the flight of the Citation. This would then be the decisive call, as times of departure and anticipated arrival in Nogales would be set. To avoid delay at their end, Jeff told Juan to expect calls from him on the hour, from nine in the morning.

"Okay, gentlemen, to the dining room. And let us hope it's not the last supper." Jeff meant to sound encouraging.

CHAPTER NINETEEN

Once again the girls were conspicuous by their absence and this time Franco was genuinely relieved. They ate in silence as an air of anticipation lingered around them. Finally, it was Driscoll who could always be relied upon to break even the thickest of ice.

"I imagine those broads have found fresh pastures to graze!" There was a hint of despondency in his voice.

"Perhaps they moved on to another town, another hotel." Jeff rationalized their failure to appear.

"I'm pretty sure April said they were here until Thursday. Lots of golf courses for them to try out." Driscoll never could fathom the interest in hitting a little ball around a park, then into a hole.

"My kind of women." Jeff had not played for more than a week and sorely missed it. "I mean golfers, naturally."

The meal was over without the light-hearted witticisms of the previous night. It was now time for Driscoll to bring in the heavy artillery that he left in the trunk of his Ford since Saturday morning. He removed a large duffel bag from the car and carried it into his room. Jeff and Franco were waiting with his door open to expedite the transfer. They were wary of being seen but the guests in the hotel could not have imagined the nefarious nature of their actions.

The deadbolt was turned and the door chained, the curtains drawn, and the television turned up to disguise any metallic sounds they might make. Preparations were under way for a small-scale war. As Driscoll unpacked the guns he laid them carefully on his own blanket that he spread across the bed. Magazines were placed next to each weapon. Some guns had several spares for reloading purposes. Next came the ammunition and he amazed the others with the plethora of rounds.

"We could start an insurrection with this armory." Jeff was suitably impressed by the profusion of guns and accessories.

"In a way, we are. Don't you think?" Franco also stared in awe.

"One difference, gentlemen, is that we are taking on foreign invaders on American soil. These traffickers are bringing poison to our country and destroying millions of lives. They care about one thing, and that's making money. No matter what the price paid by our people. What we are about to embark on is in the service of the good old U.S. of A." Driscoll was setting up his soapbox and feeling a patriotic association with their deed.

"Ask not what your country....boy, I'm moved, Driscoll." Jeff actually got goose bumps from his fellow officer's speech.

"I was looking for the flag in order to salute it." Franco was equally touched.

"Well, it's true. When this little matter is over, we shall be richer and so shall the American people." Driscoll had spoken his peace and was ready to assemble the tools of their revolt. As he picked up a square-looking handgun with a dull finish to it, his eyes began to glaze over. "This, my friends, is a Gloch nine millimeter. As you can see, it's not all metal. Great for smuggling through the x-ray machine at the airport. When it's dismantled, many of the pieces don't show up because they make them out of a kind of plastic, I think. Anyway, the end result is that they are much lighter. So, you should take one, Franco, since you've only got your two-inch."

Together they loaded six magazines; three for Franco and three for the Gloch that Driscoll was going to carry.

"Of course, we should only use our handguns as a last resort." It was Driscoll's turn to direct the action. "If we want to convince these guys to stand back while we take their bucks, we gotta instill the fear of God in them immediately. That's where the M-16's come in. I figure we don't need fully auto with just four or five guys to confront. Shit, you could be reloading every two seconds, but that's not our aim."

Franco started the arduous task of loading them up. “Man, what are these, thirty round clips?”

“For your information they are magazines! A clip is an illegal tackle in football. Don’t confuse the two.” The authority on firearms was mildly irritated by Franco’s commonly made error.

Franco smiled at Jeff, knowing that the street cop was experiencing a sense of superiority through his quite basic knowledge of weapons.

“Finally, we also have a Remington twelve gauge shotgun each. And for those of us who mistake these for sewing machines, that’s okay. The same Remington company made them both.” Driscoll continued to lecture.

“I’m glad you cleared that up. We wouldn’t want to have the bad guys in stitches now, would we?” Franco was on a roll and Jeff felt better about the overall atmosphere.

Driscoll purposely ignored the sarcasm and went on to show how the elasticated sleeves fit the butt of the shotgun. Into these sleeves they slipped six rounds in addition to the five loaded in the weapon. Shoulder straps were then attached to the rifles and shotguns.

“This is more like I expected things to go.” Franco came up with a surprising remark.

“Compared to what, Franco?” Jeff was as perplexed as Driscoll.

“Oh, nothing really. It’s just a weird dream I had, that’s all. Things are moving along according to plan and I feel better now.” He was slightly embarrassed over his dream once again.

A discrete knock at the door was barely heard over the volume of the television. Each of them looked at the other two, showing an assortment of shocked expressions.

“Was this in your dream?” Driscoll queried nervously.

“Fuck no! Who the Hell can it be?” He asked this of nobody in particular.

“Quick, the guns.” Jeff acted swiftly. He tossed a Gloch to Franco and took the other himself. Then he started to wrap the blanket and oversized bedspread on top of the remaining guns. Jeff and Franco hid in the bathroom and made it clear to Driscoll with hand signals, that they would cover him while he answered the door.

There was a peephole in the door that Driscoll utilized before opening up. As he unchained and unlocked the door, he looked back at his comrades and winked knowingly.

"April, hi. Oh, and Jeanette is with you." He spoke rather loud for Franco's benefit.

The two girls giggled and held each other, primarily due to their intoxicated state. April looked beyond the doorway and seemed happy to see he was alone.

"Can I come in?" There was no mistaking her intentions but Driscoll held reservations about her capabilities.

"Actually, I'm not alone. Sorry darling." He shrugged his shoulders and was sincerely sorry.

For a variety of reasons Jeff jumped into action. He handed his Gloch to Franco, flushed the toilet and stepped out of the bathroom. He quickly moved close to Driscoll's side and gave April a huge smile.

"Don't get the wrong idea, ladies. We are having a serious business discussion. Perhaps you'd like to call my buddy here in about ten minutes. I'll be gone by then."

This made extremely happy people out of April and Driscoll. Jeanette persisted with her girlish giggling.

"I'm sure that would be most suitable." April attempted to be the proper lady but also burst out laughing herself.

The girls swayed down the hallway and Driscoll popped his head out, giving a far from subtle reminder. "Ten minutes."

With the door closed, he turned to Shackleford. "I owe you one, Jeffy baby. That's very considerate of you."

"Don't mention it. Just make sure you get some sleep too." Jeff started to put the loaded weapons into the duffel bag.

"Looking at her condition, I figure she should last maybe twenty minutes before passing out." Driscoll helped his most generous friend with the packing.

Franco came out of the bathroom after actually using it himself. "Why on Earth would you need twenty minutes?"

Driscoll put his arm around Franco's shoulders and hugged him. "I got their room number if you want it."

"That's okay. I'm gonna watch the Tonight Show if I can find which channel it's on here."

Jeff decided it was best to take the bag of goodies to his room since Driscoll was expecting company. He wished the big guy well with his enterprise and left the room with Franco.

If he was supposed to be gone in ten minutes, then why not simply stroll over there. This was April's line of thinking. She was making the corner at the far end of the hall when she heard their voices. She stayed just out of sight but caught a glimpse of Franco leaving the room too. With tremendous concentration April was able to see which door Franco keyed. She knew Driscoll would not let her call Jeanette and give her this valuable news, so she returned to their shared room and proudly told her girlfriend. Jeanette was ecstatic and made up her mind to go directly to Franco's room instead of calling.

Jeanette hid at the end of the hall while her roommate knocked at Driscoll's door. The instant it opened, she was grabbed and unceremoniously yanked inside, shrieking excitedly all the way.

Franco was shocked to say the least when he opened his door. Jeanette labored to behave as sober as possible and Franco was unable to resist her request to join him. Her black stretch pants and brightly decorated, loose-fitting red top left far more to the imagination for most people. However, Franco had seen her scantily dressed form at the pool and rapidly formed a mental picture of the numerous delightful curves.

She flopped lazily onto his bed and her head was sent spinning for a moment. This was a long enough distraction for her to miss Franco taking a seat in one of the two armchairs.

Jeanette patted the bed next to her and simulated a pout. "Sit by me, Franco. I want you near to me."

"Maybe I should stay right here." He in turn patted the arms of the very comfortable chair.

"Have it your way, you hunk." She stood and swayed precariously before taking the three short steps to his side. Her very trim figure was lighter than he envisioned and it stimulated latent feelings when she settled on his lap. She threw her right arm around his shoulders and nuzzled up to his neck.

He wrapped an arm around her body as she closed in on him, ostensibly to stop her from sitting on the edge of the chair and falling back. They were now in an intimate embrace and she wriggled as if to get even more comfortable. This movement aroused him instantly and unexpectedly. It was a feeling he missed because of the tensions that were imposed upon him back home.

The spark of desire did not go unnoticed to Jeanette and she breathed gently and warmly into his ear. "I want you, Franco. I want you so bad." If her lips had not been so close he would not have heard the soft, pleading voice.

His heart was pounding, his arm tightened about her slim waist and the sweet fragrance of her delicate perfume toyed with his senses. He wanted to turn to her and quench the fire with his lips. His body ached for the passion that Jeanette offered so freely.

He could not have conceived the inner strength that was needed to resist this exquisite temptation. All he knew was that it pleaded with his decency and propriety.

"Jeanette. You can't imagine how much of a fool I feel when I tell you this." Franco tenderly pushed her a few inches from his neck so he could speak to her. "You are a beautiful young woman and under other circumstances I would not hesitate to make love to you."

"But….." It was Jeanette who started the crucial sentence.

"But, I'm married and love my wife dearly. She would never know of this night, but I would." He took a deep breath and was thankful she knew his true feelings.

More than a minute went by while Jeanette absorbed this revelation. Neither of them moved an inch. It seemed as if neither of them breathed more than once or twice.

"I hope she knows what a lucky girl she is. You're a special person, Franco. If I promise not to move, not to blow in your ear, can I sit here just a little while? I'd like you to just hold me." There was heartbreak and admiration in her voice simultaneously.

He said nothing, but placed a hand on her soft cheek and tenderly drew her head down to his shoulder again. They sat for a long time as barely a trace of a tear appeared in her eye.

Two rooms away there was considerable commotion as April surpassed all expectations. She was able to go full tilt for thirty-five minutes and amazed Driscoll with a performance that exceeded the previous night's passion.

Almost as quickly as she had swooped upon his portly form, she fell into a deep and satisfied sleep. Driscoll lay next to her and admired the voluptuous curves as she breathed more steadily by the minute. She seemed content and at peace with the world. Her chubby, rosy face displayed a countenance like that of a cherub.

Driscoll's life had drifted aimlessly for several years. However, when he looked back over the previous two days, it was a rich gathering of memories. Two close friends with similar outlooks, engaged in a great adventure; a woman who not only admired him but also desired him; it was the best forty-eight hours he had lived for a very long time.

CHAPTER TWENTY

"Damn, you look awful! Didn't you get any sleep?" Jeff was partly concerned but he was also mildly amused.

"I feel great. And I got plenty of sleep." Driscoll was even more disheveled than usual.

"Is that bad news, then?" Franco spoke with a mouthful of breakfast. They had not waited for Casanova to join them before ordering, and Jeanette had informed Franco that the girls were playing another course early again.

"Not at all." The street cop was a little unsteady as he slid into a seat across from the other two. "We did it before we went to sleep and once more when we woke up."

"I'm impressed. You've got staying power, partner." Jeff tilted his coffee cup at Driscoll as a form of salutation.

"I think I should have suggested we brush our teeth first, this morning. Don't you hate that furry taste? Especially when it's someone else's mouth." Driscoll took Franco's cup and rinsed his mouth with a little coffee. It was a purely symbolic gesture intended to disgust the others, since he had already brushed before showering.

"We had a pretty appealing image until you mentioned furry mouths." Jeff's opinion of his colleague slipped just a notch.

"Any update from Nogales, Jeffy baby?" It was an unpredictable change of direction, as they expected him to revel in his sexual prowess for a while.

"Twenty minutes before I call him." Shackleford took his turn at speaking while chewing.

Driscoll nodded then placed his order when the waitress showed up. For the next few minutes he used the salt and pepper shakers, together with several packets of Sweet 'n Low, in an apparent attempt to simulate the tactical situation at the airstrip. He quietly moved them all around the tablecloth in front of him, mumbling incoherent directions to each of them.

Franco finished his meal and could not resist an observation. "The pepper must be me and the salt must be our blond confederate here." He alluded to Jeff Shackleford. "But don't tell me you're one of the sweeteners!"

Driscoll was probably not going to be disturbed by Franco, except that his own breakfast arrived at that moment.

"I'm sweet enough, buddy. Just don't worry your Hispanic little brain about who's who." The big guy swept the condiments out of the way and picked up his knife and fork with gusto.

Long before Driscoll was finished with his rather large plate of food, Jeff excused himself to make the first telephonic contact of the day. Franco sat and drank more coffee, giving Driscoll a long, puzzling stare. He wondered if his friend was as scared as himself. He also speculated silently if any of them would admit their true feelings to each other.

Several more minutes passed in silence and Driscoll ignored the attention he was getting. It was becoming something of a challenge to Franco who took more and more smaller sips from his cup, eyes drilling Driscoll. Tension was building but it was primarily in one direction.

The response was disguised as the food was cut into tiny pieces, with each one being deliberately chewed and the swallowing motion so pronounced. Not until Driscoll was down to just a cup of coffee did anyone say a thing, and it was he who spoke.

"Let's cut the crap, buddy! I'm scared as hell about our little excursion this afternoon. Does that satisfy you?"

Franco was caught totally off guard. The last thing he expected was a confession and he did not know how to handle it. Minutes passed while he stared into his cup for a change, feeling a churning through his stomach. He could not fathom if it was because of the verbal confrontation with Driscoll or the prospect of an all out battle near the border.

A heavy hand clamped itself onto Franco's shoulder from across the table and squeezed roughly. "It's natural to feel this way, buddy. If you're too cool then you might take things for granted and get sloppy."

Driscoll's words instantly soothed the aching that was spreading to his gut. He felt sure his feelings were the same as Driscoll admitted to, and realized they were probably for the good.

"What's this? You guys not getting too friendly, I hope." Jeff returned at an awkward moment.

The hand slid off the shoulder, both parties pretended to sip at their coffee cups, now long empty, and no reply was forthcoming.

"Okay, gentlemen, I guess I'll never know what you two were up to. Maybe I don't want to know. Anyway, there's nothing new as of nine o'clock."

"Here's to ten o'clock." Franco raised his cup high in the air as he said this. Driscoll tapped his cup against the other in an acknowledgement of the salutation. Both simulated the completion of the toast by tipping their dry cups. Franco even went so far as to wipe his mouth with an exaggerated back handed movement.

Some nervous quips followed as Jeff picked up the check. He shook his head as he examined it, but the perplexed look came not from the charges, but as a result of the eccentric behavior around him.

When they returned to the rooms they actually flipped coins to see who would ride together. Jeff had tails and the other two turned up heads. Franco and Driscoll were so ecstatic at this outcome that they had to explain about the moments spent together in the dining room, in order to avoid hurting Jeff's feelings.

Much to Franco's relief, yet again, they planned to arrive hours ahead of the crooks and set up their final game plan. This necessitated a stop along the way to pick up some supplies; plenty of liquids and some snacks were considered essential. For obvious reasons they chose not to use the mini-market around the corner from the hotel.

Jeff was going to transport the bulk of the weapons in the Toyota, while the others traveled in the Jeep. Since they had made no substantial plans for the period after taking the cash, it was decided to keep the rooms. They may need to bed down one more night after the exhilaration of the campaign.

When it came time for the ten o'clock check-in, Franco and Driscoll sat on Jeff's bed and listened intently. The call was long and it seemed as though most of the talking was being done at the other end. When he hung up the phone Jeff held out two upturned palms towards his companions.

"Gentlemen, start your engines. We have a load ready to take off." He was smiling and unashamedly displayed some relief.

The other two men each gave five to Jeff simultaneously and then shook hands with him in turn.

Jeff went on to explain that shortly after the previous contact with Juan, word was received from the air base that the Citation radar plane was in the air just after seven-thirty. When the call came in from Mexico, Juan informed his contact of the takeoff. They were obviously anxiously waiting down south since the response was swift. The load would leave at ten forty-five, he was told, and be ready for it's arrival around three forty-five.

Juan confirmed that both the money men and those designated to pick up the dope were contacted in the same manner. He never had any communication with these other players, even to the extent that they talked very little at the landing site. Everyone reached the area between fifteen and thirty minutes ahead of the plane.

Do not show up at the site, he was asked one last time. But Juan insisted that they might get suspicious if the plane approached and he was not there. If they have ground-to-air radios, maybe they would tell the pilot to turn around. Juan wished Jeff the best of luck and told him to concern himself with his own safety.

Jeff suggested they drive down to Nogales immediately, pick up what they might need from a store, then have a leisurely lunch. Just as they were leaving the room, Franco came up with the notion that they should leave any form of identification behind. Jeff was not sure why this sounded a good idea but they took their cash and left the wallets in Driscoll's Ford. With these plans agreed upon, wheels were set in motion.

Most of the forty-five miles to the Maricopa off-ramp presented a relaxing panorama of the Santa Cruz Valley. The river carrying the same name meandered lazily alongside the freeway but never showed itself, often running beneath the ground. However, its influence upon the land was more visible, creating a lush and fertile valley.

Franco drove and Driscoll soaked up the local scenery, speaking only periodically when he pointed out something of interest. Jeff set the pace in front with exactly sixty-five miles per hour as a safe speed.

An eastbound turn when they left the freeway took them to a large shopping center, which provided the market and several places to eat.

CHAPTER TWENTY-ONE

It was twelve-thirty by the time they ate and Jeff convinced his companions that it was not too early to head for the side road. He wanted to make absolutely certain they could hide their vehicles from the view of the crooks when it was their turn to arrive. There was no dissension from Franco who was now satisfied that his dream was not a warning of things to come. Driscoll looked at his watch and sighed heavily, but eventually relented.

When Jeff reached the landing strip he checked all around. There looked to be a knoll just west of the mesa that was close enough to approach from quickly and an adequate size to conceal their vehicles. He made a brief reconnaissance and found it to be ideal for their purpose. Upon his return he sent the others with the Jeep to ensure it would be completely hidden when someone else arrived at the site. Within seconds he joined them and verified his satisfaction.

"Glad we got that settled, Jeffy baby. Now, what do we do for the next three hours?" Driscoll squinted toward the early afternoon sun that was already making him sweat profusely.

"It might be less than two and a half hours to the arrival of the money. And we still have some work to take care of." Jeff flipped open the rear hatch of the Jeep, displaying the equipment they used when a genuine narcotics bust was about to go down. Naturally, they intended wearing their bulletproof vests and on top would go the raid jackets. These were the lightweights nylon coats that clearly displayed the police insignia and badge. There would be no mistaking who these three men were supposed to represent.

Franco was going to approach by going around the side of the knoll. This would put the Jeep coming somewhat from behind the position where they expected the target vehicles to stop. They based this upon the only safe approach the bad guys could make, which was along the primary dirt road onto the mesa.

Jeff was to drive the Toyota over the top of the hill to gain high ground from the outset. They would have a Spanish speaker coming from each direction. Driscoll would be his passenger, since he had more experience handling the rifle. It was necessary to get the drop on their opposition to prevent any needless gunfire.

The trucks were positioned for attack, guns propped against them and all of the other equipment set on the ground in order. They laid out the gun blanket in the shade of the Toyota and sat down for what promised to be a very long, two-hour vigil.

Even in the shade it was uncomfortable. Driscoll was on his back, staring at nothing in particular, when he saw a bird circling lazily overhead. They were in the desert, it was incredibly hot and they perhaps appeared not to be moving at all. It took very little to talk himself into believing it was a buzzard that was awaiting its chance to swoop down on them. He took out his Gloch 9mm and stretched an arm straight up, pointing the weapon at the bird. It was actually a hawk that sought to plunge not upon Driscoll but a desert rat nearby.

"I trust you aren't going to fire that thing!" Jeff had been scanning the horizon towards the border and turned to see a gun pointing skyward.

Driscoll pulled the trigger one time. "Bang." He whispered it with conviction as the barely audible sound of the trigger action slid smoothly through its paces with the safety on. He took the safety off, making the weapon deadly and ready for use, and then returned it to his holster. Minutes ticked slowly by and seemed like hours. Nobody had anything to discuss for a very long time.

"One thing we ain't talked about is what we're gonna do with the cash." Driscoll tossed this out for openers then took a long swig of lemon-flavored ice tea.

"Three way split, or course." Jeff thought he had the obvious answer.

"I should hope so! Actually, I meant how you gonna spend it?"

Franco inhaled deeply, then let it out slowly as he looked to the delicate, wispy clouds that scudded by above them. There was much thought behind his response when it finally came. "I'm getting my family outta Dodge. No reason for me to stay in California." A trace of bitterness showed through and Jeff nodded as if to approve of the resolution.

"Where, specifically?" Driscoll persisted.

"South of the border, I guess. Buy me some nice beachfront property at Cabo. Somewhere like that. Shit, I'll finish raising my kids in Mexico. At least they won't have to visit their dad in jail."

"What about you, Jeffy baby? You're awful quiet."

"New Zealand." Jeff gave no reasoning along with the prompt reply.

"Why the fuck would you want to go to New Zealand?" What he heard from the senior detective came as no surprise to Driscoll, but his reaction was equally as predictable.

"Oh, I don't know. Perhaps buy a sheep farm or ranch, or whatever they call them."

"And the beautiful Mrs. Shackleford would love being up to her armpits in sheep shit!" Kirk Driscoll pulled no punches and painted a scene that made Jeff think again.

"Well, there's always other kinds of businesses we could get into. I just think it's a neat country." His train of thought was more focused. "We'd get a house on a private golf course. That would be my ultimate aim."

"Those country clubs can eat your money up real quick." The street cop tried an ineffective ploy to disillusion his friend.

Jeff shook his head slowly. "We're talking maybe four million dollars each. Takes a lot to spend that much cash. We should probably invest a substantial portion of it."

"Oh, yeah, I can see it now. I'm a retired cop and would like to invest a million dollars cash in the stock market. Can you help me, please? Next stop, Club Fed." A lopsided grin snaked its way across Driscoll's chubby face.

"How about you? You've been doing all the asking and criticizing. What would you spend it on?" Jeff turned the tables at long last.

"Let me see. You mean other than the usual charitable donations?" This brought groans of derision from the other two. After Driscoll gave it considerably more thought, he came up with something that topped the existing suggestions. "First, I'd get me to a country that's got no extradition treaty with the US. Brazil would be perfect. They got nice beaches and gorgeous women. Then I'd set me up a company that deals in arms, selling to countries that got nothing except more cash than they can handle. You know, like a small Arab nation that's friendly but they're worried about defending themselves. That's what I'd do for starters."

"Sounds like you got it all figured out." Franco was fascinated by the detailed deliberation he just witnessed.

"One of the many possibilities, that's all. Been thinking of nothing else for days, actually." It was a side of Driscoll they could not have visualized.

"Even when you were screwing April?" Franco was curious.

"Nope. I was the perfect gentleman. Didn't even think about someone else when we did the wild thing."

"I hope she appreciated that thought." It was the last thing Franco said for some time. Jeff was also silent as he tossed ideas around in his head. He tried to picture all of the possible directions this conspiracy could take in the next hour or so.

Every now and then Driscoll would come up with a country from which to operate his gun-peddling business. "Switzerland! Nope. Too damn cold."

The sun continued to beat down relentlessly, baking everything in its view. Not a sound broke their self-induced silence. It seemed as if there were no animals nearby that they could hear. If there were any, then they were probably smart enough to take cover from the unseasonably hot September sunshine.

"New Zealand! That's it. I'm gonna go to New Zealand too. I like that line of thinking, Jeffy baby. Which island were you….."

"Shhh. Did you hear that?" Jeff's reactions included grabbing Driscoll by the arm as he hushed the big guy.

"Hear what, for Christ sake? There's nothing moving out here except my lips." The street cop failed to grasp the urgency in his partner's voice.

"Listen. Just listen."

They all held their breath for what seemed an eternity. Then they all heard it simultaneously. A heavy, throbbing and metallic, grinding sound, far off in the distance. It demanded to be heard, as it got slowly and painfully closer to them.

"Jesus! It sounds like something out of War of the Worlds. Nothing like I've heard before." Driscoll announced his feelings in a typically exaggerated manner, reflecting those of his comrades.

Close to the top of the knoll was a clump of mesquite bushes that gave adequate protection while they spied on the airstrip. All three crawled on their stomachs in order to view the offending machinery.

"Looks like one of them tankers that fills the planes at the airport, only smaller." Once again, Driscoll spoke for the trio.

That was indeed what they were watching. Juan Maldonado eased the ancient, rusted tanker along the narrow track towards them. It lumbered over the crest of the final hill and slowly, deliberately made a very wide turn until it was facing the route out. All of the hoses and connections were at the rear, closer to the area where the plane would be able to taxi up to it.

When it finally stopped, the dust clouds surrounded the vehicle for a few minutes. Juan did not wait for the sand and dirt to settle. Instead, he stepped down from the cab and stood in the murky haze, looking all around. As if satisfied with what he saw, or did not see, he proceeded to unhook some of the lines at the back of the truck. He busied himself as if it was a normal drug run, engaged in the duties he was expected to perform.

They watched him for several minutes before Jeff suggested at least one of them should return to the trucks, watching both the artillery and their backs. Franco volunteered to continue the observations of Juan and to look out for the rest to arrive. Jeff considered putting his vest on at this stage but it was too hot even for him. There would be time to prepare before the confrontation took place. He convinced himself of that.

Driscoll slung one of the rifles over his shoulder after making sure it was ready for action. He took out a pocketknife and nervously scraped at invisible dirt beneath his fingernails. Every so often he would look up and stare off at the horizon, fixing a stern look on his face. The rest of the guns were checked and double-checked by Jeff. Then he verified the keys were in the ignition of both vehicles. Lastly, he stood the vests up on end and leaned them against the Toyota. Time was on their side but it was also eating at them as surely as the circling vulture would, given the chance.

The Arizona desert air got even heavier, breathing became labored and time seemed to almost stand still. Then a small rock rolled across the blanket between them and scared the living daylights out of two seasoned cops.

"What the….." Driscoll started loudly, but quickly remembered how close he was to Juan Maldonado. He stopped himself from finishing the expletive.

It became apparent what the source of the rock was, as they both looked in Franco's direction. He had rolled a small rock quite gently on a course destined to pass close to his friends. He held an index finger up to his lips to silence any other outburst. Then motioned for them to rejoin him. Stealthily, they moved next to him but saw nothing new. Then Franco pointed down the trail and it became clear why he attracted their attention. A dust cloud was swirling way off in the distance from the area where the side road began. No noise yet; but lots of ground being stirred up.

Jeff looked back every few seconds for reasons of safety but if anyone wanted to pick them off from the rear, it would have proved a simple task. It was the last thing they expected, given the rough terrain and difficulty gaining access to the area. An interminable amount of time passed before they could see the cause of the disturbance. Only seconds later they could also hear it. The smallest size U-Haul moving van was headed their way, taking the twists and turns of the precarious route at a prudent speed.

Barely whispering to himself, Driscoll murmured his thoughts. "U-Haul. You do the moving. Huh, I love it."

"This must be for the dope that's coming in." Franco directed a few hushed words at Jeff, who nodded in silent agreement.

As the van topped the hill and leveled off it appeared as if the cab held three men. The trio of cops watched in silence as it took a similar turn as Juan had made with the tanker. A significant difference was the speed with which the driver completed this maneuver. He spun the wheels unmercifully, tossing sizeable rocks in all directions. When it came to rest next to Juan's vehicle, the van created such a cloud of dust and debris that it took fully five minutes for it to settle. Three Hispanic men jumped from the cab and approached Juan Maldonado. They were laughing and joking with each other. There were also bottles of beer in their hands. One of them carried a cooler.

Juan was surrounded and his back slapped very roughly by each of them in turn. The cooler was flipped open and a bottle thrust towards Juan. There were uproarious screams of mirth as he refused the offer and three empty bottles were tossed through the air. It may have been significant that the direction in which they were thrown was south, towards the border. Jeff surmised they would find a whole slew of broken beer bottles on the south side of the mesa.

It was the driver's side of the van that could be seen from the knoll. It had stopped short of the tanker but a little further away from their watching eyes. As the party moved to the rear of the vehicle one of the newcomers pushed open the roll-top back door. He was the tallest of the three and sported a huge, black mustache. The one with the cooler was short and fat, his face was dark from several days without a shave. He flung the ice chest just inside the tailgate area and removed some items from the van that sent a chill down three nearby spines. This was what the cops had feared but naturally expected. Automatic rifles were passed around and each crook shouldered his own.

Another beer for each of them and many more laughs all round. If the drug lords could see how their product was about to be handled, they would probably annihilate these lower level workers. For his lack of interest in the alcohol, Juan was ostracized and no further contact was made with him.

Jeff mouthed his apprehension and barely uttered a sound "Three of them to pick up the dope and the money guys aren't even here yet. That could make five plus the pilot."

"Maybe they'll get so drunk they'll all pass out." It was the ultimate in optimism from Franco.

"These are real Mexicans, *amigo*. They can drink even me under the table." Driscoll had never been more accurate than with this characterization.

It was now three-thirty and the sun was behind them continuing to warm the back of their necks. The airstrip stretched out away from them to the east and their targets were less than two hundred feet from the bushes on the knoll. Minutes dragged by laboriously and still nobody else arrived. The greatest fear was that they had gone to all of this trouble and no money was to be transported this time. What they had been through already amounted to a serious crime. It would prove to be an immense anticlimax if the conspiracy was a failure by default.

It seemed as if Juan was also somewhat agitated. He looked at his watch every thirty seconds, but still gave the appearance of being busy with the tanker. Twice it seemed as if he looked right at them through their concealment. He could not have been sure of their position but he knew they must be close by. Logic dictated he might arrive at the conclusion they were behind the knoll.

A sound that first excited the sober trio and drunken group alike, toyed with the senses. Three Los Angeles police officers turned their heads slightly to the left. The main road was a mile away in that direction. They searched the horizon for a telltale dust storm but none was forthcoming. Strangely, the U-Haul threesome were staring off to the Mexican border, now quietly sipping their beers. As this incongruous image registered with Jeff Shackleford, he turned to his right. He realized from his auditory perception that the sound was from the south and was an all too familiar one.

"What is it?" Franco asked in the most general sense.

"The timing is beginning to worry me, but I'm pretty sure it's a plane." Jeff could not fathom out why the cash was not here yet. What would they do if the other vehicle did not arrive soon? Should they just let the shipment of cocaine be transferred and allow it to continue on its deadly journey?

"Shouldn't we at least get dressed up?" Franco was also confused but remained calm and practical.

Without a word Jeff nodded for the others to put on bulletproof vests and raid jackets, while he maintained observations. It was done in a great hurry and there was barely a dark speck on the horizon when they returned. It grew gradually and at an even pace until they could make out the approaching Piper Chieftain.

As soon as it could be distinguished as the plane they had all waited for, the crooks let out a rousing cheer. They saluted the arriving dope with raised bottles, drained the contents, and then tossed them among the distant, growing piles of broken glass.

Jeff was equally as quick to don his protective gear and retrieve a rifle for good measure. The plane's arrival was an integral part of the operation, since they would have to start their engines at some point, it would serve to drown out the noise. However, they were baffled by the absence of the two men with the money vehicle. No contingency plan allowed for this setback. Franco and Driscoll were unaccustomed to the flustered expression on Jeff's face. He was the mainstay of the organization and their faith was failing as rapidly as the Chieftain was approaching.

"Any bright ideas, Jeffy baby?" Driscoll spoke at a normal level now that the plane's engines were so close.

He shook his head in dismay. "Perhaps it's for the best. If there's no cash to steal, then we don't commit the crime of the century."

"Screw it! I say, take their dope instead." Franco spoke out of frustration and fear for his future.

"Brilliant idea! And spend the rest of our lives trying to peddle cocaine?" Jeff talked down to Franco for the very first time.

"So we're going to sit this out and watch the show. Is that your best idea?" Franco was mad enough to grab Jeff by the lapels and spit the words at him.

"Hey, you guys. We'd better do something soon." Driscoll was pointing at the aircraft, looming almost overhead. It had swept to the west and was making its approach to touch down at the end of the strip closest to them. He added the obvious. "That pilot is certain to see us."

As the plane reached a distance of a few hundred feet it veered sharply to the north, pulling up from its landing pattern. The pilot had evidently observed the strangers lurking next to his landing strip. The question was: did the ground crew have communication with him?

It conducted a distant circling operation and came back southward at them. Without question, it came at them. The pilot displayed no intention of landing as he buzzed their knoll at less than a hundred and fifty feet. The sand and dust they had seen being stirred up earlier was nothing to what engulfed them now.

Within minutes he was headed back once again from the direction of the border. Driscoll was as engrossed by the performance as were his colleagues. Fortunately, he glimpsed some movement out of the corner of his eye. What he beheld was a truly shocking sight. The large mustache and the fat one were marching defiantly across the rugged terrain, guns at port arms.

"Boys, we got us some company." The street cop was shouting at the top of his voice. The plane was directly overhead again, kicking up a storm and deafening them all.

Jeff and Franco heard the desperate warning and viewed the advancing Mexican forces with astonishment.

"Remember the Alamo!" Driscoll prepared his rifle by tucking the butt in tight to his right side.

"Showtime!" The reference to General Santa Ana's bombardment of 1836 was lost on Franco, who was the first to advance around the bushes and into the fray.

Jeff said nothing but his mind flashed to his favorite classic: Butch Cassidy and The Sundance Kid. This was hardly a huge Mexican force they were facing, but one bullet or hundreds of them, either could be deadly.

Because of the lack of cover, they were grateful for the dust activity the pane had kicked up. The crooks' reactions were slowed partly by their earlier imbibing and their poor tactics. Three cops literally had the drop on them. Whereas, mustache and the fat one had their guns pointing to the sky.

"Polizia! Suelte le arma! Manos ariba." Franco ordered them in clear terms to drop the guns and raise their hands.

It was with immense relief that Jeff and Driscoll watched the results of Franco's commands. None of them wanted a shoot-out unless it became absolutely necessary, but the immediate and unconditional surrender of arms came as a welcome surprise. In the distance the third crook was about six feet from where he had propped his rifle against the van. There was a moment of hesitation where he thought it was close enough to retrieve and use upon the intruders. However, the swift actions of the *polizia* showed a determination that he lacked himself even when sober.

Stepping over the abandoned firearms, Driscoll and Franco marched the first two malefactors back towards the U-Haul. Juan behaved appropriately and sent his arms above his head. He stood rigidly behind the tanker and was relieved the arrest was going so well. When they all got within ten feet of the last culprit there came an eerie scream that echoed unnaturally.

"Aaieeeeeeeee…." The otherwise unobserved fourth bandit leaped from inside the cargo area of the U-Haul, automatic rifle pointing at the group.

"*Vamanos, amigos*!" His call was for the benefit of his compadres, indicating they should get the hell out of the way. It was all for show. He saw instantly that his life was on the line and saving his friends became a mere hindrance.

There was no time for anyone else to think or react. Bullets sprayed the whole scene. Holes were punctured in the tanker resulting in numerous miniature streams of fuel spraying outward. It was a miracle that the liquid did not ignite from the rounds that perforated the metal.

Juan Maldonado was cut in two with a dozen rounds striking him in the back. There was never any feeling of pain, with death arriving instantly. His part in the great plan was over. His extensive family would mourn the passing without understanding the implications of his departure.

Mustache was standing in front of Jeff Shackleford and shielded him from the few rounds that headed their way. At least one of them proved fatal for the crook. As his lifeless form slumped to the ground, Jeff dropped directly behind him continuing to use the body as protection.

Driscoll and Franco were not so luckily positioned. The fat Mexican presented plenty of cover but was not situated exactly between the mad gunman and themselves. Several bullets hit Franco; direct hits in the ten ring, every one. He was lifted off the ground by the impact and thrown six feet back.

The fat crook and the fat cop miraculously stood unharmed after the first barrage of rounds. Driscoll reacted instinctively as he fired over and over again. The driver, who was the cowardly one that could not reach for his gun, was still standing just a few feet from his reckless associate. He placed his hands over his ears when the firing began, remaining in that posture until one of Driscoll's projectiles pierced his heart.

The Mexican assailant stood his ground as he replaced the thirty round magazine with a fresh one. He stepped back to gain some minimal cover from the van and, incredibly, remained unscathed from Driscoll's weapon. Even Jeff fired at him but the U-Haul bore the brunt of his assault.

There was perhaps a second where Driscoll had time to head for the tanker for his own cover. His concentration was broken by the sight of Franco lying on the ground, motionless. It was his downfall.

Given some encouragement by the inattention of the only adversary still standing, the desperado stepped out into the open once more. He carefully leveled his weapon at Driscoll.

"Look out Kirk!" Jeff's warning came too late.

The captive drug trafficker and Kirk Driscoll were knocked down by a constant volley of rounds from the rear of the U-Haul. The firing stopped only when the magazine was empty. The single crook was protected from Jeff's weapon by the van, and took even better cover by spinning sideways to the far side of the vehicle.

A mechanical spluttering emanated from a far off location. The plane had continued to circle but at a safe distance. Calculations for the fuel needed on the trip were accurate. However, the twenty-minute delay in landing the load had taken its toll. About two miles west of the battlefield, the Piper Chieftain plummeted unceremoniously to the earth and created a spiral of thick black smoke.

Jeff chanced a quick look over his shoulder at the crash and was elated that the cartel had at least lost a substantial quantity of cocaine. There would be no gross or net profits, just a total loss.

The trio of conspirators had fared almost as poorly. Only Shackleford remained to face the final showdown. He had a slight advantage over the fourth culprit whose legs from the knee down were vulnerable beneath the chassis of the van. He took the time needed to aim as carefully as he had ever directed a weapon at any human. Unknown to Jeff, his target was struggling to release the second magazine, which had jammed due to past abuse.

A single gunshot brought his enemy crashing to the ground as his right ankle was broken by the blast. He lay immobilized, facing Jeff's direction. Although Jeff remained still for fear that a burst of automatic fire would end his life, the crook made eye contact with him immediately. There was the look of a hunted fox in his eyes; a trepidation of meeting his maker. Jeff swore he recognized a plea for mercy that reached out to touch his very soul. The man grasped his fractured extremity with both hands and was indisputably unarmed.

For Driscoll; for Franco; and, yes, for Juan Maldonado. Jeff Shackleford never imagined he could kill someone in cold blood. But he did just that. He would be a different person from that moment. His destiny, although uncertain, would always be in his hands alone.

It took just one remarkably small missile, strategically directed at the man's head, to end his wretched life.

For a very long time it was peaceful. Nothing stirred. Jeff was devastated and the impact of five minutes of utter chaos left him drained emotionally and physically. He waited for a sign. Something to tell him it was okay to be alive.

He rolled over onto his back, still resting partly on the mustachioed corpse. The distant smoke rising inexorably to the sky was strangely relaxing.

He hated being alone. He hated being alive.

CHAPTER TWENTY-TWO

He was normally a decisive man. When the plane first approached he was as at a loss as to the course of action to take. Although their hand was forced by the curiosity of two crooks, it pained him to think of his momentary lack of determination. Now he faced it again. There was every reason not to go on; nothing to encourage him to even stand and face the consequences of the failed campaign.

A bird circled overhead once more. Was it really a vulture this time? Did they even have vultures in this part of the country? It certainly seemed interested in the carnage that lay around him. Around and around; he gave it credit for its patience.

A few feet away a Gloch 9mm was raised up high and pointed at the bird. One round after another, firing in a steady, determined sequence, the reports were deafening and startling, while at the same time comforting. Driscoll was trying his damnedest to shoot down his vulture, but had difficulty aiming as the circling made him dizzy. Only when the magazine was empty did Jeff scramble to his feet and approach his friend. Both hand and gun dropped to his side in acceptance of the bird's superior flight pattern.

"You okay, old buddy?" Jeff knelt by the side of the injured street cop. Vicious looking wounds were evident around Driscoll's neck just above the protective shield of the vest.

Jeff looked around hoping to be inspired by finding something to press against the bloody mess. The recumbent cop let the firearm slip from his hand and grasped Jeff Shackleford's right wrist firmly, pulling him closer.

"Did we get 'em all?" He wanted to know the score

Jeff nodded and gave the full accounting. "Looks like they're all dead."

"What about Franco? He didn't look so good."

This time Jeff lowered his eyes and barely shook his head.

"Fuck! Well, I'm outta here, Jeffy baby."

"No! Driscoll, you asshole. You don't….." Jeff's words trailed off as the grip on his wrist slipped away. Driscoll had cursed his last curse. He was gone.

Losing such a close friend was hard on Jeff. It seemed almost easier to accept before the firing at the bird, but literally watching him die was tough to take. He was not so sure he wanted to check on Franco, although it had to be done.

It looked as if four bullets had torn at the blue material covering Franco's vest. Blood was significantly absent as Jeff felt for any vital signs.

Franco was breathing. Evidently the bulletproof fabric had done its job well. He had been thrown back by the high velocity rounds and hit his head upon landing. Even as Jeff conducted his examination, Franco began regaining consciousness.

"Take it easy, Franco." Jeff gently restrained his sole partner from rising up too quickly.

"Man, does my chest hurt. Do I have any holes in me?"

"None that I can see, my friend." Tears welled as he helped Franco slip the heavy vest off.

"Feels like I was hit in the chest by a sledgehammer." He rubbed his sternum and took several deep but slow breaths. He was eventually able to stand with a little assistance.

There was more pain as he saw the lifeless form of the third member of their company. They had all grown so close over the last few days. Each of them with their own reasons for being a party to this insane conspiracy. A venture that turned sour and ended with appalling results. They both examined Juan Maldonado but it was a mere formality. It was also a distressing moment, particularly for Jeff who believed he should have insisted that the informant not show up.

Franco came close to throwing up after viewing the gory mutilation of the tiny Mexican's body. "I need a beer. I just hope there's one left."

The cooler still had a half dozen full bottles inside, and Franco removed the twist-off cap, shooting a twinge of pain across his chest. As he put the bottle to his mouth he all but spilled the amber fluid down his shirt.

Jeff was giving a cursory inspection of the two crooks they had originally captured. When he started towards the U-Haul he saw Franco standing with his mouth open. The beer bottle was held just inches from his mouth and he was staring into the rear of the van. The look on his face was not immediately a familiar one and Jeff suspected a fifth drug peddler was holding Franco at gunpoint.

He made sure his own rifle still had ammunition and slowly crept closer to Franco's position. At the last moment he stepped briskly to a point where he could fire at anyone still inside the van. There was nobody there. What he saw left him as speechless as his partner.

Stacked at the front of the compartment were six bales each about three feet on all sides. Thick plastic covered them and sealed the packages tightly. It was clear plastic and they could see the contents with ease. Bundles of US currency were compressed against each other in quantities that sent their minds swirling.

Both cops stood for about thirty seconds until Franco regained his composure. "I don't believe it. There's millions…..and millions."

When he came to his senses he took the longest drink from his bottle.

"I'd better have one of those." Jeff reached into the cooler and joined his buddy in celebration.

"So it was here all the time. That's why there were four guys with the van. They sent the extra men but only one vehicle." Franco deduced this from the conspicuous facts.

As a symbolic gesture they tossed their empty bottles in the same manner and direction as they had seen earlier. Then they climbed into the van and rolled one of the bundles close to the tailgate. With more light available they saw the contents appeared to be made up of twenties, fifties and hundred dollar bills.

"I've heard that when money reaches this level within the organization they toss out the smaller bills. They take up too much space." Jeff speculated on the reason for the large bills being the only ones visible.

"How much do you figure in each parcel?" It was more of a passing thought than a realistic inquiry.

"I can't begin to imagine. But you know something, Franco, it doesn't really matter just how much is here. This is more than we'll ever need." The first impression of all hard-working, middle-class people over an imaginary amount of cash so huge, is that it is an ample sum.

Jeff suggested they get to work quickly because the plume of smoke from the plane crash might bring search and rescue teams to the area. Both cops strode between the bloodshed to retrieve their vehicles. As they made their way over the knoll they fixed their gaze on the distant crash site. It was too far for them to make out the debris on the ground but the fire raged as five hundred kilograms of cocaine burned out of control.

"Heads are gonna roll when they learn everything is lost." Franco sneered at the prospect.

"I was going to say that all of the heads that could roll, did so here today. But you have to reckon somebody higher up the ladder will be held accountable." Jeff rationalized. "You're most likely right about that, Franco."

The guns were wrapped in the blanket and placed in the Jeep which Jeff drove, followed by Franco in the Toyota. Both were then backed up to the U-Haul truck in preparation for the transfer. As soon as they reached for the one bundle that was within reach, a problem occurred to Franco.

"If we put three packages in each truck, how do we hide them from prying eyes?"

Jeff thought about this issue for a moment. "We could use the gun blanket for one load but it won't help for the rest of the cash. Damn, I wish we had rented something with tinted windows at least."

"And what about the bodies? What about Driscoll? We just leave him?" Franco was full of questions but struggled to find any answers.

Jeff was now back in full control of his faculties and the mind was churning over at a considerably enhanced speed. He came to some very devious conclusions as he outlined the new and improved game plan. It seemed unlikely to Jeff that the six bodies would remain undetected for long and so Driscoll would be recovered by the authorities. If he was going to be found at all, it might as well be right there.

Any attempt to bury or cover up just one of the dead would suggest a friendly action. This might lead to unwanted inquiries at the police department. If the underlying view of the scene left a thought that Driscoll was involved with the crooks, so be it.

The best way to transport the money would be the U-Haul. They should drive off in one four-by-four and the moving van. Park the cash at a lot in Nogales then return quickly for the other rental. It would be a case of shuttling them back to the hotel, then eventually to Tucson.

They played with the notion of using the fuel tanker to destroy the bodies and the tanker itself. Although Jeff had killed one of the men himself he was unsure if he could set fire to any of them. There was no doubt that he could not do so to Driscoll. Abandoning them seemed the preferred method.

"What about Driscoll's Ford?" Franco was good at posing the predicaments.

"Maybe we should bring it close to Nogales. We have to get it away from the hotel so there are no inquiries there." Something struck Jeff about the discussion over Driscoll's car. They needed the keys which were in the dead man's pocket.

Jeff performed the unpleasant task of searching Driscoll's pockets. He double-checked to make sure there was nothing to identify the man. It would only be a matter of time before they found out who he was from his fingerprints, but any delay might prove precious for the duo.

Franco shut the rear door of the U-Haul and was relieved to find the keys in the ignition. He did not relish the thought of searching a dead man's clothing himself. They took the rifle that Driscoll had used to eliminate the driver just in case their prints were still on it. His Gloch 9mm was wiped clean, as were the magazines, and replaced in the holster for appearances.

The moving van led the way, followed by Jeff in the Jeep. Franco took things more carefully than he had in the smaller vehicle. Other than the danger to himself, he was concerned about the valuable load.

Four hours had passed since they left the shopping area on Mariposa Road. A myriad of experiences had cut through their lives like a carving knife. Things could have turned out much better, but they could also have ended with greater tragedy. Franco parked the U-Haul in the middle of the busy lot and walked as if he were going to a store. Jeff picked him up as he cruised the perimeter. Nobody would make the connection between the conveyances or become the slightest bit suspicious.

As rapidly as the Jeep would safely take them back to the site, Jeff drove without a word. He dropped Franco at the Toyota and prepared to leave immediately. His Hispanic associate grabbed the passenger door before Jeff could set off.

"Shouldn't we say a few words for Driscoll. I mean, when the authorities do find him, he doesn't have anyone who might care. Except maybe an ex-wife or two." It was a heartfelt plea that Jeff could not decline.

They stood over his tranquil form and looked ahead to the west. Smoke still spiraled upward some two miles away and there was no sign of a plane or helicopter above the disaster site. Both simply stood stiffly with arms hanging to their side. They were at attention and thinking fond thoughts of their courageous friend.

"You want me to speak?" Jeff asked weakly.

Franco nodded. He could not bring himself to say anything as tears filled his eyes without warning.

"If there is a place after this that Driscoll goes to, then I hope it is a place without prejudice or bigotry; a place without hatred or discrimination; a place without animosity or spite. I hope that whoever is in charge will see Driscoll for what he is, not what intolerant people perceived him to be. He was a dear and valiant friend. I am proud to have known the real Kirk Driscoll. We will both miss him."

Franco knew that Driscoll would not have wanted any direct references to God or religion. He would have appreciated the words that Jeff used. Franco Perez put his arm around the shoulders of Jeff Shackleford and hugged him warmly, nodding his approval.

"Let's get going, Franco. It's our survival we have to think about now."

"Okay. Hey, Driscoll, I hope they find you real soon." Franco could not bare the thought of Driscoll's vulture swooping down on him.

Actually, it would be six long days before the bodies would be discovered.

Officially, that is.

CHAPTER TWENTY-THREE

It was the fastest journey they ever made along the treacherous trail. Now that they were so close to escaping the scene of the crime, it was as if the chase was on. Both vehicles came within inches of sliding over the edge and tumbling down steep hillsides. Franco had a flashback to his dreadful dream at the pool and slowed down a little. Jeff was ahead and saw the distance between them growing, so he sensibly reduced his speed too.

At the shopping center they dropped the Toyota and Franco walked a hundred feet to where he left the U-Haul. Jeff passed him slowly, and strongly advised him to keep pretty close to the speed limit. Franco's response was a simple nod in the affirmative.

The trip back to the hotel was uneventful and six-thirty had come and gone. Jeff insisted he make his usual call home before they drove back for the other truck.

"Hi, Honey. Anything exciting happen today?" It seemed a remarkable question for Jessica to ask under the circumstances.

He was tempted to say it was extraordinary in its own way but gave the predictable cop response. ""Just the usual. Spent a lot of time watching the crook's house. He only went out for a little grocery shopping." Jeff tried to make it sound as routine as many of the surveillances he had worked.

"When are you coming home? I miss you so bad." She really meant it and sounded a little desperate.

"Maybe tomorrow, Honey. This case isn't working out like we expected." At least that was substantially true.

They said their loving goodbyes and Jeff hung up the phone. He wondered to himself how he was going to explain what he had done. Fifteen years as a good cop and now he was party to a horrific chain of events. They would work things out somehow. She had to understand the pressures he was feeling; the unfair lawsuit when he had risked his life to save another.

Franco knocked at the door, anxious to pick up the Toyota. There was one other call to be made and it was an onerous task indeed. Since Juan was not going home, Jeff would have to speak with Cornejo. During the phone conversation he told his informant they must meet tonight. Cornejo was troubled by Jeff's avoidance of his questions about Juan and wanted to know if he was in the local jail. Jeff continued to insist he would explain everything at the Burger King in one hour.

The rear of the U-Haul could not be locked and they had backed it against a wall for safety. Before leaving in Driscoll's Ford, Jeff moved the van and took a small suitcase as he climbed in the back. He cut open one of the bundles and filled the case with a huge sum of cash.

Franco warmed up the Ford and was more than curious about the visit to the moving truck. "Is that what I think it is?"

"Franco, we know Cornejo can find the landing strip so he has to know what happened. This should be more than enough to keep him quiet."

"Look what we've come down to. Everything we do now has a criminal element to it." Franco was upset and confused.

"We're alive and we have the money. If there is something we have to do to keep our heads above water, then we must do it. As long as we don't resort to killing anyone else." Jeff felt comfortable with that rider.

When they arrived at the Burger King they were fifteen minutes late. Cornejo was waiting impatiently, soda cup in hand.

"What is it? What has happened to Juan? Did you make the arrest and get their money and cocaine?" He had a million questions and barely gave Jeff a chance to speak.

"Calm down, Cornejo. Things did not go as we expected." Jeff went on to explain how there was a shootout and one of their own men was killed. He told of the crooks all being wiped out and that Juan had been caught in the crossfire.

The Mexican was stupefied. He wondered out aloud if he could gather the nerve to attend Juan's funeral. Did someone from his family need to identify him? He asked this because he had seen it on many American television shows.

Jeff had not planned how to tell the most difficult part and his hand was now forced. Plain and simple was the way he did it. No frills and unfortunately no sympathy. This time Cornejo said nothing. He was trying to work out how he fit into the scheme of things. Was he really a party to the disastrous events? Finally, how much was it going to be worth to him?

"Cornejo, I don't know how much is in this case. It's probably many more times what you expected from the police department for this job. Just take it and hide, for a long time."

The informant peeked into the suitcase and his eyes almost popped out of their sockets.

Jeff was thinking fast and added something close to a threat. "This is the only payment you will receive. There are many higher-ups who have to get their cut of the money. We get about the same as you. Breathe a word to anyone and we'll make sure the cartel know of your participation. Understand?"

His answer came in the form of a slight nod. As Cornejo fastened the clasps of the case he declared he was not even returning to Juan's house. He would travel east, maybe New Mexico and start anew there.

Jeff was satisfied with Cornejo's reaction and asked for Juan's address in Nogales so his family could be informed. Although he did not know what they would be told, or who would tell them. They said farewell to Cornejo who in turn wished Jeff and Franco good luck.

It had been a long day and too long since they ate. Double burgers and large fries sounded as good as anything. Particularly since they were right there just feet from where they were preparing the food. Two tired multi-millionaires sat down to a five-dollar fast food meal.

Following the nourishment they dropped the Ford off at Mariposa Road and continued north in the Toyota to Green Valley. Franco pondered the question as to exactly how much cash there was. It intrigued him so, having such a vast sum and not knowing what it amounted to.

As Franco locked up the car at the hotel parking lot, Jeff again moved the van and acquired two wads of money. Although it was nearly eleven and fairly dark in the lot, he was taking a chance of being seen by another guest. Franco told him he was crazy and rushed to open his room door ahead of time. Once inside the room the bundles were thrown unceremoniously onto the bed.

"There! You count those two so we can get an idea of how many bills are in each stack. I counted six packs across the top and twelve from top to bottom. It was difficult to tell how many of those were from front to rear because of the rubber bands around them. But I have a pretty good idea, so start counting. You want to know, then we're going to work it out, buddy."

Jeff was deadly serious and Franco stripped the bands off the first pack. This consisted of twenty-dollar bills, the other was hundreds. Give or take a couple of bills they had a thousand in each pack and Jeff had his rough estimate of the quantity of packs. Several minutes followed of scratching numbers on the notepad they found in the nightstand drawer.

"Eight million dollars. Give or take a couple hundred thousand." Jeff waved a hand to show his figures were somewhat arbitrary.

"We've been swindled, partner! That's a lot less than we were led to expect." Franco surprised himself at first with his grave concern over the amount of cash. Then immediately began chuckling as the absurdity of the moment struck him.

"Wait a cotton-picking minute. That's in just one of those bales. Six times eight.....fuck! That's forty-eight." Jeff was on the bed and at this point he flopped backwards and rubbed his eyes with outstretched fingers.

"You mean forty-eight million dollars?" Franco was now laughing almost hysterically as he said this.

"Naw. Must be something wrong with my figures. It's probably much less than that. Hey, Franco, we may never know how much we have. But what does it matter?"

Franco did something he always dreamed of doing. He grabbed all of the money he just counted and threw it wildly at the ceiling. Bills showered down on him and he repeated the estimate because he liked the sound of it. "Forty-eight million dollars. **Yes**." There was emphasis on the yes, similar to when a sportsman makes a score; similar to when the gambler rolls the dice. "**Yes. Yes. Yes.**"

CHAPTER TWENTY-FOUR

Room service seemed in order. They were millionaires so they might as well spend a few dollars. Breakfast was sent to Franco's room and he was about to tip with a twenty before Jeff stepped in.

He's new to our country. The bills all look the same to him. Here, this is for you." Jeff explained the situation to the young man that delivered the tray of food and handed over a five-dollar bill.

After the door was closed Franco shrugged his shoulders and laughed. "Just thought it would be fun to see his face."

"Actually, I think five is too much but it is easy to be generous when we have so much. It would be in our best interest to try and behave the same as we always have. Any extravagance might attract the wrong kind of attention." Jeff was secretly having difficulty himself with his bid to behave normal.

Both cops had a considerable appetite for the vast array of food they ordered. This was not surprising since the last meal they consumed was a basic hamburger the evening before. Virtually every scrap was gone when the phone rang. Franco twisted his face into a puzzled expression as he headed towards the nightstand.

"Hello." He tried to sound as generic as possible.

It was Jeanette. The girls were preparing to leave for the Sedona area and she asked if she could see him just one more time. Franco quickly came up with an excuse, stating he was shaving and about to jump in the shower. She playfully suggested they jump in the shower together and he laughed this off as a further example of her teasing nature.

He was thrown for a loop when she asked about Driscoll. April had called his room without any response and was concerned about her "lover boy." Franco suddenly felt a greater pain for the loss of his friend than even when he was standing over the bloodied corpse. Despite his brown complexion he turned instantly ashen. For a moment he was unable to speak. This was not for lack of a rational explanation, but for fear that he might break down when speaking of his late buddy.

Jeff had easily grasped the thrust of the conversation and rightly determined the reason for his partner's hesitation. He whispered in Franco's other ear, giving a scenario that might sound plausible. It involved Driscoll being called back east for a new assignment.

Franco seemed not to hear the advice and continued to stare ahead, glassy-eyed. Jeanette's demeanor at the other end of the line must have aroused suspicion with April, who took the phone and spoke with Franco herself.

"Is there something wrong? Where is Kirk?" She sensed the uncertainty in Franco's voice when he mumbled incoherently at first.

"Tell me, Franco! What happened to him?"

He wanted to tell her the truth; some of it, at least. He wanted her to share in his grief as if this would ease his own, just a little. However, the uncompromising manner in which she demanded an answer helped him resolve the issue far more compassionately. Even though he lied through his teeth.

"Nothing is wrong with him. I simply can't tell you about his whereabouts. He left us yesterday and won't be working on the same case." The vague reference to half-truths failed to bring him peace of mind.

She persisted for a while and only relented when Franco became a little irate. It was clear to her that wherever Driscoll was and whatever he was doing, there would be no further contact between them. Disappointed, she said goodbyes for herself and Jeanette, and then hung up.

"It's tougher now than it was yesterday." This was an understatement.

Jeff Shackleford sat next to his closest friend and examined his own hands as if looking for a fitting remark. They lingered, shoulder to shoulder, unwittingly giving each other great comfort at a crucial moment. Neither was able to verbally express his feelings on the subject of Kirk Driscoll. From this moment hence they would only **feel** their mourning individually, without sharing those times with the other.

Silently, they stowed their belongings in the U-Haul, together with Driscoll's effects. After checking out of the hotel it was time for more shuttling of vehicles. Even though it seemed risky to leave the cash behind, they figured that the less time they were on the road with it in an uncovered condition, the safer it would be.

They took both rentals back to Tucson but before returning the Toyota, they bought a Ford Econoline van from a used car lot. Their latest form of transport cost a little more than seven thousand and they handed over hundred dollar bills in payment. The dealer was somewhat cautious when Jeff stated he did not have his driver's license with him. However, the prospect of losing an uncontested sale proved too much for him. He never pressed for more than an obviously fictitious name and address. Before heading south one last time, they purchased several blankets to use for covering the cash. The new van had no side windows but there were small, clear ones in each of the rear doors.

Jeff dropped Franco off behind the Quality Inn and waited until he was ready to follow with the U-Haul. Just six miles after rejoining the freeway they pulled off at Pima Mine Road. It was the ramp that led to a nearby casino and presented a potentially busy road. However, it was the first they came to with the freeway crossing overhead, and hidden from the passing interstate traffic they parked in some seclusion.

Franco parked first and Jeff maneuvered the Ford van so it was backed up to within three feet of the tailgate. The open doors of the van blocked out almost any view of the transfer, and the level of the floor was just lower than the inside of the U-Haul. With both of them working on the bales of money together, it took less than ten minutes to load up the Ford and cover the cash.

They had already discovered the rental documents in the cab of the moving truck. It showed a starting time early in the morning on the previous day out of a Tucson office. It would not take two brilliant detectives to deduce that the crooks that died, actually rented it for their illicit deed.

As two experienced cops they knew that unless the van could be immediately tied to a robbery or more serious crime, then there would not be any search for fingerprints. With this is mind they stopped in Tucson and made a call to the U-Haul office and anonymously tipped them off to the abandoned vehicle. They hoped by the time the carnage was discovered in Nogales and the identities of the dead became known, the truck would have been cleaned and hopefully rented out again.

They devoured a late lunch, gassed up the van and carefully checked the water and oil levels before setting off for Phoenix. Jeff was driving and the oldies played one after another from the radio. Franco simply watched the landmarks slip by during the rather boring trip. Nothing stirred his imagination until they approached the suburbs of Phoenix. On the west side of the freeway several ultra-modern buildings caused him to wonder how many millions of dollars were sunk into those construction projects. Soon afterwards came Sky Harbor International Airport and the thought that he might take up flying lessons.

"Hey, dream boy, you gonna take the wheel for a stretch?"

His fantasy was dashed by reality, and he was about to offer Jeff a hundred dollars a mile if he drove the rest of the journey. The absurdity of such a proposal struck him just in time.

"Whenever you're ready, Jeffy baby." Franco could not imagine why he used Driscoll's term of endearment when he addressed Jeff Shackleford.

Jeff was startled by the comment and almost swerved into the next lane, which was full of traffic at four on a Thursday afternoon. The lanes twisted through the downtown area before setting sights for the west once more.

"For Christ's sake! Don't ever do that to me again, Franco."

"I'm real sorry. I don't know how that happened." Franco was apologetic and also very much aware of the danger posed by a freeway accident.

Jeff pulled off at the Thirty-Fifth Avenue ramp and they switched seats without getting out of the van. Franco's concentration was suitably directed to the rush-hour traffic as he left the metropolitan area. His grip on the wheel remained tight until the numbers of the Avenues were in the hundreds. On the left was a long-abandoned sports arena and on the north side was a prison camp. He chuckled to himself as he saw a sign at the side of the freeway. It advised drivers: do not pick up hitchhikers.

"Man, they're not kidding!" He spoke for the first time since taking the helm.

Jeff had also spotted the sign and nodded in agreement. A few seconds later he was to pose a question they had both avoided since the relative success of the operation.

"What do we do next? We've got the money. How the hell do we get away from L.A. without getting caught?"

"And where do we go?" Franco squinted as he drove towards the falling sun, wishing they had at least one pair of sunglasses between them.

"One thing's for sure: we won't be able to get home tonight." Jeff concluded this from the distance, time and their physical condition. "Might as well stop in Blythe, or somewhere around there. That will give us this evening to think out the plan from here."

It was Franco's turn to nod in tacit consensus.

One hundred and twenty miles later, Franco was becoming weary of the miles they had put behind them over the last couple of days. The state border crossing was ahead and Jeff had his head resting heavily on the window next to him.

"Anything to declare?" It was an inquiry that related to produce being unlawfully transported into California. However, Franco felt his sphincter muscle tighten automatically as he answered the border crossing guard.

"Nope. Except that my partner's snoring is keeping me awake." He decided that some mild humor might help work on his own anxiety.

In seconds they were safely on home turf and the van steered down the second Californian off-ramp. This one housed most of the restaurants and motels in the area that were freeway close. It was after six by now and they agreed to find a room before any other business. A Motel Six was within walking distance of several eating establishments and became the next recipient of confiscated twenty-dollar bills. A payphone in the lobby attracted Jeff's attention after they paid for the rooms.

"I'm going to call Jessica. Let her know I'll be home tomorrow, maybe early afternoon."

"I'll use it after you. I've called home once since we left on Sunday. Don't want her worrying, particularly now we are so close." Franco knew he wanted Teresa to understand why he had done this deed, but had not the slightest idea how he would explain it.

The phone rang six times as Jeff became impatient and a little concerned. The answering machine kicked in so he hung up. He could not think of anything appropriate to say and was perplexed as to why Jessica was not home at six-thirty-five.

"How do you leave this kind of message?" He asked himself and expected no answer from Franco who was sitting in the only chair in the tiny lobby.

"My turn now. You should try later. She's probably just working late at that salon of yours." He took the handset before it was hung up. After dialing his home number he thought he must have pushed a wrong button or two. He had no machine at the other end and allowed the ringing to continue for what seemed an eternity. Finally, there was an end to it as the phone was picked up. Franco considered a sarcastic remark about the time it took to answer, but he held his tongue.

"Hello." It was a man's voice.

Franco was shocked and asked if this was his number. He recited his home number slowly, including the area code.

"That is correct." What few words he had heard belonged to a Hispanic male who spoke fairly good English.

"Who the fuck is this?" Franco was worried and infuriated, simultaneously.

"Ah, this must be Francisco Perez…."

Before the intruder at his home could say any more, Franco wanted to lash out with a tirade of futile threats, but his intentions were quickly thwarted.

"You listen, Mister Francisco Perez. We have your wife and two precious boys. You have our money." The man was educated but Franco recognized the accent was from Mexico.

While this apocalyptic disclosure sunk in, Franco visualized this barbarian in control of his beloved family. "What do you want?" It was a simplistic response, but the obvious inquiry.

"You are not a stupid man, Francisco Perez. We have something you cherish and the money is all that we care about. Call this number after you have slept on it."

Despite Franco's protestations, all he was given was a seven-digit number. He frantically waved to Jeff for a pen and one was retrieved from the clerk at the desk. Franco wrote down what he remembered as the number and read it back. There was confirmation that he had recorded the number correctly.

"Is that eight-one-eight area code?" He wanted so desperately to ask other questions but felt this was monumentally important under the circumstances.

"We do not live in the rich man's part of town like you. It is two-one-three. And if you think you can find your family by tracing the number, they will be killed one by one if you make a wrong move. Tell your partner that we also make the same promise about his beautiful blonde wife." This final threat was followed by a click as the phone was hung up.

"What's up, Franco? It sounds bad from where I'm standing."

"It is. Real bad. They have Teresa and my boys…..Jessica too." He replaced the handset slowly, automatically, staring absently at the instrument that had relayed the devastating news.

"Jessica! How? What in hell's name led them to our families?" It was an understandable, near-hysterical outburst.

The clerk was also agitated by the disturbance in his lobby. He asked them to leave or he would call the police. They convinced him it was nothing to worry about; a personal tragedy. They would take their grief to the rooms he just rented to them. As they left, he thought it might have been a mistake to let them have those rooms. The police would be his first option if they caused another commotion.

In Jeff's room the drab décor seemed even more depressing, given their state of mind. The roller-coaster ride they had experienced over the last few days was proving to be a severe shock to their mental and physical well-being. Any consideration that might have been directed towards the final stages of their conspiracy was now placed firmly on hold.

Not being able to take any further positive action was the ultimate stumbling block. The message had been loud and clear: sleep on it! With the lives of their loved ones at stake, they knew that the ground rules must be followed; at least until they could develop a position of advantage. Faith was in short supply as they considered their options. They toyed briefly with the prospect of driving to Los Angeles that night, but common sense won out since they were both too fatigued for the journey.

Franco left for a few minutes and returned from a brief visit to a nearby mini-market. A brown paper sack held a six-pack of cold beers and Franco popped two before Jeff could pass judgment.

"Look, Jeff, I'm sure you have lost any desire to eat just like me. So this might make us feel a little better. I have no intention of getting drunk, but what else are we gonna do tonight?"

Jeff displayed a dejected look of resignation. Following a deep sigh he took one of the open containers and drank long and hard from it.

"Tastes pretty good, Franco. Thanks for being there for me."

"We need each other more than ever. This is likely to be tougher than the rip-off." Franco extended his right arm and tilted his beer can slightly in Jeff's direction.

Jeff tapped the can with his own and swore a solemn oath.

"I know this is going to work out okay. We can be bigger assholes than them, if necessary."

CHAPTER TWENTY-FIVE

It was a long and frustrating night after they each drank three beers in the first hour. On empty stomachs, the alcohol had an immediate effect on their attitude, providing a display of bravado. Originally disheartened by the prospect of turning over the cash to the cartel, Jeff and Franco jovially described horrendous shoot-outs with the crooks; imaginary scenarios that left everyone dead except the twin conspirators and their family members.

"We'll kick some ass, man! Just wait and see." Franco's intoxication was more advanced due in part to his slender frame.

"Like we did yesterday. Oh boy, do they have something to look forward to!" Jeff was in the same groove.

Franco remained in his partner's room until he fell asleep. It was as much for the comfort of being together, as it was the inability to walk steadily. They slept for more hours than they might have expected. Since the drapes were left open, it was the early morning light that roused them. Mild hangovers were the order for the day. Since it was too soon to think of making the call, they felt a hearty breakfast would set them straight for the daunting task ahead.

Franco went to his room to shower while Jeff used his own. It was the first time they had been apart for nearly twenty-four hours. In spite of the adjacent rooms, both of them felt their respective levels of courage and determination drop to an unacceptably low point. As they soaped themselves it seemed such an immense burden had been laid on their shoulders. Things improved rapidly once again, when they set off across the road for the earliest meal they had consumed since each of them had worked the graveyard shift.

"Do you think we're more dependent on each other than ever before?" As they waited for the waitress, it was Franco that voiced his concern first.

"I know what you're feeling, 'cause I'm feeling it too." Jeff attempted to put the matter in perspective. "Even though we talked some shit last night, we both realize the cards are stacked against us."

"At least we do have something they want. In fact, they want it bad enough that they take four people hostage. That shows we have so much of their money, it hurts them." Franco took a long drink from the ice water brought by the bus boy and felt a hundred percent better.

"That's true, Franco, but these people are ruthless. They have no morals, no standards of behavior."

"Sounds like us, huh?" Franco turned his attention to the menu as the waitress arrived. Orders were placed and more water requested. Then they were alone again.

"I think we have more respect for the sanctity of human life than these thugs ever will." Jeff was convinced and sought to clear Franco's mind of any doubt.

"Yeah. Even after all we've been put through by the city, the department and even the people of L.A., I reckon we'd come out ahead of the average Joe in a popularity contest."

"And remember what we stood up to in Nogales. I know we had our backs against the wall, but all three of us showed as much intestinal fortitude as any cop."

"Or maybe we were simply stupid for being there in the first place." Franco Perez shook his head as he was reminded of the battleground.

"I don't regret being a part of it. Except I'd give just about anything to bring Driscoll back. Here's the food. I'm glad we ordered plenty to eat; we might be heading for some serious kind of showdown when we get back in town." Jeff had his knife and fork in hand as breakfast arrived.

The meal was devoured without further conversation. As they closed in on the dreaded moment when Franco was to call the crooks, there was only room for thoughts of their loved ones. Where were they? How were they being treated? And the question they tried so hard to avoid: were they still alive?

"Let's use the phone here by the restrooms. I don't want that hotel clerk getting jumpy again." Jeff's suggestion was accepted as he handed over a pen and some paper for the anticipated instructions.

"It's ringing." Franco felt his heart pounding as if it wanted to escape from his chest.

It was still very early, barely seven o'clock, but the phone was picked up after a couple of seconds.

"Who is this?" The voice was the same as the night before.

"You know who it is. Just give me the game plan."

"Ah, detective Perez, still thinking like a cop. In spite of stepping over to the wrong side of the law." When the crook said the words cop and law, he snarled with contempt. "But of course you are now as bad as we are. Is that not correct?"

"Don't play word games. What do you want?" Impatience was bubbling at the surface.

"There can be no doubt what it is we want. The only matter to be resolved is how you must get it to us." The exceedingly calm tone was just as annoying as the words.

Jeff saw Franco's face reddening as his eyes narrowed. Nothing was said for what seemed an eternity to Jeff. The silence sent a message to the crook who ultimately ended it.

"Let me speak with the *gringo*. He may not be so emotional as you, detective Perez. After all, he has only one family member to lose."

Before he responded with an outburst he would regret, Franco handed the phone to Jeff. He could not even bring himself to explain to his friend what had transpired so far.

"This is Shackleford. But then, you probably know that."

"Ahah! I like the way you think, *gringo*. Please be sure to remember the strength of my position." He utilized the same tactic with Jeff as he emphasized the derogatory term.

"The ball seems to be in your court, so let's hear it."

"Okay. How long will it take to get to Third Street and Vermont?" He named an intersection just west of downtown Los Angeles that was well known to Jeff from his days working Rampart Division patrol.

"We're still a ways out. Could be four or five hours, depending on traffic." It was as accurate an estimate as Jeff could give.

"I don't believe you two did not drive closer last night. You must be at the Arizona border."

"You could have been a good detective." It was Jeff's turn to show disdain.

"You could have been a good dope dealer." This time it was a genuine compliment. After he received no response to his misplaced praise, the crook went on with a list of conditions that the cops must adhere to. They would call as soon as they got within a mile or so of the meet location and be prepared to hand over the cash. They, in turn, would be reunited with their families.

"There's just one problem with those arrangements." Jeff and Franco had agreed the night before on a course of action that might prove deadly. However, it was based upon the sound conclusion that these men could not be trusted to keep their end of the bargain.

"I see no problem, detective Shackleford, unless you want to make one."

"When we arrive, we shall have two of the large bales of money. Not six. The exchange will be for the boys. If this goes well, then you can expect us to deal for the rest of your cash." It was a risky ploy. However, they had to find out if there was any chance of their wives and the twins being handed over alive.

"We do not agree to any terms you may dream up, detective. We have the people you love, and you do not." It was an uncompromising stance.

"The way we see it, you lost a large load of cocaine and many of your men too. So, even if you got your money back, we expect retribution and our family members are too easy a target." Jeff gave the rationale behind their position.

"Ah, yes, the cocaine. There will be many more shipments and those fools will be easy to replace. Of course, it was a valuable plane and will take some time to fit the extra tanks on a new one. But, we forgive you all of that. Just bring the money and we will keep our end of the bargain." He sounded as if he meant them to bring all of the money. Jeff was not about to argue the issue at this stage.

"And don't try to find us as we head towards L.A." This was a further ruse. They had assumed that if this organization was smart enough to find their homes in such short order, then they could calculate which vehicles were five hours away. They probably found Driscoll's apartment and saw Jeff's car there. Since Franco's car was at the supermarket lot, they might expect them to have that one plus Driscoll's big Ford.

"If I give you credit, you must do the same for me. We cannot hope to find you before the meet. It is obvious you know about counter-surveillance techniques if you work major narcotics section. And you have to work at that level of investigation to have learned so much about the Nogales Crossing. We have talked more than necessary and you have many miles to drive. Please, be careful."

The phone went dead before Jeff could wish him the same.

"So did he go for it?" Franco was anxious for the welfare of Teresa and the boys.

"He doesn't like our proposal one bit, Franco. But we expected resistance at first. Hopefully, when the cash is closer to them, they will come around. We should get on the road right away."

After collecting what few items they had in the motel rooms, they headed for the interstate, then westbound towards the Chocolate Mountains. In little more than an hour they were cruising down the steep approach to the Coachella Valley, which sports the stylish Palm Springs at its western-most point.

It is a decline virtually to sea level and many drivers find themselves exceeding the sixty-five speed limit by too great a margin. The Highway Patrol tend to give people the benefit of the doubt but there are times they cannot ignore the worst offenders. So it was with Jeff's careless and rapid descent.

"Franco, we have company. Chippy, probably." Jeff used the term made famous by the television series *Chips*.

The sleek Ford Mustang was some distance back with its red light illuminated, but their Ford van was the only vehicle within a half mile. As it got closer there was no doubt he meant for Jeff to pull over.

"Play it cool, partner." This was Franco's best advice.

"I don't think we should ID ourselves as cops. It might take more explaining that way." Jeff felt uncomfortable with the enormous sum of money looming in the rear of the van.

"Good morning, gentlemen. Are we in a hurry to get somewhere?" It was an inane yet harmless opening comment. The patrolman was a typical model of perfection. The uniform was sharply pressed, leather gear spit-polished; even his mustache could have been no more neatly trimmed.

"Sorry, officer. I guess I didn't realize how fast I was going down this long hill." Politely repentant seemed to be the best route.

"Driver's license, registration and insurance, please." He retained an air of formality, stopping well short of arrogance.

Jeff handed over his license and reached into the glove box for the papers from the dealership in Tucson.

"I'm afraid I don't have the proof of insurance with me right now."

The cop looked beyond Jeff's seat at the load in the rear. It was completely covered by the blankets, giving no clue to what was hidden from sight. He checked the papers, and then returned his attention to the load.

"This Terrance Maddox who owns the van, where is he right now?" He referred to the fictitious name used by Jeff when he made the purchase.

"Oh, Terry? Well, he's back in Tucson." Jeff was getting worried over the scrutiny given to the cash.

"What's in back, that's so important you have to speed wherever you're going?" He was not going to let it rest and clearly wanted a closer look.

"It's a special load of paper we have to deliver to a business associate in Los Angeles." More stares even while Jeff was explaining. They both knew this Highway Patrol officer needed a little more probable cause to demand the back doors be opened. But this cop did not know when to give up. Jeff took a calculated risk at ending his curiosity.

"Hey, look, if you're gonna write me up, just give me the ticket. Then we can be on our way. We got a living to make too, you know." He tried hard to balance his indignation with a minimal amount of respect.

This took the attention from the back of the van. He looked hard and long into Jeff's eyes. For a second, Franco thought he might wrench the door open and tell Jeff to step out. The heat from the low desert outside was adding to the sweat that streamed down the sides of Jeff's face.

"Just as you wish, sir. You were doing eighty-five in a more than generous sixty-five zone. I'll be back with the citation."

When he was back at his patrol car and busy with the ticket, Franco gasped a huge sigh of relief. "My God! I was certain he was going to look in the back. That was quite a gamble."

"You said it, buddy. And I think I lost about five pounds in perspiration."

With due consideration to the driver's statement and obvious hurry to get to his destination, the *chippy* took five minutes more than he usually did for a simple speeding ticket. When he returned to the van to present the citation for signing, he was no longer interested in what was behind Jeff.

"Sign here and I'll give you your copy." It was signed without protest or comment.

"Have a nice day and watch your speed, sir." The venom was gone from his voice now that the deed was complete.

In comparison to this incident, the rest of the journey was uneventful. Except when Franco tried to urge Jeff to take the fifty-seven freeway to Diamond Bar. He wanted to check on his house: the scene of a most terrible abduction.

Jeff was able to convince him that it would serve no purpose. There was also the slight possibility that members of the cartel were watching the place for just such a mistake. Franco submitted to his more cautious partner as they continued west through Pomona and over Kellog Hill.

They needed a safe place to store the bulk of the cash while they made their offer of one third. With incredible foresight and imagination, Jeff came up with the idea of the parking structure at

Central Facilities. This building was home to Central Division patrol as well as Major Narcotics. Jeff worked out of this location daily.

They rented another van in the downtown area and proceeded to the roof of the police parking area. Both of them were aware that they need only flash their badges to gain access. On the top level they were unlikely to be seen by anyone other than a police helicopter crew landing on the adjacent portion of the roof.

When they could see that nobody was driving around the parking spaces, they transferred four of the unopened packages of money into the new van and secured it. They were confident it could stay right there for many weeks, even months, without being disturbed.

With the weight of the crimes they had already committed it was an easy decision for Jeff to take his regular surveillance car from the roof. His blue Mercury Cougar had been sitting in the same spot since the previous Friday. Because of a full week off work, he was expected to leave it downtown and use his personal car. The spare set of keys was in a small magnetic box he hid under the rear bumper.

He drove his Cougar and Franco moved the Ford Econoline with the two packages of money. They purposely went directly to the meet location of Third Street and Vermont Avenue. With such a long delay expected by the crooks, they were not likely to be waiting patiently anywhere other than the phone location. This gave the duo a chance to case the area and set a game plan of their own.

There was only one obvious corner for the exchange, and that was the northeast. It was dominated by a Vons supermarket and provided an extremely large parking lot. They decided to leave the Ford van on the east side of the Vons, somewhat north of Third Street. This was done even prior to the call being placed. Their meet would take place on the west side of the lot, giving the easiest route for escape, north onto Vermont Avenue.

Just a block away they found a phone that was both working and not currently being used by any small time drug dealer. Jeff dropped the dime, although it was actually a thirty-five cent call. It was nearly three in the afternoon and they fully expected the crooks to be impatient.

CHAPTER TWENTY-SIX

On Wednesday evening, when the load of cocaine was not delivered to the next staging point, wheels were set in motion at a furious pace. Critical and confidential contacts were made and a well-oiled machine was activated. Preparations were made throughout the night and a game plan, more intricate and detailed than any law enforcement operation, was formulated.

With the ultimate in precision, three homes were raided simultaneously; in Van Nuys, Valencia and Diamond Bar. Teams were armed not only with superior weapons but also with background information that would leave the FBI blushing.

A three-man team hit Driscoll's apartment and found nobody home. In his parking space they found a vehicle that should have been at the Valencia address. Ransacking disclosed nothing of value except several firearms, which were taken for good measure.

A similar team visited Jessica Shackleford long before her departure for the beauty salon. Bound and gagged, she was able to show little resistance as they placed her in a car and whisked her away.

Significantly, there were more men who took down the Perez residence. It was as if they knew there would be a requirement for greater control at this location. Franco's boys struggled more through a desire to stop the manhandling of their mother, rather than for self-preservation. They were taken in a windowless van to the same location as Jessica.

Each vehicle they used was displaying out-of-state plates as a form of disguise. Less than three miles from each residence, the teams stopped and removed the plates, disclosing the genuine California plate for that particular car or van. It was an incisive attack completed in less than fifteen minutes in each instance.

One might be excused if the campaign was believed to have been masterminded by an elite group of police officers or a covert federal team. It was, however, the result of funds from the bottomless coffers of the Medellin cocaine cartel.

In a dingy apartment close to Seventh and Union Streets, they met for the first time. It was on the third floor and many of the other units were vacant. Jessica Shackleford had attended the last three Christmas parties thrown by Narcotics Group. However, she did not recognize Teresa Perez. This was not surprising since Teresa did not frequent police gatherings because of her devotion to the twins. A babysitter during the day while she worked could be rationalized, but the nights were for her family.

Two workers from the lowest levels of the organization were assigned to watch over the women and children. They spoke not one word of English and so their contact was primarily with Teresa Perez. For the first several hours all four captives remained bound and gagged. It became apparent that this arrangement would not work indefinitely because of feeding the prisoners and calls of nature.

It was made quite clear to Teresa that if anyone tried to scream or otherwise call out, there would be retribution dished out promptly. Only one of the four could go to the bathroom at any given time, and with that exception they would be handcuffed to a pipe that ran the length of the grimy apartment. Food could be easily eaten with the free hand, they were informed.

There was to be no talking allowed between the hostages. Teresa took the rare opportunity to speak with Jessica when something had to be translated. She gave the shortest English version of their commands, and then proceeded to chat about the situation. It gave some small comfort to all of them as the boys listened intently to their mother.

She persisted in asking questions of her captors that were beyond their knowledge. Why were they there? What were the demands?

How long could they expect to be in the apartment? Again it was a much needed chance to pretend to interpret for Jessica.

One of the jailers let it slip that he hoped the money was given up because he did not want to harm any of them. This puzzled Teresa who could not imagine what money he referred to. The castigation meted out by his partner-in-crime for disclosing this fact gave the girls a few minutes to discuss the issue. Teresa asked Jessica if her husband had a lot of cash and her response was predictable. Neither could fathom who might pay such a large sum for their release, particularly considering the scale and sophistication of the kidnappings.

It was a miserable day and the night was worse due to the apparent nightlife outside. The majority of the bedlam came from the noisy purveyors of drugs and their equally inconsiderate customers, with horns honking if a vender was not at the car door before the vehicle stopped. A few of the occupants within the building also added to the din by playing radios at the highest range of volume. Their first taste of the area often referred to by the media as South Central was a traumatic one indeed.

Breakfast was served very early. It consisted of menudo and tortillas which were quite acceptable to Anthony, Daniel and their mother. However, Jessica was not used to the Mexican delicacy and turned her nose up at the breakfast soup. She correctly guessed it was probably not produced in the most sanitary conditions anyway.

Unknown to all of the hostages, at the very time the food was offered there was a telephone call being answered in the adjacent apartment. The husbands were conducting the first stages of negotiation with a man that desired to see all of them dead. There would be no concessions made if he had his way. Fortunately for the cops and their families, he answered to a higher authority.

That Friday was a scorcher in Los Angeles and the tiny, roach-infested room had no air-conditioning or other fan to circulate the heavy atmosphere. With the windows closed tightly, the crooks were impervious to the stifling heat that bore down upon the reluctant guests. An aroma from the unwashed bodies began to nauseate all but their keepers. Even if they had been allowed to use the shower there was only one hand towel hanging from a nail in the bathroom.

This was already so filthy that they eventually stopped using it to dry their hands. Cleanliness was obviously far from the minds of the men assigned the task of watching over them. Unkempt hair, unshaven faces, dirt hiding under each fingernail; this was the standard set by both men.

Shortly after three that afternoon there was a knock at the door and one of the jailers spoke excitedly with the visitor. The person could not be seen from inside the room and the hushed voices were barely audible to Teresa. She caught the occasional word or phrase as she strained to hear. The story was relayed to the other man in the relative privacy of the bathroom. This gave a chance for Jessica to learn what little had been comprehended by her fellow hostage. It amounted to some reference to the money being nearby and the whole matter being over with very soon. There was an air of excitement and also trepidation when the men returned to the room.

Both sons and wives prayed for the comfort of their own homes as soon as possible. The devious laughter that the two men engaged in was not as encouraging as they had hoped.

CHAPTER TWENTY-SEVEN

"It is so long since we have heard from you. You must drive like a snail." This was the initial response to Jeff's telephone call.

"Actually, I got a ticket from the Highway Patrol for speeding. So you should be thankful we got here at all." It was a mild attempt at sarcasm.

There was uncharacteristic laughter at the other end of the line. Finally their contact was able to speak. "Lucky for you that the policeman did not check the load you are carrying."

"Lucky for you. I know how much you want this cash. Anyway, we are close to the meet location." Jeff's exterior composure was commendable in spite of his gut feeling of a potential tragedy.

"Ah, the meet location. I love the terms you cops use. Actually, we have a new location for the…..meet. It is now….."

Jeff jumped in on the dialogue. "No way! You think you can call the shots? We are close to Third and Vermont, and that's where it will go down. Like it or not."

"I do not like it….." He was about to say more but was interrupted yet again.

"Listen, I've had enough dealing with a nobody. I want to speak with someone of importance in your organization." Jeff hoped he could push some buttons with this remark.

"Let me tell you, detective, Federico Sanchez is not a nobody!" Even after saying this he was so infuriated that he did not realize what he had done.

"So, Federico Sanchez, you are a big wheel in the machinery. Is that what you are saying?" Jeff was taking control in a less than subtle manner.

There was silence for many seconds before Sanchez could contain himself.

"You are good. I will give you that, detective. Let us get back to the matter in hand. I am the one designated to deal with you, so let us talk." There was a concerted effort to keep a level head during the remainder of the phone call.

"Rico. May I call you Rico?" Jeff's rhetorical question was meant to be a slap in the face for Sanchez. "We have two bales of cash ready to exchange. That's a third of your money. We want Franco's boys for this first move. If you screw things up, you lose the rest of the cash. We know you people are ruthless but your objective is to get all of it back. This is the way to make certain everyone gets what they want."

There was silence while more thinking went on at one end of the call.

"If you try to double-cross us you should know that your wife and the entire family of detective Perez will be killed." Federico Sanchez made an attempt to regain lost ground.

"We have no intention of doing anything to jeopardize our families." Jeff was confident that he had the upper hand with the negotiations but worried about the actual outcome. "When can you be there with the boys?"

"Twenty minutes. At the Vons parking lot." Sanchez picked the predictable quadrant at the specified intersection.

"See you then. Drive carefully." It was Jeff's turn to hang up first.

Franco had been intent on picking up the whole conversation but was missing small pieces of the jigsaw. Jeff filled in the blanks and added his own summation without regard for Franco's somewhat tenuous faith.

"I don't trust this man. We have to be as careful as we've ever been during any operation we were involved in."

"Do you think we can expect to see my boys at the meet?" This was Franco's main concern.

"If he wants to get all of the cash back, I don't see how he cannot bring them." It was hardly an encouraging reply.

Jeff and Franco set up quickly in the lot and sat in the back of the Cougar surveillance car. There were dark windows all around except for the windshield. This was not legal, but then neither was jumping red lights and running stop signs. These were necessary infringements when following major drug dealers; on an official basis, at least.

One minor omission had been the question of how to recognize Sanchez when he arrived. Jeff wished he had raised the point but felt sure his instincts would kick in at the relevant time. This time came more rapidly than expected, as a dilapidated Dodge van entered the lot from Third Street. A red Nissan Sentra closely followed it and both of them cruised the lot for a minute or so.

There were two men in the Sentra and one man driving the van. If there was anybody else in the back of the van, they could not be readily seen. With the tinted windows and their lowered position in the rear seat, Jeff and Franco were virtually invisible.

As the Nissan continued to circulate around the very busy lot, the driver of the van parked and stepped out, looking in all directions. He was tall and slender with a confident bearing. Clean-shaven and well dressed, he was too neat to be driving such a clunker. This was certainly their man Sanchez.

He walked slowly yet deliberately to the payphones in front of the store and waited. It was Franco's turn to set off on foot.

Jeff was in a good position for viewing the encounter and his experience told him to stay put. Moving around such a lot without leaving it, this would tell a good observer who he was.

There was instant contact between Sanchez and Franco Perez.

"Rico?" Franco needed immediate confirmation.

"Ah. Detective Perez, I presume. You are not pale enough to be Shackleford." Sanchez could not be the straight man for any length of time.

"Are my boys here?"

"But of course. We have an agreement. Do you have our money?" This was now a strictly business meeting for Federico Sanchez.

The Sentra rolled within a few feet and Sanchez simply smiled in the direction of his associates.

"We have what we promised to bring. Here are the keys to the Ford van over there." Franco nodded towards the vehicle that had served them well all the way from Tucson.

"It is a pleasure doing business with you, detective. Our vehicle is in the middle of the lot. A sorry excuse for a Dodge van, I'm afraid. The keys are in the ignition. I hope to do this again quite soon." As Sanchez strode briskly towards the Ford van, the Nissan closed in on his position.

Timing seemed to be of the essence. That was Jeff's view from a hundred feet away. Sanchez was at the money vehicle an instant before Franco could reach the Dodge. Just out of sight of anyone else, Federico Sanchez confirmed that there were indeed two bales of money in the Ford. He gave a signal to the occupants of the Nissan with a subtle gesture of his right hand. It gently stroked the front of his own throat in a cutting motion, sending a clear message to his compadres.

A second later, Franco was the recipient of the greatest let down of his life. The Dodge van was devoid of any children. At first he looked in the direction of Jeff Shackleford with dismay. His second reaction was to turn to Sanchez and call him a son-of-a-bitch. However, the vision of the Nissan racing towards him told him that name calling was secondary to survival.

Franco's reactions and the approaching Sentra painted a picture that could not be any clearer to Jeff. He was already in the front seat and cranked up the Mercury Cougar in preparation for serious action. If it had not been for several shoppers with loaded carts blocking their way, the crooks would have reached Franco first. Luck would have it that Jeff was able to pick him up and reverse wildly until he had a lane available for their escape.

"Motherfuckers!" Franco spat the profane title at the fast approaching Japanese car.

"You got your piece ready, Franco?"

"You bet." Franco Perez had the Gloch nine millimeter poised for action. "They didn't bring my boys. Those assholes! What kind of game do they think they're playing?"

"I can't understand their reasoning. But then I gave up trying to figure out dope dealers years ago." Jeff could shed no light on his partner's dilemma.

The Mercury sped from the lot, northbound on Vermont, joining a steady stream of cars. It was closely followed by the two men, one of them driving the Nissan with reckless abandon.

Jeff weaved in and out of the typically sluggish Friday afternoon traffic as carefully and as swiftly as he could. There were complaints from many drivers, some simply waved a clenched fist, others screamed obscenities through the L.A. smog. Without a set of rules to govern his conduct, the driver of the Nissan intimidated those same drivers to such an extent that they feared for the safety of their vehicles. There were no thoughts of challenging this maniac. With the atmosphere the way it had been in Southern California for years, he was as likely as not to be armed.

Jeff and Franco were far more certain of this last perception through personal experience. What they could not fathom was the ultimate intent of their pursuers. As Jeff Shackleford spun the wheel, turning east onto First Street, two shots rang out close behind them. If they had any doubts as to the purpose of the chase, they were dispelled in that one instant.

Pedestrians ran in every direction not knowing the source of the gunfire. Several of those more experienced in street survival flattened themselves to the sidewalk. Babies cried and women screamed as more rounds were discharged. An unsuspecting commuter held up the Nissan from its turn and became frozen at the wheel when he heard the gunfire. Eager to keep the Cougar in sight, the fanatical crook rammed the car ahead three times until he pushed it into the intersection. His front bumper was left behind as he raced towards downtown, intent on closing the gap at any cost.

If Jeff had noticed the slight delay via his rearview mirror, he could easily have made a quick turn and ended the chase. However, his attention was directed at surviving the treacherous course he was taking. Franco had been silenced by the shots and was frantic over the thought that he might never see his wife and children again. A sudden change in direction with a right turn on Alvarado Street tossed Franco almost into Jeff's lap, and his nine millimeter handgun slipped from his now moist grasp. It fell beneath Jeff's feet and under the brake pedal but his driving was so intense that he was unaware of its presence.

"Shit! My piece. It's by your feet." Franco chanced a look back himself before deciding how to retrieve his gun. It was a shock indeed to see the little red car only a couple of hundred feet to their rear. At first he considered the darkly tinted windows might be playing a game with his eyesight. However, the foolhardy manner in which it was being driven told the whole story.

"Jeff, you're not losing those fuckers!"

"Well stand by to stand by, buddy." Jeff shouted this as if to impress upon his partner the magnitude of his intended maneuver. As the light turned red for their southbound lane he was in the number one lane. Jeff ran the light and made the left turn onto Third Street, crossing in front of the regular left turn lane which was loaded with cars. For a second there were only two wheels making contact with the road surface and Franco was positive they were about to flip onto the passenger side. Defying the laws of gravity, the Cougar regained its total grip upon the pavement and headed once again in the direction of L.A.'s high-rise area.

The insubordinate action of the Cougar caused most of those drivers headed east and west to brake as they started to enter the intersection. Taking advantage of this momentary lapse, the chase car swerved across two lanes while still southbound and into the northbound number one lane. The possessed driver was now on the wrong side of the road closing in on a red traffic signal. He applied one hand to the horn and held it there as he sped between protesting drivers, then he also started the left turn. His momentum took him sliding sideways into the south curb of Third Street, and his two passenger side wheels struck hard. The impact took away virtually all of the forward motion and both occupants were launched towards the right door window.

The driver was fortunate having someone next to him to soften his blow. But the passenger's head slammed into the window so hard, it almost rendered him unconscious. The chaos left in the wake of the crooks sent notice to the two cops that anything goes. Now that severe damage had been inflicted upon the nearside wheels, there was some doubt as to their ability to continue.

"Take Westlake, Jeff. It'll be faster and we can put some distance between us." It was the next road on the right and sported two generous southbound lanes, usually with light traffic.

As Jeff tightened his grip of the wheel in preparation for the turn, he moved his right foot to the brake pedal. It was imperative that he reduce his speed before the corner. There was no response to this action and when he glanced down he saw the reason. Franco's weapon had slid directly under the brake during the last violent shift in direction. It was firmly wedged under the mechanism and no significant slowing was likely in their immediate future.

"We got problems right here, Franco." It was an understatement. Jeff reached down with his right hand and held onto the steering wheel with the other. Even though he had taken his foot off the gas, he was racing past Westlake Avenue. He could not quite get a grip of the gun at first, and took his eyes off the road for a second to help his mission.

"Jesus! Look out, Jeff!" Franco saw the traffic in the number one lane was stopped for a young Hispanic woman crossing from the north. She was pushing one little baby in a stroller and held the hand of a laughing toddler next to her. With westbound traffic stopped and the first lane on the south side allowing her to cross, she was not expecting to see a car speeding towards her.

"Oh, God, no!" Jeff had his right elbow between his knees, his chin pressed against the wheel and just the fingertips of his left hand guiding the car. He was not prepared for this misfortune, and the tragedy that loomed ahead spelled greater misery than he could imagine. The slightest motion of his left hand changed the direction of travel barely enough to miss the woman and her babies by inches. She screamed in fear of being slain and other drivers held their breath and shook their heads in amazement. The joy that her older child displayed was gone in an instant as the scream of his mother scared him more than the passing car.

Meanwhile, the cause of the cops' imprudence was gaining impetus yet again. The stalled Nissan was restarted and despite two wheels bent under the frame, it headed after its quarry. It had the same deranged driver but the passenger was not completely back with the program. He held the side of his head and moaned from time to time.

An instant after Jeff passed so close to the woman, he was able to dislodge the gun and apply the brakes.

"Here we go. I'm gonna take this alley." This time Franco was determined to retain the gun as Jeff handed it to him. They made the southbound route into an alley that runs parallel with Westlake Avenue, and increased speed as they passed between the towering apartment buildings. Closing in on the tee intersection where Maryland Street meets the alley, they could see a car stopped after partially entering the alley. A drug deal was in progress at the driver's window as an opportunist seller was exchanging a small rock of cocaine for twenty dollars.

"Want to make a bust, Franco?" It was the closest they had been to a lighthearted moment for many hours.

"Just watch you don't take out the car. I'm beginning to wonder about your driving." Franco's left hand reached out for the dash and grabbed it as firmly as his right hand was holding the Gloch.

There was actually very little room to spare. So little, that the mirror on Jeff's side was unceremoniously knocked clean off by a low windowsill jutting out from the wall.

"Man, that was close." Franco had been watching his side.

"Don't use those things anyway." Jeff made reference to his absent mirror. It caused him to check in the rearview mirror and he saw the poor excuse for a Japanese car, still in hot pursuit. It was now severely damaged to both the front and the right side, but still careened wildly down the alley. The drug deal was complete and the driver saw the flash of red approaching. He backed away into Maryland Street to give adequate room for the second lunatic headed his way.

With everything that had happened during the incredible race, Jeff was now acquiring a little confidence. He had to stop at the end of the alley where it joined Sixth Street because there was no way to see traffic until the last second. Miraculously, it was clear enough to cross to the south side and head inbound for the city center for what proved to be the last time. Unfortunately, the gap in traffic was sufficient for the Nissan to follow suit without slowing.

"These guys never give up." Jeff was traveling against the main flow of commuters and accelerated to around fifty miles per hour.

"Maybe we should try and catch **them**. We could find out where our folks are even if we have to torture them." Franco sought solace from his misguided plan.

"Nice try, Franco, but you know as well as I do that those idiots would shoot it out until the bitter end." It was an accurate statement from Jeff.

They stayed well ahead until the business district provided a heavier load of cars and buses. Several times they passed through intersections with only a second to spare before the red signal. Each time they were also disheartened to see their would-be assassins creating havoc by ignoring the color of the light.

Without realizing he was headed there, Jeff steered the Cougar towards the relative safety of Central Facilities. As he passed the long abandoned Greyhound Bus Depot, he jumped one last red light himself. This gave just enough space to make a turn onto Wall Street and then into the security of the police parking structure.

When the Nissan finally arrived at the same spot, the driver was confused for the first time since Third and Vermont. He knew the fortress-like configuration on the west side of the street was a police station. What he could not believe was that the two fugitive cops would dare hide inside.

Ascending to the roof, Jeff hoped they would not meet anyone he knew. He was supposed to be on vacation for a week and here he was, driving his city car with a mirror torn off. Add to that, a suspended officer next to him holding an unauthorized weapon. This would be tough to explain. They pulled in next to the money van and saw that it was still secure. There was no doubt that it was safe, but with so much at stake it deserved their attention.

At the wall surrounding the east side of the lot they both leaned over and saw the battered Nissan parked across from the entrance below. They were four stories up but it was obvious that the driver, now standing on the sidewalk, saw them. There was also little doubt that he saw Franco flip him the finger.

CHAPTER TWENTY-EIGHT

It took about five minutes before they came to the realization that their predicament was getting worse with every move. They had just experienced a ride more terrifying than any at Disneyland. The evidence was clear that one of the rounds fired at them had struck the trunk. There was no hole, simply a deep gouge where it ricocheted from the top of the lid. It must have narrowly missed the rear window as it flew over their fleeing vehicle.

"They obviously wanted to scare the crap out of us." Franco felt the smoothness of the groove left behind by the bullet.

"I can't understand it, Franco. It sure seemed to me like they were trying to kill us." Jeff was unnerved for the umpteenth time since the money came into their hands.

"Another thing that has been bothering me: how the hell did they find out who we all are? And how did they find out so fast?" For some strange reason it was a question neither of them had posed until now. Since they became fugitives, they had expected almost anyone to be chasing them.

Jeff slowly ran the fingers of his left hand through his fair hair. After shaking his head he tossed around an idea that barely held any substance. "Perhaps they were able to ID Driscoll from fingerprints, or something." He also shrugged his shoulders as he offered the floor to Franco.

"Even if the authorities had found him, they would take much longer than this to find out his identity. These crooks must have been moving on our homes within twelve or fourteen hours after we split from Nogales." Franco was mystified by the swift and precise assaults that the cartel had undertaken.

"And what tied us to the cash, anyway? There's something we aren't seeing in all of this. Not even the most sophisticated criminal organization is capable of such clinical efficiency."

Enough time had passed for them to take another look over the wall. The little red car was gone, together with both of its occupants. A check around the north and west walls failed to tell them where the Nissan had moved to. It was impossible to view Sixth Street to the south, because a helicopter landing pad took up that portion of the roof.

They were unsure of the best move to make next. The most likely course involved a telephone call to try and find out what Sanchez' state of mind was. Remote though it appeared, the two goons in the Nissan may have overstepped their authority. Wires may have gotten crossed in the Vons parking lot.

Even so late on a Friday afternoon, there was too great a chance of Jeff meeting somebody he worked with on the third floor. They took the stairs down to the first floor, which was occupied by patrol and the divisional detectives. The large office at the west end of the building was home to detectives who investigated most crimes. Burglary, robbery, sex crimes and auto theft were handled in this office; primarily during the day watch hours. They were fortunate that it was virtually vacant, given the nature of the telephone call they intended to make.

Two detectives were seated next to each other at the far end of the room. They were diligently studying crime reports from a stack of papers positioned between them. For the pair to be so industrious with the weekend fast approaching, it must involve a serious matter. The potential for solving a crime, or string of them, might be the cause for such persistence.

"Remember when we were so conscientious?" Franco whispered to Jeff as he reflected on the not so distant past.

"It's all ancient history now, Franco. You won't find a single person on this department who will give you credit for the good you've done. And, quite frankly, I wouldn't expect any now we've broken through to the other side." Jeff finished his profound view of their state of affairs, and then picked up the phone.

"What are you gonna say to that idiot?" Franco was not sure if there was anything to discuss before the call was made, but asked his friend anyway.

There was a brief silence as Jeff looked to be staring straight ahead. Franco thought that the other detectives might have been paying them some attention, so he glanced over his shoulder to look at what Jeff could see. He should not have concerned himself with the hard working duo; whatever they were engaged in was far more important than the discreet actions of a couple of strangers.

After what seemed an eternity to Franco, the fingers of his cohort skipped over the calling buttons. Jeff could think of nothing pertinent to confer over, and so he made the connection.

"Sanchez?" Jeff had to speak first, since there was total silence at the other end when the handset was lifted.

It was reasonable to assume someone else answered the phone as a muffled conversation took place in the background. When a voice finally took over it was the same arrogance that Jeff had become used to.

"Who is this calling?" It was in English and this showed that he was expecting Shackleford to call.

"You know damn well who this is, Sanchez. What kind of double-crossing game are you playing?" Jeff showed obvious signs of strain but held short of the anger he felt inside.

"We were short by a few thousand dollars, *gringo*. One of the bundles was opened."

"That's a bunch of bullshit! With the millions you got back, you don't have any reason to complain about chump change. Besides, there's no way you could have seen there was some missing; at least, not before you set your incompetent thugs on us." He was hoping for a better feel for the situation than he was getting so far.

"Ah, yes. They were, as you say, incompetent. I will accept your description of their conduct. Maybe we can try it again. Okay?" Sanchez was cooler now than he had been since the onset of the negotiations.

"Look, Rico, we kept our end of the bargain, so far. It's your turn to keep yours. We want the boys before you see another dime." It was a valiant attempt on Jeff's part to keep the upper hand.

"I think if we are to meet again, detective, we should both bring with us what we originally agreed upon. We will deliver the precious children and you will give us two bundles of the money; unopened this time." These were Federico's ground rules for a second time.

"We never did trust you and now we have good reason for our suspicions. Bring…..us…..the boys." Jeff almost spelled it out for him.

"This is becoming tiresome. If you decide to comply, then call me back soon."

Jeff was stunned when he heard the click that ended the call. He slammed his own handset down, furious with both Sanchez and himself. Negotiations should have gone on indefinitely even if agreement was not in sight.

The inconsiderate abuse of the instrument caused the two detectives to jump and they looked at Jeff and Franco with scorn. There was a brief period when they looked as if they might inquire into the legitimacy of their presence in the detective squad room. Jeff endeavored to avoid eye contact with the rightful occupants and began his hushed recounting of the call to Franco.

"He isn't going to deal fairly. I figure he will try and recover as much money as possible. Then at any time during this one-sided transaction he will have us all killed." This was a summary of the contents of the call.

"That doesn't sound like any kind of deal to me. If he harms my wife and kids, I'm gonna hunt him down and kill him, if it's the last thing I do." Franco had these feelings, right from the moment he knew his family was in the hands of the opposition. This was the first time his gut reaction had manifested itself.

"That's very commendable, Franco, and I'll be right there beside you. However, I pray it never comes to that." Jeff had reached across the desk and grasped Franco's left wrist firmly with his right hand. It was a symbol of their solidarity during the most demanding period of their lives.

Seconds after Federico Sanchez abruptly ended the call, he entered the adjacent room. It was with his familiar, indifferent words that he addressed the families of the cops he so hated.

"Your husbands do not care for you enough. They would rather see you die than give up the money they stole from us." Sanchez uttered this statement more to prepare the women and boys for the worst, than to intimidate them. Although his words were in excellent English, Teresa responded in Spanish. She felt a misguided need to protect Jessica Shackleford from the answers she expected.

"What money could you possibly be talking about? Our husbands have no amount of money that would justify this." As she spoke the last word she swept her hand around the wretched scene in the squalid room.

He answered her in English because he wanted each hostage to understand fully the weight of the situation.

"Your two men, together with a third who is now dead, stole more than forty-five million dollars from our.....company. All we want is our money to be returned and all will be well for each of you." His announcement was so compelling that he gave no further explanation.

"Liar! Nobody says such things about my father." Daniel's outburst was a reflection of how both twins felt.

Teresa was next to Daniel and she reached out with her free hand. The distance between them was such that she could only place her hand on the back of his neck. She squeezed gently, comforting the distraught child. There was a tirade of expletives from the mother that basically said the same as her son's protestations.

Jessica simply cried softly to herself. "No! No! No!"

The results of Federico's bombshell brought tremendous amusement to the two guards. There were few words of the English exchange they could make out, but the theme was apparent.

Leaving the hostages in varying states of skepticism and alarm, Sanchez closed the door behind him and avoided further indignant criticism.

"We have to take the risk." Franco was now desperate and willing to put his own life in jeopardy at least one more time.

"If you mean trust Sanchez to bring along the boys, you're not thinking straight." Jeff knew he had his hands full with his partner's extreme point of view.

"What else is there? Even if he isn't going to keep his promise, it may be the only chance we have of finding them. Your wife too, Jeff. Are you thinking of her?"

"She's been on my mind since we tried to call yesterday. It's hurting more than I've admitted, just knowing some dope fiends have her holed up somewhere." The thought was tough, but now that he had voiced his fears there was a trace of moisture in his eyes.

"Sorry. I know you feel the same as me. I'm sure it doesn't make it any less distressing, just because they're only holding one person who's close to you." It was an honest overflow of compassion from Franco, particularly given his own anguish.

"So you figure we have to follow these morons to the place where they're hiding our folks?"

"Jeff, it has to be the only way. Especially if you're right about Sanchez and his ultimate goal." Franco saw that his partner was beginning to adopt the same line of thinking.

"How can we do it, with just the two of us? We need help and we can't ask for it." It was a realistic conclusion of Jeff's part.

"I've done it before, once or twice. And you have loads of experience on surveillance cases. Hell, nobody can fault your driving ability under pressure, particularly after that awesome performance. I thought we were dead in the water but you got us back to home base."

Jeff let the praise sink in for a while. He knew better than to agree to it with only two people. There was also the matter of only one car being available. Using the money van was out of the question. It would not perform to the standards they needed if the crooks drove at the same breakneck pace as before.

"I have an idea, Franco, and you'll think I'm insane when I tell you." Jeff was not quick to rush into an explanation of his notion. Instead, he tried to justify what he was about to propose. "We agree that Sanchez will probably not bring anyone to a meet other than his own henchmen. Therefore, it leaves us with the only option of conducting a surveillance, in the hope that he will lead us to our families. Needless to say, a full squad would do the job more proficiently."

"You sound like a politician, Jeff. I concede all of those issues. So what's your bottom line?"

"We must have help to be successful." Jeff paused momentarily to convince himself it was a rational scheme. "I know one person we might contact."

When Jeff projected a distinct lack of eagerness to bring up his main point, Franco closed his eyes and tilted his head backwards. After he drew in a deep breath, he let it out slowly in a bid to compose himself.

Jeff spoke first. He hoped to forestall a frustrated Franco from drawing more attention from the two detectives again. There was some concern that the actual suggestion itself would inflame his companion.

"Montgomery." The spoken word was even more unpalatable to Jeff as was the original idea.

"I wish you meant Field Marshal Montgomery. That famous English soldier." Franco nearly choked on his words as he considered the real meaning of Jeff's utterance.

"Yeah, me too. That would be the guy to guide us through this mess. But, unfortunately, I mean the commander, Neaville Montgomery." Jeff was speaking in a very low tone to insure they were not overheard.

This caused Franco to whisper in his own strained manner, while wanting to shout at his deranged partner in crime.

"You must be mad. You've finally lost it, Jeff. He's such an adorable character; he's the one that wants me put away for the latest shooting. I can see it now: 'so you two stole millions in cash, killed several men and cause the death of another police officer. Plus you left the scene of this catastrophe. Certainly, I'll give you all the help you need, boys.'" Franco could barely restrain himself from raising his voice. The effort made him red in the face.

"Look, we use the info that Driscoll gave us to get him to help. Maybe we can come out of this alive, with our families intact. If we stay out of prison, then that's probably a bonus." It was an awful comment on how far they had come in so few days.

"Jeff, I don't see how the story about the commander can serve us. What we gonna do, blackmail him?" Franco wanted to reach across the table and grab Jeff by the scruff of the neck and shake some sense into him.

There was no love lost between Franco and Montgomery. The ruling to prosecute the detective over the shooting of Gregory Rowland had started with a spineless decision from the commander. It was made as much to protect his elevated position in the police department, as it was to avoid the difficult questions that would be asked if he took a stance in the officer's defense. Some leader. That was the widespread, but generally secretive views of most narcotics detectives.

"I guess it's a kind of blackmail. We tell him we did something wrong, but we know he's been a bad boy too. Help us or we tell." Jeff simplified the situation dramatically.

"He's going to wonder how we know about his fraudulent banking practices." Franco was so far from being on the same wavelength that he would throw any number of stumbling blocks in the way.

"That's obviously something we must use to our advantage. The less he knows about our source, the better. Keep him wondering and he will not be sure just how much we know."

"I'm almost ready to take my chances with Sanchez right now. I don't like it, Jeff. How's he going to get men to work on this case, anyway?" The fact that Franco was asking such a question indicated he might be willing to accept the equally treacherous course that Jeff recommended.

"He can pretend it's some federal caper where they need our expertise in surveillance. That kind of thing happens all the time in majors. The local cops do all of the dirty work, then the feds take the credit when the story breaks." Tentatively, it was a plan with some small degree of promise. He was not sure himself if they could convince the commander to go along with it.

For another ten minutes they thrashed it around and fine-tuned the details. First they would try to persuade Montgomery over the phone. This would hopefully eliminate the chance of being arrested on the spot if they confronted him personally. The exact manner of dealing with Sanchez would have to come from a meeting with the number one man in Narcotics Group.

Now that Franco was satisfied they had to get Montgomery involved, he insisted on being the one to meet face to face with his nemesis. The reasoning behind such perilous conduct was that if the commander failed to go for the deal, then Franco was already in deep with the legal system anyway. Jeff would still have a chance of escape; a remote one, but a chance, nevertheless.

"If he busts me right away, then you take the money and…..well, do what you got to do." Franco was forgetting about Jessica.

"If that happens, old buddy, then you have to convince the feds to move on Sanchez. They will undoubtedly be brought in immediately, if Montgomery tells them what you admit to."

"Promise you'll take the cash somewhere safe. You know there will be an all out effort to free innocent victims of this whole mess." Franco gave his friend specific instructions. "You've admitted we cannot do it ourselves, so be patient and let them set the wheels in motion."

"Hey, we're talking like it's a done deal that you get arrested. We have to make the call first." Jeff shook off the despondent feeling that engulfed him briefly. "I'll do that. With me speaking to him on the phone, then you having the meet, it might keep him off guard longer."

They were not sure if he would still be in the building at such a late hour on Friday. If he were at work, he would be two floors above them and at the far end of the hallway. Franco picked up a phone on the same line so he could eavesdrop. Jeff dialed the five digit internal number and waited for the ringing to be countered by a secretary answering the phone. It rang for much longer than the commander would appreciate. He did not tolerate poor telephone etiquette, and that included picking up before three rings.

"Commander Montgomery, Narcotics Group. Can I help you?" There must have been nobody else around to answer, as the boss himself acknowledged with a proper greeting.

"Is this the commander?" Jeff wanted to be sure. The absence of a secretary running interference was disconcerting.

"That's what I said. Who is this, please?" He was brief but still quite courteous.

"That's not what I'd like to talk about first." Jeff wanted his senior officer to be aware of some ground rules. "I know something that….."

He was abruptly cut short. "I don't speak with anyone on the phone unless they identify themselves first. Naturally, if you want to make a Wee-Tip call, I can direct your call to the correct number." He was still polite but firm with his own rules, as he made reference to the number used by people who want to make anonymous tips about drug dealing and other crimes.

"You really should speak with me. I know something about you that is not common knowledge. And you probably would not want anyone else to know." Jeff attempted to get things on the right track.

"I don't take crank calls either. If you really must spew out some dirty tale, why don't you get to the point?" He suddenly became agitated and impatient.

"I know about the banking arrangements you had with your brother over a period of years. Large sums of money going your way that should have been returned to various police agencies. You kept the interest on the seized assets of drug dealers." This was the turning point if he was to be of any use to them.

"Who the hell is this? I don't react well to idle threats." Montgomery was now at boiling point.

"Like I said, I don't think I should tell you who I am right now. But I would point out that I have made no threats, yet." Jeff emphasized the final word.

"So I suppose you're going to ask for money. Is that it?"

Jeff and Franco made screwed up faces at each other. The thought of getting more money illegally was too much for them to consider. It almost made Franco burst out laughing.

"No, I don't want money. Not a dime. But rest assured, the public will find out about your deeds if you cross me." The position that the commander held was placed in perspective for him.

"Go on. I'm listening." This was a slight encouragement for his two subordinates.

"I need your help. I've done something pretty bad myself and I'm in a little jam. You know what it's like to be on the other side of the law. You might not know how it feels to have the whole matter blow up in your face. But I'm seeking the kind of assistance only you can organize." Most of Jeff's cards were on the table, so he waited for a response.

There was simply silence for a period of time that was magnified many times for Jeff and Franco.

"You still there?"

"You one of our cops?" Montgomery came back immediately with his own question.

Jeff held his breath a while before owning up. "You wouldn't be where you are if you couldn't figure that one out."

"What exactly do you mean by pretty bad? Just how far have you stepped over the line?" There was an unpleasant smugness about his manner. If Jeff had time to analyze it, he may have been even more uncomfortable with the dialogue.

"Far enough. There is a large sum of cash that is no longer in the possession of some drug dealers, and they want it back. Funny, really, you should know what that is like."

"We are talking about you, right now." Neaville Montgomery focused on the subject that interested him. "Where is this large sum of cash?"

"You don't need to know that at this stage. But you should be aware that these crooks have taken some people as hostages. They want to deal cash for bodies." Jeff was sure things must be clear enough for the commander.

"I don't want to sound simplistic, but have you given consideration to complying with their demands. That may get you your loved ones back."

"Commander, I said nothing about loved ones. How would you know that?" Jeff looked apprehensively at Franco across the table. The look was returned with increased consternation over the safety of their families.

"It is quite logical, really. If they were not loved ones, you would surely have taken the money and run to some far away land." It was sound reasoning on the part of their boss.

"Okay. You're right about that. We want the loved ones back and I think they may be in danger of being killed. It might not matter what we do with the money because the guy that is running their end is crazy." Jeff was feeling better about sharing the pain.

"Let us assume for the moment that I will help you. What is it you expect me to do?" Caution continued to be a primary factor at his end of the discussion.

Franco nodded to Jeff as the tension was eased for both of them.

"A surveillance of the crooks, so we can find the location where they are holding their prisoners. That's what I hope will resolve the situation." Jeff sketched out a crude game plan for the commander.

More silence. This time Jeff waited patiently.

"So you are saying that if I help you get back these folks that have been kidnapped, you will refrain from telling on me. Is that the general idea?" Montgomery certainly had a grasp of the basic scheme.

"Yes, sir. That's about the size of it." Jeff could not believe he actually used the civil term of address, considering the content of the discussion.

"Then why don't we meet and get the firm points down to our mutual liking." It was definitely a statement not a question.

"How about one hour from now?" This was a rhetorical question from Jeff Shackleford.

"In my office. Oh, I'm sure if you know so much about me, you know where my office is." There was the merest hint of sarcasm as the commander felt more comfortable than perhaps he should.

"See you then." The call was over.

Jeff's face sported a frown with deep ridges between his eyebrows. He slowly shook his head and looked at his partner's reaction to the telephone call.

"Franco, there's something I can't quite put my finger on. It just seemed to go too smoothly. What do you think?"

"I think we have no choice. It's going to be repulsive, dealing with that asshole, but I can do it. We have to think of Teresa, Jessica and my twins." Franco was able to speak more freely now, since the other two detectives left during the phone call.

"You're right. We had only one objective since we started back from Blythe. And that's to get our families together again. Screw the money. I just don't want that damn commander to get his hands on it."

They were in harmony over this last point and made a pact that he would not even see the cash. If it had to be handed over to anybody, it would be the crooks or the feds.

Jeff explained to Franco that he had given an hour for the meeting but they should move ahead right away. If Franco went directly to the commander's office, it would give more momentum to their side. Montgomery would have little time to arrange any double-cross.

They parted with a firm handshake and a vow to meet real soon. Jeff told Franco that whatever the outcome, he would make sure Teresa was safe, together with his precious boys. Franco, in turn, reminded him that the safety of everyone was about to leave Jeff's control.

It was further agreed that Jeff should remain in the detective squad room for at least thirty minutes. If there was progress that Franco could communicate to Jeff, he would contact him on the number at the desk they had used. With this decided, Franco set off for the third floor.

CHAPTER TWENTY-NINE

There are moments in one's life that fears must be challenged, demons met head-on, and roads taken that are less traveled. And so it was for Franco. As he climbed the stairs to the third floor, the weight of the world was heavy on his shoulders. Good deeds he had performed recently, passed without recognition; a history of heroic service seemed distant and without substance; a family he had cherished and nurtured diligently, was in grave peril.

One man stood between Franco and a sense of survival. Commander Neaville Montgomery demanded nothing but total dedication from the men and women under his command. He was feared for the power he possessed and grown men groveled for the favoritism he flaunted. One thing lacking for a man of his stature and position within the police department was respect. It was a word alien to him. Money, authority and larger numbers of personnel subordinate to him; these were the possessions that motivated Montgomery.

An outsider might be forgiven for comparing the upcoming meeting with the lamb visiting the lion. And in the lion's den.

There were still no secretaries or other staff members present in the commander's outer office. In anticipation of a quiet few hours leading into the weekend, he had allowed them all to leave early. This was strangely significant, given the upcoming encounter.

Franco walked past the desks of staff members he had only spoken with on the telephone. A short hallway led to a conference room on the left and a sizeable office straight ahead. The door was slightly ajar and silence reigned inside.

As he came within a few feet of the door, Franco could see the commander busy with his own flow of paperwork. He was glancing over documents and then signing them with a flourish. This was not the posture of a man about to set attack dogs upon his visitor and have him arrested.

"Commander Montgomery?" Franco was sufficiently intimidated by the seat of power for him to use his senior officer's title.

"You're early. Come in and sit down." He was congenial. Too much so in Franco's mind.

Franco checked all around the room. There were no hiding places for internal affairs. There would have been no time for the room to be bugged, unless it was set up for recording at all times. This was a most uncomfortable meeting indeed.

"I want to say that I don't trust you, and I would try anything before resorting to this allegiance. But here I am." Franco held nothing back. His contempt for the commander was unquestionable.

"Let's get something straight right away. This is no allegiance. It is a meeting of necessity. Nothing more." Montgomery had a mutual disrespect for the serf that had the audacity to confront him in such an insolent manner.

Franco was unsettled before they had begun discussing the operation. He was frozen in place; sitting like a mannequin, waiting to be bent into any shape that Montgomery saw fit.

"You're not the one I spoke with on the phone. I see he sends his Mexican lackey to do the dirty work." There could be no doubt that Montgomery sought to antagonize Franco from the outset.

"I was born here, but you don't really care about that. You just want your way, no matter what the consequences." Franco's utter disgust for the man was as apparent as the mutual feelings from behind the lavish oak desk.

"Wait a minute! I know this wimp I see before me. You shot a defenseless man about two weeks ago in Southwest Division. Yes, that was you." Recognition came from the senior officer's visit to the shooting scene.

"That man had a gun and he shot me first. The word defenseless has no place in that incident." Franco was certainly on the defensive, with the man that Jeff hoped would save them from their seemingly doomed situation.

The finer details of the investigation conducted by internal affairs were tossed back and forth. Points of view were scrutinized and conclusions were challenged, until both sides were as convinced as ever that they were right.

"Detective Perez, let us get to the reason for your intrusion here today." This was hardly an acceptance by the commander that he was about to help them. Except, perhaps, under duress.

"Just like my.....colleague told you, there is a substantial sum of currency that was taken from a band of drug dealers. Now they have taken our wives and children as hostages, until the money is returned. We tried to trade a portion of the cash for two kids, but they double-crossed us and nearly succeeded in killing us too."

"Now you want me to get you out of this bind. Is that the general idea?" There was the hint of a snarl as Montgomery summed up the predicament.

"Basically, yes. If we call them again and agree to their terms, I feel sure they will renege. They probably have no intention of turning over our people until they have everything. And that might well include finishing us off." The hopelessness of the detective's position was completely exposed.

"So for miraculously solving this impasse, all I get in return is a vague promise not to tell some wild story about me. Do I have that right?" He was giving Franco second thoughts about the decision to involve him.

"That's all I can say. Look, if you don't like it, why don't you call someone to come arrest me?" Franco's back was pinned securely to the wall.

"I would like nothing more than to throw your sorry ass in jail. However, since you have not told me where this money came from, I cannot imagine what I could have you arrested for. Of course, your pea-brain had probably not computed that fact. There has been nothing in the papers about such a theft, albeit from drug dealers. So my hands are somewhat tied."

The commander gave Franco a huge break in the negotiations by his comments. He was certainly a difficult person to fathom.

"Does that mean you'll help us?" Franco was still unsure as to the line of thinking behind Montgomery's words.

"Tell me about the money. Is it in a safe place?"

Franco resisted a wide grin that threatened to give away so much. "Yes, it's….you could say it's in a safe place. Don't worry about the money."

For more than twenty minutes they traded comments and suggestions over the manner in which the operation should proceed. Every now and then, the commander would pitch in with a query about the money. Franco wisely sidestepped the issue with a claim that he need not concern himself with its current whereabouts. There seemed little doubt that the senior officer was sincere in his concern for the safe recovery of the hostages. This puzzled Franco because the extent to which they knew about his money mismanagement was never raised.

"I told my colleague not to be surprised if you refused our request for assistance. Tell me, commander, why has it been so easy to get you this far?"

"I see a vision. It incorporates all that I can wish from this whole mess. Me being responsible for the ultimate safe return of your families so they can watch you rot in state prison." He was back to sneering again and felt quite comfortable with it.

"Seems reasonable, under the circumstances. And one other thing: why haven't you asked what we know about **your** criminal activity? We may have hardly anything on you." It was time for the subject to be discussed, and Franco went to the heart of his curiosity.

"If you would take such a risk as coming to me with the amazing story you have related, you must know enough. Anyway, a little knowledge can be dangerous. I believe that's how the saying goes." Montgomery made it sound elementary.

"Damn! I didn't realize we'd been talking that long." Franco checked his watch for the first time since he entered the office.

"Do you have somewhere to go, perhaps?" There was an effort at sarcasm from behind the elegant desk. However, unease over Franco's exclamation added a little apprehension to his voice.

"No. It's just that I was supposed to call.....well, make a call within thirty minutes. It's been at least that long." Franco picked up the phone without a hint of asking permission to use it.

"Is your.....colleague going to turn into a pumpkin, or some such thing, if you fail to call?"

Franco ignored the ridiculous comment as he dialed. To avoid letting Montgomery know Jeff was in the building, he pushed nine first. This gave him an outside line before completing the call as if he were dialing to somewhere else. He also insured that the numbers he punched in were not visible from across the desk.

Jeff had waited patiently for about twenty-five minutes. Then he became anxious for Franco's freedom and safety. If there had been carpet in the detective office, he would have worn a ten-foot strip clean through. The phone barely had a chance to complete the first ring, before he had the handset to his ear.

"Yes!" It was a command for the calling party to give him news: good news.

"This is detective Perez. I'm calling from the commander's office."

"What the hell happened to your voice? And why are you detective Perez? Is there someone listening in on the call?" Jeff's stress level had reached its limit while waiting for the call. The floodgates were opened as he insisted on answers.

"Everything is okay. I'm okay. You can speak freely. I just forgot the time, that's all." He put Jeff's mind at rest but failed to calm him down.

"That's all? Now I know how our wives feel when we work late and don't get around to calling home." The agitation was natural and Jeff eventually composed himself.

"Listen. The commander has agreed to help. He will have a squad ready later this evening to follow the crooks away from our next meet. As soon as he has them assembled, we drop the dime and arrange the time and location. The info will be relayed to the commander and hopefully we come out of this unscathed." It was the briefest summary of a game plan, but it was all they hoped for.

"Great! Franco, when you leave, go out through the front lobby onto Sixth Street. Walk west, that way they can't follow you in a vehicle." Naturally, Jeff was telling him to go one way when the flow of traffic was eastbound only. "When you get to Main Street, wait on the northeast corner. I'll pick you up in the Cougar."

"Sounds fair to me." Franco wanted the conversation on the other end to seem innocuous.

The commander was now leaning back in his comfortable, leather chair with a smug grin on his face. He was mildly amused by the surreptitious telephone contact.

"Are you done with him? You gonna be leaving real soon?" This would be Jeff's final inquiry.

"I guess I'm done here. Any other details can be handled on the phone." As Franco was telling this to Jeff, he was eyeing the commander to solicit his endorsement of the remark.

With the slightest nod of the head, Montgomery gave his seal of approval. He then crossed his arms, confident he had the pathetic wretch opposite him under control. After Franco hung up, Montgomery set one more rule for the affair.

"Obviously we must take all steps to avoid the men I call in from seeing either you or you colleague. While I set things in motion you might want to call my office each half hour, just to see how I am progressing. Unless you wish to give me a number where I can contact you."

"Nice try, but we'll be on the move, I'm sure. So if there's nothing else, I'll be going." Franco stood and as a gesture that was meant to seal the enterprise, he held out his right hand.

Montgomery remained motionless, arms crossed, leaning back. It was an uncomfortable few seconds; for Franco, at least.

"Right. Then I'm off." On reflection he was pleased that he had not shaken hands with the unscrupulous senior officer. Jeff and Franco may have stolen from drug dealers, but the commander had scorned the public's trust in him. The distinction was a fine line but Franco was easily able to picture it running between them.

As Franco left the outer office, his boss stood and closed the door to insure privacy. When he sat down he immediately turned the phone around to face him again. He picked up the handset and began setting wheels in motion. The ringing at the other end went on for longer than he would normally tolerate. To his relief it was finally answered and commander Neaville Montgomery spoke to the other party.

"Sanchez. You have business to complete. I don't want any mistakes this time. *Comprende*?"

CHAPTER THIRTY

Franco Perez was never one to display paranoia. If anyone was watching him as he left the fortress that doubled for a Police Station, they would not accept such a statement.

He viewed every lost soul in the lobby with suspicion. Trying to determine which of them was an operative with internal affairs. He gave the few passers-by in front of the building the same scrutiny. When he reached the intersection of Sixth and Los Angeles Streets, he took several minutes simply looking back eastbound.

Almost satisfied that he was not being followed, he next crossed south with the pedestrian signal. After further examination of both sidewalks, he strode west across Los Angeles Street. To completely throw off his would be trackers, he crossed to the north side of Sixth Street one more time.

Just a short block west of him was Main Street, where Jeff stated he would pick him up. Things looked all too easy up to this point, so he decided to really throw them off. He took Los Angeles north until Fifth Street and then headed west once again towards Main. Although it was small for a downtown city block, it still had a north/south alley. He came close to falling flat on his face as he missed the step down at the alley, since he had been looking back over his shoulder yet again.

"Hey, little wetback, yo' should be watching where yo' walking." A filthy bum, commonplace in the downtown area, prevented his fall. The six-foot, black man was holding Franco by the shoulders.

"Can yo' spare some change for a po' nigger that saved yo' Mexican ass?" There was more than begging involved, evidenced by the man's intimidating tone.

Franco was infuriated by the term wetback and the closeness of the man brought a repugnant odor to his sense of smell. He was about to turn on the offensive but the absence of his firearm demanded more tolerance. Since he was suspended from duty he had left the Gloch nine millimeter in Jeff's Mercury Cougar. It seemed more prudent at this moment to behave like a wetback.

"Cat got yo' tongue, Mexican? Hey, what yo' think brothers?" The solitary male now had several black friends in the alley. They all jeered and shouted their advice.

"Take the little shit to the cleaners, Walter."

"Screw his fucking Mexican ass."

"Probably got nothin' but Pesos. Take 'em anyhow."

There was no sympathy from the spectators.

Without realizing how he produced it so quickly, Franco was now looking at the business end of the four-inch blade from Walter's pocketknife. It rested against his chest gently, but in a most threatening manner.

"Got anything for me now, you slimy little asshole?" Walter's words and actions did not in themselves pose the greatest threat. His adversary was probably in his late forties, dimwitted and under the influence of some incredibly cheap wine. This last point was determined by the obnoxious breath that Walter directed towards his target. While Franco was evaluating all of these factors, he failed to notice two of Walter's cohorts approaching. Suddenly, Franco was virtually lifted from the ground as each took an arm with great force.

"Perhaps yo' Mexican ass should step into my office." Walter leaned ever closer to Franco's face.

On one of the busiest blocks downtown, here was an innocent victim being accosted by at least three black males. People were passing by without paying attention to the assault taking place before them. Nobody dared to stop it from happening. Los Angeles: the armpit of the Earth.

Franco was half dragged, half carried into the alley where several more bums surrounded him. They all looked as if they would tear him apart for the change in his pocket. Little did they know, he had more than five hundred of the drug money in a back pocket.

"I saw him first, genelmens. Stand aside." Walter was bigger and stronger than the others. Besides, he had the knife. Walter unceremoniously jabbed at Franco's chest with the blade. It sliced his tee shirt and penetrated the skin. There was just enough space behind Franco for him to step back. This prevented a more serious wound but left him against a wall with no way out.

Even if he handed over all he possessed, it was apparent that Walter was performing for the benefit of the crowd. He had something to prove to his peers and Franco was the guinea pig.

The basic instinct for survival fed its way through his veins, bringing with it the much needed adrenaline to fight off his attacker. A swift kick to the groin sent Walter complaining and whimpering to a neutral corner. It was a signal that the others should join in the free-for-all. Fists and elbows were tossed towards him and he needed his wits to fend off the blows. Most of his assailants were older than Walter and somewhat feeble. However, they grew in strength as the impetus of the fight gave them increased courage.

When a kick landed sharply behind his left knee, Franco buckled and fell to the ground. It was at this point that he became aware of the reek of human feces and urine that was so pervasive in the alley. Many more blows landed on his body and he needed his arms to protect his head. There were too many of them for him to fight back. Walter could be heard in the background, shouting for his pound of flesh.

"Get back. Get back. I'm gonna kill this fucking wetback. Let me at him."

Fortunately for Franco, the mob would heed Walter's words no longer. He had lost control and they were doing whatever they pleased. Very few kicks found their way through the melee and complaints were directed at those who tried such tactics. His foes were their own worst enemies, but there was no end in sight as he concentrated on shielding himself.

There was just so much he could take and with so many areas experiencing intense pain, he now felt that consciousness was slipping away. If this happened he knew he would be lost. None of them were trying to take anything from him. The frenzy was directed at injuring him and incapacitating him.

He wondered where Jeff was. Probably just a short block away and wondering himself why Franco Perez was not at the corner. Jeff would be oblivious to the fracas in the nearby alley, and yet so close to helping Franco live long enough to see his wife and boys again. Now that he thought of them, their faces swam in front of him. They all had puzzled looks and seemed disenchanted with the head of their family. This was the way he remembered them when he left home aeons ago. It was not the way he wanted them to remember him. He did not want to die in a squalid, rat-infested alley at the hands of a bunch of derelicts.

A siren shrieked in the distance and he believed it must be the sound at the other end of the tunnel. Directing him to the everlasting light. However, it seemed to mean more to the vagrants around him than it did to Franco himself.

As the black and white swung into the alley from Fifth Street, the two street cops saw the fight. It was nothing unusual to see the local vagabonds scrapping over some seemingly invaluable item that had been thrown out as trash by a vendor. A sudden burst on the patrol car's siren was all that was needed to disperse the crowd. This time there was a victim, who lay motionless on the ground. He seemed to have taken the brunt of the battle. The uniformed cops casually climbed out of the vehicle and gave a cursory check of the prostrate body. They had to insure they did not have yet another homicide scene to protect.

Franco groaned softly, his hands reaching for his ribs on the left side. It hurt to breathe and so he tried not to. There were two people in dark clothing leaning over him. They were not trying to hurt him; they just looked and then spoke to each other.

"You okay, sir?" One of them finally addressed him personally.

If breathing hurt so much, then he knew for sure that talking would be worse.

"Here, let us help you to your feet." It was well meant but the lifting motion that they engaged in was more harmful than helpful. As Franco leaned precariously against the wall that had prevented his escape so solidly, he was able to focus on the red light facing him. With less than fifty percent of his faculties back to normal, he could still identify a Los Angeles Police Department patrol car. Thank God for the uniformed officers.

"Were they trying to rob you, sir?"

How come when you have fifteen years on the job, every street cop looks young enough to be your much younger brother? Except Driscoll, of course. Franco's mind raced back to Nogales and he wished he could forget. The vision of his close friend's body with gaping bullet wounds around his neck was too much. Franco felt the blood draining from essential parts of his brain. Both cops reached out together and prevented Franco's limp frame from hitting the ground for a second time in as many minutes. Realizing he would require medical attention, they decided to place him in their back seat while waiting for a paramedic unit.

Meanwhile, Jeff had performed some very elaborate, and superfluous anti-surveillance techniques of his own. After driving out of the parking structure he set off at great speed, north on Wall Street. A quick right turn at Fourth and another at San Pedro put him southbound. He just made the light when he crossed Fifth Street and immediately pulled to the curb. If anyone was following him, they would be trying to jump the red signal and would give themselves away. He gave it a couple of seconds and then continued south until he made another right at Seventh; this, after his light turned red.

Plenty of traffic moved in behind him that came directly from the east. He was confident that anyone other than a helicopter pilot would have lost sight of him by now. He need not have spent those reckless two minutes pushing his car to the limit. There was never any surveillance of his vehicle and there never would be.

At Main Street he made his northbound turn, just one block from the spot where he would pick up Franco. There should have been ample time for his partner to reach the corner but he was nowhere in sight. In spite of so many people coming and going, Jeff fully expected to make out the waiting pedestrian. It would be no surprise if Franco was a little impatient because of the potential for being followed.

He was far from frantic as he neared Sixth Street, but there was a sinking feeling when he reached the intersection and had yet to see a familiar face. Slowly, Jeff cruised past Sixth and there was no sign of Franco to the east, back in the direction of the station. Maybe his frenzied driving had brought him to the meet location too quickly. So he took Fourth over to Los Angeles and then started to backtrack along Fifth. This was taking him directly past the entrance to the alley. Mid-block he was crawling along, barely moving. The flashing amber lights at the rear of the black-and-white attracted his attention. He was virtually past the alley when he saw the two street cops helping someone to the patrol car. Jeff's reactions almost caused a serious accident.

As the early evening light was fast fading he could not be positive, but it looked like Franco being held up between two uniforms. At such a slow speed he did not affect anyone when he braked sharply. It was the sudden change of direction that brought pandemonium to the cautious but irritable commuter drivers behind him. As Jeff caught the slightest glimpse of the man he believed he recognized, he immediately slammed the gearshift into reverse. Without a glance in his mirror or over his shoulder he backed up. A horn blared its angry message at him and this was followed by several more. Brakes squealed, tires screeched and a few disgruntled voices could also be heard.

Jeff saw in time that he could not reverse far enough to make an easy turn into the alley. The car closest to his was certainly not going to budge and it left him only one alternative. It took four or five maneuvers of forward and backward movement but he eventually made it.

He drove towards the officers where they had now placed their victim in the back seat. Since they had witnessed Jeff's erratic driving they were wary of potential danger from his approach. One had his hand on his weapon, although it remained holstered. Under other circumstances Jeff Shackleford would have viewed this as commendable. Too many police officers were needlessly killed or wounded because of poor tactics and a disregard for caution.

There was no reason that Jeff could think why he should not identify himself. It seemed the prudent course to take for both his safety and that of the two officers. He was able to reach his detective card and he held it out the window in plain sight.

"Detective Shackleford. I'm with Narcotics."

Tensions were eased. The grip on the weapon was released. One of them even smiled.

"We're okay. Just a bunch of bums attacked this feller. He should do fine when the paramedics clean him up." As the officer was explaining this to Jeff it became clear it was indeed Franco.

"That's an old partner of mine. Let me take a look at him." Jeff was out and moving to the black-and-white.

"You mean he's a cop? With LA?" There was great concern that they had allowed the suspects to flee after one of their own had been savagely beaten.

Jeff examined Franco and saw numerous abrasions to his hands, together with a couple of dark spots on his face that would inevitably bruise and swell up. The blood on his shirtfront was barely visible, so he did not associate it with a wound that lay beneath the clothing. Franco was still dazed and he held his left side around the bottom of his rib cage. His breathing was shallow but only to avoid the pain in his side.

"Have you called the ambulance yet?" Jeff hoped the answer was in the negative.

The cop that had already spoken to him was worried that Shackleford intended to be reproachful over their slow pace. "Taking care of it right away." He directed the obviously junior officer. "We only just picked him up. Looked like a simple dispute among some local street people."

"Don't worry about it. Everything's okay, guys. Tell you what: I'll take him to the hospital myself. I'll go to California since it's only a short distance away." Jeff made reference to the hospital on Hope Street just south of Pico Boulevard. "Besides, you know these paramedics, they'll probably take him to County and there'll be a million people waiting in line." He hoped this last remark would convince them to let him take care of Franco.

"Whatever you say, it's okay by us. He definitely needs attention, though." It would be an easy way out for the uniformed officers. They could get on with other calls for service, and they would not have to make out a report on the attack.

"Great. Can you give me a hand with him?" Jeff leaned into the car and took a careful hold of the right arm.

Franco was coming back to his senses and was aware of Jeff's intentions. He swung his legs out and winced with pain as his left hand shot to the ribs again. With the assistance of one of the officers, Jeff got Franco into the passenger seat of the Cougar.

"Thanks again, guys. Be careful out here." Jeff hoped they continued using sound tactics as they fought the front line battle.

They both waved as they retreated to the patrol car.

"What the hell, Franco! I let you out of my sight for thirty minutes and look at you."

"Don't make me laugh, Jeff. Whatever you do, don't make me laugh. I'm sure those scumbags broke a rib or two." Franco was gingerly fingering each of his left side ribs, one at a time.

The Cougar cruised down the rest of the alley. Jeff waited for a summary of the events that had filled Franco's life since they were last together. However, his injured passenger was intent on finding any of the culprits who had beaten him unmercifully.

"You want to tell me about the meeting with Montgomery first, or the trouble you had walking these dangerous streets?"

"If we see any of those cowardly bums I want you to run them down. Okay?" Franco had seen nobody resembling the suspects by the time they had driven three blocks away.

"We really should get you to the hospital. Especially if you have ribs broken."

"What for? All they do now is tell you not to do anything strenuous and send you home. They don't even wrap you up anymore." What he stated was basically the truth.

"But you look awful, Franco."

"Well if it's my looks you're worried about, maybe we should get a room real quick. I can shower and I'm sure that will make me feel better. I might even look better too." Franco started to chuckle at his own humor but managed to restrain himself.

"Good thinking. How about the University Hilton across from USC. We can use it as a base for making our calls to the commander." Jeff saw the obvious advantage of such a move and the Hilton was close, clean and within their price range.

"We got a little chump change in our pockets, so might as well put it to good use." Franco was at least talking with a little more comfort. "I need a new shirt 'cause there's a blood stain on this one. All our stuff is in the van and I can't see going back to the building right now. Perhaps we could pick one up on the way to the hotel."

Jeff had made several turns and was now headed south on Broadway as he frowned at the request.

"Where the heck we gonna pick up a shirt at this time?"

"For crying out loud! Do I have to do all the thinking for this duo? You're about three blocks from the garment district. There must be some of those places still open." Franco pointed east with his right hand and instantly placed it on top of his left, still comforting his side.

"Your wish is my command." Jeff steered the Cougar towards the five or six square block area that was crammed with small stores selling everything from socks to party dresses.

They bought a complete change of clothing for each of them. With nearly a thousand in cash between them, they decided their last hours of freedom should be in moderate comfort. In keeping with their new found lifestyle, the hotel room was quite luxurious and sported two king size beds. Franco remained in the car while Jeff checked in. The clerk might have cause for alarm if he had shown his now bruised face and tattered appearance.

The first order was for Franco to shower. If he thought unscrewing the cap off the complimentary shampoo was an ordeal, there was more severe pain when he applied it. Every few seconds he had to rest with his arms at his sides, allowing the hot water to beat down on his suffering torso. It was the longest shower of his life. There was the prospect that it might be his last. It quite likely might be the last without a hundred other inmates showering next to him.

Because at least a half hour had passed since Franco parted company with the commander, Jeff checked in with their boss. There was no news on the availability of squad members but many of them had been summoned to work. This was what Neaville Montgomery told Jeff. He also gave out his pager number and instructed Jeff to use that for contacting him. This would avoid Jeff's calls from being answered by someone else.

Before Franco appeared from the steam filled bathroom, Jeff called room service and placed an order for dinner. When he originally paid for the room it was with cash and the clerk informed him that an additional deposit would be necessary. This would cover any phone calls or room service that might be incurred. Without first asking the amount needed Jeff simply handed over a hundred dollars, stating that it should cover their anticipated expenses. It was a rarity that the clerk received cash up front and he made a mental note to keep track of Jeff's room charges. Jeff sensed the curiosity and smiled as he asked if there was a problem.

"Not at all, sir. We are happy to have your business. If there is anything you need, please feel free to call." There was a hint of a bow as he sought to assuage Jeff's concern.

"Not at all, sir." Jeff mouthed to himself later when he dialed room service.

Franco's chest wound might have been worse if he had not stepped away. However, it was about a half inch deep and the majority of blood had run down to his waistline. His pants and under shorts were ruined, so he dumped all of his clothing in the bag provided for laundry and dry cleaning.

"Out with the old and in with the new." He made this declaration as he tossed the bag into a corner.

"We'd better take those when we leave and dispose of them elsewhere. Don't want any maid getting nervous over a few drops of blood." Jeff was headed for the bathroom himself.

"A few drops of blood! Man, I must have lost at least a pint." Franco's indignation was exaggerated.

"Yeah. All of it from your head too, by the way you were behaving for those patrol cops." There was no chance of a comeback for Franco as the bathroom door swung almost shut.

A few minutes later the food was delivered to the room and Franco took the opportunity to tip with a twenty. The eyes of a fellow Hispanic showed caution at first as he spoke in broken English.

"Sorry, sir. We have no change."

"In that case, why don't you keep it? Go ahead, it's all yours." Franco chuckled and immediately felt guilty for behaving so uncouth.

"*Gracias. Gracias.* Thees, it is too mush."

To avoid the spectacle of seeing a grown man grovel, Franco made a waving motion with one hand and closed the door swiftly.

"Did I hear food arriving?" Jeff came out with a towel wrapped around him to find Franco digging in heartily.

There was a chicken dish that demanded a French title. Jeff had difficulty with the name when he placed the order. Neither of them had such difficulty devouring the delicacy. Two sizeable slices of cheesecake sat waiting for them on a china plate with a pot of hot coffee to compliment the dessert. As Franco sat back carefully in an easy chair he held a fork poised to cut into the second course.

"The last supper. That's what this reminds me of." He hesitated before sinking his fork into the generous slice.

"Yeah. Except there were twelve of them." Jeff still had some chicken to finish.

"Heathen! There were thirteen of them, with Jesus." Franco shook his head solemnly as he forced a large piece of cheesecake into his mouth.

"I guess they needed him along to cover the check." Jeff felt that a little joviality was good for them both.

With his mouth still stuffed full, Franco's response was predictable but very difficult to understand.

"Man, you're going straight to hell! That's if lightning doesn't strike you down right now." He almost choked in his efforts to pass judgment, and spat out a tiny piece of food as he coughed and spluttered. This, of course, hurt his ribs considerably and made Jeff laugh too.

When seven-thirty approached it was time to try the commander again. Jeff looked at the notepaper on which he had written the pager number.

"This isn't right. He gave me his pager so I could make sure we got in contact direct. That means I have to send him our number here at the hotel. With the resources available to him, he could find us in no time. We have to drive a few blocks away at least and use a payphone."

"Is that what they give you detective two pay for?" Franco was swilling down the final bite with some coffee.

"That's okay. You just rest your weary, broken bones in the comfort of our luxury suite. I'll go make the call. Just don't touch my cheesecake while I'm away."

Franco licked his lips. "If you leave me here I don't think I could control myself."

"In that case I'd better drag your ass along with me." Jeff began putting on his new clothes.

"Hmm, and they say clothes make the man. I'm not so sure." Franco's comment was supposed to be derogatory.

"I'm sure a woman coined that phrase. Let's go check in with the boss."

"Boss is not the word I would use." Franco's good humor faded as he pictured Montgomery.

"I don't think I need to ask what word you **would** use."

CHAPTER THIRTY-ONE

Neaville Montgomery wanted to be Chief of Police. He wanted to be Chief of the Los Angeles Police Department so badly that he was prepared to do whatever it takes. Unfortunately, he was not the only one. Several commanders, assistant and deputy chiefs also aspired to be the Chief.

It was not the additional thirty or forty grand a year. Hell, they could keep the damn paycheck. He was set for life. Due primarily to strategic investments, made during his years of handling the assets seized from major drug dealers. And only three people knew of his deeds.

One had been paid so handsomely and was close to being a partner. The intimidation that Driscoll believed was keeping that mouth shut was, if fact, a pay-off. A senior detective in the asset forfeiture section was now helping Montgomery with any and all of his continued illegal dealings.

The other two were about to meet their maker. He would have given the order for their families to be eliminated, if it were not for the possibility that their voices might be needed. Perez or Shackleford were likely to ask to speak with their loved ones before complying with any demands. Either way, they would all be dead soon.

He received the page around seven forty-five. The third floor of Central Facilities was now virtually deserted, particularly at his end of the hall. He was even smart enough to recognize the number on the pager display as a payphone. The first number of the final group of four was a nine. This was not a sure fire guarantee that it was a payphone, but the odds were in favor of it.

"Glad to see you are being careful." It might have sounded like a compliment but Montgomery tried his best to avoid acknowledging the cunning that these two detectives possessed.

"How does it look?" Jeff wanted the lowdown and nothing else.

"All set. We only have a squad of six so they will be able to follow just one vehicle." The commander wanted his lies to sound authentic so he embellished somewhat.

"Okay. Call me back at this number in ten minutes. I should have a location by then." Jeff felt more confident than ever, now that he believed a squad of majors detectives was going to follow Federico Sanchez.

"Ten minutes, and counting." He hung up. Montgomery would know exactly when he should call. After Shackleford made contact with his man, Sanchez, the commander would receive a call himself from the guardian of the hostages. The web was being spun and the prey was about to take the bait.

"Amazing." Jeff was actually amazed. "I can't believe he got so many guys to come in on Friday evening at such short notice."

"I take it we are ready to go." Franco had waited patiently next to the payphone.

"Six cars. That's what we have to follow Sanchez. I might as well call right away." Jeff punched in the numbers for what he expected to be the last time and waited.

"*Si*?" A Spanish speaker.

"Yes. I need to speak with Federico Sanchez…..please." Jeff spoke slowly to help the person on the other end understand him.

"Ah, detective, it is good to hear from you again. And thank you for using my correct name. I suspected you might have taken the money and forgotten your families. Are we ready to do business?" Sanchez continued to grasp the upper hand.

"Whatever you say. But it had better be an honest swap this time." Jeff tried hard to be congenial while displaying a firm façade.

"Or what…..? You will kill our money? Let us waste no time, my friend. You will bring two of the bales of money and we will give you the young ones. At Seventh and Union there is a swap meet building on the southwest corner. Be in the lot just south of that business in thirty minutes." It was final. Sanchez set the rules and they had no choice in the matter.

"Okay." Jeff was weak in the knees at the prospect of meeting him again.

When the call was completed Jeff relayed the details of the meet to Franco. A couple of minutes later the phone rang. It was Montgomery, ostensibly calling to get the particulars for himself.

"Remember. I don't want any of the squad to see you. Go into the lot and make contact. Then give an excuse to leave; maybe you have the cash nearby, or something. When this guy leaves he will be tailed by the best." The commander sounded sincere.

"I hope they can do the job. We're relying on them." Jeff was talking about people he had worked with during his years in majors. At least, that is what he thought.

"Okay, I'll get them set up around the area." Montgomery hung up first.

"Franco, there's something too pat about this whole business. That asshole sounds a little glib for my liking."

"We gotta go with it now. There's no other choices to make." Franco hated the commander but he was not the one who just spoke with him. He did not grasp the same deceitful undertones that Jeff felt were present.

"For our women and children's sake, I hope we can trust his Highness. Let's move." Before Jeff got in the car he took the bulletproof vests from the back seat and handed one to Franco. They both put them on without a word.

With light traffic on a Friday evening near the downtown area, there was no dire need to hurry. Jeff took Figueroa Street north until he realized he had missed Wilshire Boulevard. The next available left turn was Fifth Street, which ran into Sixth as they crossed over the Harbor Freeway. They had the windows down as the warm September evening brought a slight sticky feeling to the desperate conspirators. Smog was not visible at this time of night but its effects were telling on the lungs. Both of them were breathing hard and their pulses were quickening. It was still several blocks away but there was about ten minutes to spare.

"What the fuck are we doing, Jeff? We're driving into an ambush and even if Sanchez is straight with us, we don't have the cash."

It was apparent to Jeff that they had no real game plan. He made a quick right turn into the parking lot of the Central Receiving Hospital. Coincidentally, this was the place where cops would be sent if they had some non-emergency medical problem.

"Let's talk about it, Franco. We got to get things settled in our own minds." Jeff pulled into a spot next to a dark blue Ford Crown Victoria.

They talked for a couple of minutes but the cause still seemed a lost one. Then Jeff glanced out of his window and was taken back by what he saw.

"That's Montgomery's!"

"What is?" Franco was unaware of what grabbed Jeff's attention.

"It's his car. What the hell is it doing here?" Jeff pointed to the vehicle so things would be clear to Franco.

"Are you sure it's his? There's a lot of those about." Franco hardly doubted his partner but wanted to believe some other explanation.

"I see it almost every day at the building. I pass it to get to our parking area." He stepped out of the Cougar to double-check. "No doubt about it, Franco. But I suppose it would be natural for him to be close on such a delicate operation."

"But why isn't he in his car? He should be monitoring everything on his radio and have his phone at his fingertips." Franco's earliest suspicions were now ringing true.

"Let's page him and see where he is. Simple as that." Jeff backed the car up first and took Sixth Street west to Loma Drive. He entered an east/west alley and they turned around so they were facing the spot where Montgomery's car was parked.

Jeff used the car phone to send his number to the commander's pager. The wait was interminable and they thought the time to the meet would run out. But then they saw the Ford Econoline van that started its long journey less than thirty-six hours earlier in Tucson. It was headed east on Sixth Street, from the direction of the swap meet, and turned into the hospital lot. As it closed in on the Crown Victoria there was insufficient light to see the occupants.

It stopped for just a second and the commander jumped from the passenger side. He walked to his car as the van left the parking lot. Jeff and Franco were overwhelmed with the thought that he knew about the crooks all along. How much he was involved was too staggering to contemplate at this moment. It was the ultimate betrayal. Neaville Montgomery unlocked his door, reached inside for his car phone and appeared to dial. Seconds later both Jeff and Franco nearly jumped out of their skin as the car phone between them rang out loud. It rang five times before Jeff summoned the courage to pick it up.

"Hello." It was all he could manage.

"Who is this?" The senior detective demanded.

"Shackleford." He figured the name alone would give his boss some cause to think.

It was a long pause, since the commander was not supposed to know who Franco's colleague was.

"So, I imagine you might be watching me right now. That puts you at a slight advantage." It was a discreet remark without an admission.

"And we were watching you as Sanchez dropped you at your car." Jeff reasonably assumed that no lower party in their organization would be driving the big man around.

"Well, well, well. This does change the complexion a little. What shall we do now?" Montgomery wanted only one thing: the end of their lives, and as soon as possible. If only Sanchez had remained while he made the call. Perhaps he could have assisted with the elimination of these two thorns in his side.

"Fuck you, sir! You were the one who arranged the kidnappings. You're an asshole, just in case nobody has the balls to tell you." Jeff wanted to let fly with more of the same.

"Come, come. These are cellular calls. Somebody might be listening and they are sure to be offended by your profanity." He was self-righteous to a fault.

"Maybe you're right. But tell me how you found out it was the three of us. I presume you hit all three of our homes the next morning." Jeff just had to know the answer.

"Oh, well. I guess it won't hurt to tell. Our people obviously checked the landing site when the delivery failed to show up. Driscoll still had his handgun in a holster and he was such a fastidious firearms dealer, he had it registered to him. That was the easy one. Now you were also fairly easy to figure, detective Shackleford. I made an inquiry, just as you had done earlier, to see if anyone was working a case in the Nogales area. Naturally, your name came up as having made the check in our computers a few days before the rip-off.

"Perez was tougher, and perhaps stemmed from a hunch at first. I thought there might be one or two others involved because of the size of the assault. When I remembered you were in on the initial Perez shooting investigation, I guessed he might be with you. Since he is on suspension it was nothing unusual for me to be calling his home. When his pretty little wife told me he was away for a few days….. bingo! The rest you can figure out. You're a smart one, Shackleford." It was time for Montgomery to rest awhile. He had told more than he knew he should, but arrogance goes hand in hand with conceit.

"Have you killed them yet?" It was a forthright question that stunned even Franco.

"Not at all. I have some scruples, you know." He lied about his character.

"Okay. This is our proposal. If you want the money back we want to speak with both our wives and Franco's boys first. Then we will negotiate and meet pretty much whatever demands you make." It was a gutsy move on Jeff's part.

"I cannot deny that is a reasonable request. Call the number you have for Sanchez in one hour. I'll arrange it." Montgomery succumbed too easily again for Jeff's liking.

"I'll do that." Jeff hung up and watched the commander as he looked all around him. When he was unable to detect their location, he made another call on his car phone.

Jeff backed down the alley and left the area for fear that Sanchez and his henchmen might soon appear. Franco was getting fed up with being able to hear only one side of the conversation most of the time. However, he listened to Jeff's narration of the call with an open mind that was being continually stretched to its limits.

Jeff covered every minute detail as he automatically returned to the hotel. They decided to make themselves comfortable during the short wait, and maybe some brilliant idea would surface before the hour was up.

CHAPTER THIRTY-TWO

DESTINY: *The preordained or inevitable course of events, considered as something beyond human power or control.*

Man will continue with attempts to control his destiny. He will often see encouraging results; frequently he will be frustrated with events taking on their own will. No matter what the adversity, there should always be the resolution to live and to create something positive with that life.

A man might believe he is doing right; it may be a case of simply being more right than the man that is wrong. This will be of little consequence if all his good deeds are forgotten in an instant.

There will be effects, repercussions and even a price to pay for a man's actions. But without the attempt, he will not be satisfied with the outcome.

Destiny may already be ahead of him, but there are great strides to take before reaching life's goals.

"It's a no-win situation." Franco sat on one of the huge beds and nursed his bruised ribs. The torment inflicted upon him over the past few weeks, coupled with his physical condition, these factors pushed him closer to total submission. He could come up with no logical course of action.

Jeff Shackleford was as determined as ever to see his wife released safely. He became more resolute even as Franco was falling in the other direction, and also envisioned the downfall of the unscrupulous commander. The problem lay in finding a plan to bring about such satisfactory results. He pondered their predicament, with no assistance from Franco, until the time arrived for the call to Sanchez. There was no discernible strategy on the table and so Jeff simply made the call.

Federico Sanchez picked up the receiver and asked which wife they wanted to speak to first. It was obvious that he expected no other telephone calls, and his conduct was that of a disinterested agent.

"Jessica Shackleford." This was all Jeff felt was necessary. He hoped beyond his dreams that his wife was still safe and alive. His heart skipped when he heard that beautiful woman on the line.

"Jeff? Is that you?"

"Jessica. My God, I never thought I would speak with you again. I'm sorry for what we've done. I wish it could all be taken back, but what is done is done. I love you and I'm going to do everything in my power to get you out of this mess."

"Very touching." Sanchez had taken the phone from Jessica during Shackleford's pleading comments. "Put that wetback on, so he can speak with his wife, too."

Jeff handed the phone to Franco without a word. His look was not encouraging, but it did not scare Franco.

"Franco, this is Teresa. I know they won't let us speak long. Your sons are okay and they have not harmed us. Do whatever they say, if you can trust them to release us."

Franco was able to hear all that Teresa was allowed to say, but Sanchez immediately got back on the line. "So, you know we are men of our word." As the double-crossing kidnapper continued his deceit, he made a waving motion with one hand in order to dismiss the guard and direct him to return the women to the next apartment.

"How will this be done, Rico?" Franco felt as much contempt towards the captor as he could remember feeling about anyone. Except, perhaps, the federal agent Martinet.

"I am getting tired of all these trips to meet you. Be at the Seventh and Union parking lot at six in the morning. I have plans for tonight." Sanchez spoke too nonchalantly about such a serious matter.

As an afterthought, he added a comment for amusement purposes. "Perhaps I will entertain one of your wives for the evening."

Franco was about to curse the insufferable tyrant but the line went dead immediately following the last word of Federico Sanchez. The details concerning the time and location of the meeting were relayed to Jeff. Franco was able to control himself sufficiently to avoid telling about what he hoped was an idle threat.

"Six tomorrow morning? Damn! If last night wasn't bad enough, I don't really want to go through another. Not knowing what's happening to them. Those slime balls holding our families." Jeff was rambling on and it did nothing for Franco's lack of optimism.

"At least we know they are alive and they haven't been harmed. I learned that much from Teresa."

"All I got was a couple of words. Then like a fool I hogged the phone until Rico came back on the line." Jeff admonished himself for not being better prepared for the call.

They discussed the inevitable ambush that they would be driving into and could see no way around the confrontation. As Franco had admitted earlier, it was unquestionably a no-win situation. By six o'clock the next morning they would have none of the cash and, quite likely, no future worth talking about.

"There must be somebody we can trust to help us, or at least to advise us." It was a continuing dilemma for Jeff Shackleford. "What about that defense rep who was in on your FBI interview?"

"Franklin. George Franklin. He's as straight and honest as they come." Franco admitted. "But that might be a liability. My guess is he can't stand crooked cops."

"That's probably true, Franco, but maybe if he was made aware of the commander's role in this whole thing….." Jeff let the idea hang in the air to see if his partner felt the same way.

"You've got a point there. I would hope he cared enough to go after the big fish. Particularly since he feels the top brass are giving us troops the shaft. Like you said, we need help from somewhere."

It was agreed that they would tell all to Franklin and see if he could come up with a suggestion. Their motive was to seek assistance, but the ultimate result was to relinquish their responsibility. They were basically at their wits' end.

Franco made the call to Detective Headquarters, where a handful of officers and detectives manned the phones twenty-four hours a day, seven days a week. If there was no other division or entity to take care of off-hours business, then Detective Headquarters either did it themselves or woke somebody up to do it. He explained who he was to the detective that answered his call and stated it was imperative that he speak with Franklin as soon as possible. When asked where he could be reached, Franco freely gave the hotel number and the room in which he was staying.

"I hope they relay the message to him. If they do, then I'm sure he will at least call." Franco was optimistic about Franklin but unsure if the effort would be made to contact him on a Friday evening.

Jeff asked if his friend wanted a stiff drink, but Franco stated a soda would suffice. A call was made to room service, and two cokes and a couple of sandwiches were ordered.

"I don't think I'm ready to eat right now, Jeff."

"Just in case the room service stops later on. I figure there's no harm in having something if we get hungry." As Jeff explained this to Franco, he turned on the late night news.

All that was showing was crime in the city. Killings, drug infested neighborhoods, and car-jackings. A sorry state of affairs for the armpit of the Earth.

"Makes you wonder how it would be without cops to stem the flow." Jeff shook his head in dismay as he lay back on the other bed.

After ten minutes of tragedy and misery, he could stand it no longer. The channel changer took aim and began its erratic journey through the local and national choices. It appeared as if the whole medium of television was geared to proclaim the woes of Southern California, just before their viewers retired for the night.

They watched snatches of various stories for a couple of minutes here and a few seconds there. Franco was oblivious to the media messages. Although he stared at the screen, he was far away mentally. Thoughts of his dear wife and precious children could not be dismissed. He knew they were probably a mile or two away but it might as well be a million.

"What the heck is taking so long? You put a piece of meat between two slices of bread and grab a couple of cans from the cooler." Jeff turned the clock radio to face him so he could watch the minutes flick by on the digital read-out. Every time Jeff changed the channel he glanced at the clock. The numbers changed but the stories did not. There came a time when the numbers seemed not to vary and so he watched carefully. The minutes did in fact move along but Jeff was so tired that he missed this event. They had forgotten to turn the air conditioning up and the heat eased them both to a deep sleep.

A loud knocking at the door awakened them with a start. When Franco sat up quickly he felt the stabbing pain around his rib cage once more. He doubled over in agony, grimacing towards his confederate.

The healthy partner was soaked in sweat, partly from the temperature, partly from the anxiety of being woken so abruptly. The minutes had been busy: the display told him it was 11:58. This seemed altogether too late. He scooped up his nine millimeter and approached the door cautiously.

"Who is it?" His finger was poised on the trigger as he peered through the peephole.

"Room service. Sorry it took so long." There was a young man clad in a white jacket just outside the door.

Jeff's finger relaxed as he returned to the table. "Hang on just a second." Both he and Franco exchanged looks of relief and the gun was placed next to his wallet. Several one-dollar bills were extracted for the tip, although there was a moment when Jeff considered zero would be appropriate. However, there was the possibility that the messenger was not the one who took so long to prepare the food.

With cash in one hand he pulled the door open with the other and began his complaint. "What the heck took so.....oh, my God! Oh, shit!"

There was never going to be any room service; only a hallway full of dark-suited men, each of them pointing weapons at him. One of them reached in and grabbed Jeff Shackleford, then unceremoniously yanked him to the opposite wall in the hallway. Four others darted into the hotel room, announcing in loud voices that they were federal agents and for Franco to "get his fucking hands in the air."

In spite of being startled, he was smart enough to comply with orders given under such circumstances. The bruised ribs demanded his attention and the motion of his hands coming back down again brought about swift retribution from one of the four agents. The mentally drained, physically abused body of Franco Perez was dragged from the bed and tossed to the floor. While an agent handcuffed the unresisting suspect, a heavy knee was held in the middle of his back, pressing down with much of the man's weight. The wind was knocked out of him and Franco groaned from the torture his ribs were experiencing.

In less than two minutes from the time Jeff opened the door, they were both sitting on the bed with cuffs. Nine federal agents were in the room and the bath and closet had been checked for other occupants. Franco was unable to speak and Jeff thought it prudent not to say anything until he was spoken to.

"So, Francisco Perez, here we are again." It was a voice that he knew he would hear again, but hoped beyond all hope that the man would fall foul of some gruesome accident. William Martinet could have been anyone's worst enemy; it just so happened that Franco was the unfortunate soul to fit that category for the moment. Still no response came from the laboring lungs, but the once lively and expectant, brown eyes simply stared into those of Martinet.

Jeff was confused, disappointed and even somewhat scared of the prospect of facing this man's wrath. He was given little time to ponder the thought as the headhunter tore into him.

"And you, I anticipate, will be indicted for harboring a fugitive." He pointed his finger squarely at Jeff's face to insure the recipient of the promise was aware of his future. This proved most confusing to Jeff, as did the next comment from another agent.

"Hey, Bill, lookey here. A couple of handguns. We got him on this too."

"Well, well, well. You know you can't possess a firearm out of your home when you're suspended." Martinet was once again concentrating on his primary quarry. "What you got to say for yourself, Perez? The charges just keep adding up."

His target had come to a decision that even when he could speak, he would never utter another word to this evil man posing as a defender of justice. Meanwhile, Jeff's mind was racing at a hundred miles an hour. The comments about him harboring a fugitive and possession of the gun were serious but not heinous crimes. It certainly seemed as if these men had no inkling of the devastation from the past couple of days.

"If you don't mind me asking, how did you find us?" Jeff risked a very tentative question.

"I don't mind at all.....mister....."

"Shackleford. Detective Shackleford." Jeff was convinced that this man was ignorant of the gravity of this situation. He really did not know how important the arrest of these two detectives could prove.

"Detective Shackleford. Well, you can kiss your career in law enforcement goodbye." Martinet was smug when it came to putting down police officers. "Anyway, to answer your query, we simply ran the phone number through the system and came up with the hotel. Your buddy here gave us the room number."

"No, I didn't mean that. What I was interested in was how did you get called by our department?"

"Your question makes no sense at all. You must know as well as everyone that Perez is wanted. That is obviously why you are helping him hide in this hotel room. Your signature is on the registration card."

Jeff was missing something in the explanation. "I know you guys have been trying everything possible to put Franco behind bars, but what exactly is he wanted for?"

"You must be working on your defense, I guess. Well, I'll humor you to a point. This poor excuse for a Los Angeles Police Officer has been indicted on several charges stemming from his association with a drug task force. We have been trying to pick him up for two days now. Even his whole family has been magically whisked away from the Perez home. When they got the call downtown from Perez himself, they were obliged to immediately make contact with my office."

"Bill, we have everything packed up. Ready to hit the road?" The other agent had been directing things while Martinet spoke to Jeff.

"Sure. Let's get some shoes on these guys and we're out of here." Martinet was all set and as he walked away it looked as though he might leave the room first.

In a last desperate bid to save the women and children of their two shattered families, Jeff took a calculated but serious risk. "Excuse me, sir. Can I speak with you on a matter of grave importance?"

Martinet half turned and grinned. "Another feeble attempt to save your hide?"

"No. Actually it could result in me going to jail for a very long time."

The federal agent's interest was stirred enough for him to approach and face the detective. "It had better be worth my time. Go ahead."

"It's a long story, but if you like putting crooked cops where they belong, then you should listen. While I tell you what this is about, could you at least cuff Franco in front? His ribs took a severe beating earlier today."

"Tell you what, Shackleford. I'm going to take the cuffs off both of you while I hear this. As soon as I tire of your tale, you both get hooked up again and off we all go." Martinet showed a miniscule shred of compassion.

Jeff told of the money rip-off and the fact that it was far from Los Angeles. He made no mention of the deaths that resulted or the specific location. With the Feds having no prior knowledge of the incident, he felt somewhat safe with this abbreviated version of events. So far he had given Martinet nothing with which he could charge the two cops. An admission of crime is of no use unless there is proof that it actually happened.

The woeful account of the kidnapping and subsequent demands held the agent's attention more than Jeff expected. Perhaps because he was rightly anticipating the news of a bigger fish involved in the affair. Montgomery's part in the double-cross was explained at length without his name being mentioned.

"I guess I have to ask the obvious question: who the hell is this main player that set you up?" Martinet played along with the detective's manner of storytelling.

Jeff Shackleford took a deep breath and let it out slowly before divulging the name. "Neaville Montgomery, Commander of Narcotics, Los Angeles Police Department."

Both men stared at each other poker-faced, while Franco stared at Martinet with contempt, mingled with the merest hint of hope. Silence reigned for an eternity. Martinet looked away first. He was convinced of Shackleford's sincerity but needed time to digest the facts before coming to a decision. Franco kept his personal vow of silence and Jeff waited as patiently as possible, hardly breathing.

"So you want me to believe that a Commander of Police is a key member in a drug cartel; that he was instrumental in having your families kidnapped; and that he directed his men to kill you. Is that about the size of it?"

"Oh, and he misused huge sums of seized assets to make a considerable amount of money for himself." Jeff figured he should toss that one in too.

"You have proof of this?"

Jeff shook his head slowly. "He discussed it with Franco, and that's why we thought he wanted us killed. I'm sure he thinks we do have some proof."

"Let me guess what you want me to do." The agent intended to display his deductive reasoning. "Take a crew of federal agents into battle with these thugs and save your women and children."

"Actually, I'd want more." Jeff could not believe what he was about to ask for.

"More? Huh, I'd love to hear it."

"Whatever this whole caper has brought about, there will be no charges brought against either of us, state or federal." It seemed fair to Jeff after he spoke the words.

"That's it?" Martinet kept a poker face so Jeff could not read his reaction.

"More."

"More?"

"Drop the federal indictment against Franco and the state charges against him for the Manhattan Place shooting." It was to be all or nothing. Jeff felt it was worth chasing while the cards were being laid out. Franco's heart was pounding. He hardly expected anything positive from this discussion, other than more grief for the two of them.

"**If** we get the commander while directly involved in this mess; **if** we get some evidence on tape from him about the money scam; **if** what you're telling me is true; this is what I'm prepared to do." The lead up sounded promising. "There will be no charges whatsoever from this caper; I'll try my damndest to get the federal indictment against Perez dropped; what I will not do is get the state charges for the killing on Manhattan Place dropped. I see Perez as guilty of manslaughter at least. And you both quit the job."

It was more than Jeff could have imagined, but it was not everything. He turned to Franco, who nodded in agreement without hesitation. Franco could see that his close friend would face no legal battles at all. For himself, it was virtually back to the point where he was when they left town.

Jeff told Martinet it was a deal, provided it was in writing and they had a defense representative with them when it was recorded. He suggested George Franklin.

"I have no problem with that. If my two conditions are not met, however, then all bets are off." Martinet summoned a couple of his colleagues closer and gave them detailed instructions. One of them was to use the phone in the room to arrange for Franklin to be contacted and picked up from home. The second agent was to use the cellular phone in Martinet's car to call out a stenographer, and then bring a tape recorder to the room.

When the notifications had been completed from the hotel phone, Martinet began making his own calls. It was his intention to cover the hurdle posed by the federal indictment, so that it could be included in the written agreement. He impressed both cops with these efforts. This was a man who detested wayward officers, but he was certainly a man of his word.

When George Franklin was ushered into the crowded hotel room, Martinet was busy with other calls. He was attempting the most difficult aspect, lining up an Assistant United States Attorney to approve his phone warrant. Yet another agent was busy writing the actual warrant necessary to record telephone conversations between Jeff and the commander. When the AUSA was satisfied with it, they could wake up a judge at home and hopefully solicit his signature on the crucial document.

The scenario was overwhelming to Franklin, who had been intimidated personally by Martinet during the first interview with Franco Perez. Now he was to be party to some admitted conspiracy and perhaps illegalities by a commander of his department. The driver that whisked him away from the comfort and security of his home at one-fifteen in the morning had relayed this much to him.

"Ah, Detective Franklin. Please, sit with us." Martinet was strangely cordial as he patted a seat next to him.

The following ten minutes of recitation by both Martinet and Jeff proved almost too much for Franklin to accept. He shook his head many times and gave frequent darting looks towards Franco, who remained silent throughout. When the essentials of what had taken place were completed, Franklin gave his unabridged opinion.

"You're all crazy. You two for thinking you could violate the law so freely." He nodded at the two detectives. "And you, Mr. Martinet, for covering for them, simply to catch someone more important."

"Let's get one thing straight here, Franklin. I don't need your views on the subject. You are only here as a courtesy to these two officers. You will not be a party to the interview, except to see that all is conducted fairly. And I can assure you I am a fair man, even though you see me through different eyes."

Franklin's response was a simple shrug of resignation.

"Before we go any further, there's a few things I should disclose before it's all written and recorded." Jeff felt it was time to come clean about the carnage in the desert.

After the revelation of numerous bodies lying about the landing strip, including a Los Angeles Police Officer, Franklin became nauseous. He left for the bathroom and was not seen for some while. Martinet spent more time thinking again. Then without another word to Jeff, he picked up the phone and made a single call. This must have been to the head man, since it was clear the accountability was entirely at the other end of the line. It must have been a weighty decision, because Martinet waited on his end for a considerable time before he received his orders.

"Very well, sir. I'll make that quite clear to both of them." Martinet hung up the phone and spoke to the trio, now that Franklin had rejoined them. "Gentlemen, the deal is still on. However, if your end is not met to our satisfaction, you will likely be liable for charges stemming from the deaths of however many souls we find in the Arizona desert."

It was no time for the weak hearted. Life sentences faced them. It was really too late to turn back. It had been too late for more than two days. Franco's hands twisted together in a ball as Jeff laid his own hand upon them. When their eyes met, Franco Perez told his partner what he already knew. "We gotta do it."

It took more than two hours to record every minute detail. Jeff was exhausted by the time it was finally over. It had passed as an unspoken agreement that he would talk for both of them, given his partner's condition. Nevertheless, even Franco felt as empty as if they had drained his life's blood from him.

The warrant had been approved and signed. Even the equipment to record the conversation was set up. It was time to go over the details of the final game plan of their law enforcement careers.

CHAPTER THIRTY-THREE

It was the ultimate in rude awakenings. The piercing beep of the pager was, in his view, more disconcerting than the phone ringing. The pager was at his bedside, but when you are elevated to such a lofty position within the department, it is rare that they call you at such an hour. The alarm clock displayed an unbelievable 4:18.

If this was not a dire emergency then heads would roll. The commander liked it when heads rolled.

The number in the pager display was unfamiliar, and it was most certainly not a city phone. Still in a daze, he tried to figure out who it could be. There was the slightest possibility that Sanchez needed to speak about some matter. His brain started to clear and he rationalized that Federico Sanchez must surely be sleeping off the effects of a six-pack of Bud.

He hoped the fool would have sufficient sense to wake early enough himself and make the appointed meet time. Could it be the two rogue cops calling him? He remembered giving Shackleford his pager number. As he was thinking this out, a second page caused the beeping to commence once again. The same number, with 9-1-1 after it.

He slid out of bed and threw a silk robe over his shoulders. It would be safer to make the call from his study, so as not to wake his wife and give her cause for concern. He was pleasantly surprised how well he had slept up until this time. It was comforting to know that two significant problems would be taken care of in the early morning hours.

At the University Hilton, ninety-nine percent of the guests were sound asleep. In room 308 there was a hive of activity. Agents bustled about their respective duties; some monitored the listening devices; others fiddled with knobs to get the balance just right for the recording equipment. Martinet and Jeff Shackleford waited anxiously for the call.

It was decided that the equipment had to be set up in the hotel room. Any remote place, such as a payphone, would pose tremendous logistical challenges. The commander might normally have the number traced, but at four-thirty in the morning they surmised even he might find that difficult to justify.

Although there were other noises about them, it startled them both, causing them to jump back from the phones. A technician first turned on the tapes then gave the thumbs up sign. Silence fell instantly about the room, except for the persistence of the telephone. Martinet silently counted down from three with his fingers, and Jeff picked up one handset as the agent did the same with their own added instrument.

"Hello." Jeff was a little self-conscious with so many listeners to both ends of the conversation.

"Who the hell is paging me at such an ungodly hour?"

"Commander Montgomery, I think you can probably guess, sir."

"Shackleford! Why don't you just call my man, Sanchez? I need a couple more hours sleep."

Martinet was undoubtedly impressed by the conversation so far. There was the recognition of Shackleford over the phone and reference to 'his man Sanchez.'

"I don't trust him. I'd rather deal directly with you."

"I find that difficult to believe. He's been as trustworthy as they come for several years. Others come and go, but Sanchez is faithful to a fault." Montgomery was digging his own grave, a little at a time.

"Even so, I think it would be safer if you were around to give the orders. I want to make sure our wives and Franco's boys are safely turned loose." This was a great lead by Shackleford.

"They will be free as the wind as soon as the money is in our hands."

"Our hands." Martinet thought to himself. This was confirmation of virtually everything the cops had recounted.

"Let's just say it is a little insurance for us both. After all, we do know about your banking scheme."

"Shackleford, I don't think you know anything other than just rumors." The high-ranking cop was taking the bait.

"We have evidence….." Jeff was unsure how to proceed and the senior officer jumped in.

"Evidence. You have nothing, punk." He spat the last word out and gave the impression the conversation was coming to a close.

"You'd be surprised. We have….." Jeff tried to think fast. He had to get the commander hooked completely, or all was lost. "….. documents from your brother's bank."

There was no response. Nothing from the other end at all. For a second Jeff suspected the commander was on to them; that Montgomery was cognizant of the listening devices and that he was being set up for the big fall.

In a soft tone, there came a cautious inquiry. "What documents?"

Jeff felt a weight lifted from his shoulders. This question meant one thing, and one thing only. There were documents of some kind, somewhere.

"They show amounts, dates, account numbers, and most important of all, they show names." Jeff was taking a risk by going so far, but he felt he needed to reel in his boss.

"You say you will bring those with you?" When Martinet heard this response, he gave Jeff a thumb up sign. This meant he had virtually completed his part of the bargain. All that remained was to insure Montgomery would come to the meet.

"I didn't say I would bring them. But if you are there, then I'll hand them over to you. If I don't see you perhaps I'll go directly to the LA Times." It was the emptiest threat Jeff would make in his life.

"In your dreams, detective. I'll be there. Six o'clock sharp. You know where to be." Jeff had his eyes closed now and a hint of a smile across his face. He was thankful that the commander was so greedy and so crooked.

"Yes, sir. Seventh and Union, in the parking lot just south of the swap meet building." He felt it was necessary to get this on tape too.

"Right." It was his final word to Jeff before hanging up the phone.

When Jeff and Martinet replaced their handsets there were a number of agents that shook hands excitedly. These were the ones privy to the details of the whole conversation. They soon brought the others up to speed and the room was buzzing with enthusiasm.

"I have to admit that I had my doubts." Martinet put his hand on Jeff's shoulder. "But now I realize what you guys have been going through. It doesn't make your own deeds any less evil, but it does make this Commander Montgomery look like the crooked cop of the century."

Jeff also filled in the blanks for Franco, and the aging process that had taken its toll on him during the last few weeks seemed to abate somewhat. There was light at the end of the tunnel. It was a grim, distant light, but it could be seen from afar.

Martinet busied himself, barking orders for his men to prepare for the impending operation.

Jeff Shackleford viewed the clock and raised the subject that had barely been touched upon. "Are you going to send a couple of your guys with us to get the money?"

"Shit! I almost forgot about the money. It would be best if you bring it along, just in case. It might likely be the catalyst needed to get them to take action." Martinet then contemplated the dire issue of manpower. "Is it close by?"

"About ten minutes this time of morning."

"I can't spare the manpower. There's a tremendous amount of work for the crew to get done if we want to be in place by, say, five forty-five. If you two can handle it, why don't you get going?"

"You mean you trust us?" It was an incredulous look on Jeff's face.

"After what you two have attempted in order to get your families safely home, I trust the fact that you aren't giving up on them at this stage. Now move it."

They did not need to be told a third time. They rushed off to the Cougar in the parking lot and Franco gently eased himself into the passenger seat. Jeff drove quickly yet safely, given the importance of their presence at the meet location.

"How about some coffee?" It was the most Franco had spoken for more than four hours.

"Sure. Good idea. There's a coffee shop at that motel up ahead." Jeff nodded towards a place on the west side of Figueroa just a couple of blocks from the Hilton.

Tired and very much pissed off at these two bothersome detectives, Montgomery made contact with Sanchez. The phone seemed to ring for an eternity before the still drunken Mexican picked up.

"*Si*?" He almost fell asleep immediately after uttering this solitary word.

"For Christ's sake, Sanchez, couldn't you wait until this whole mess was cleared up before getting bombed?"

"Hey, boss, what you doing calling me? I got things under control, don't you know?" Sanchez was suddenly alert and also worried that he had missed the meeting with the two detectives. His eyes gradually focused on the forty-dollar digital wristwatch that he swapped for ten dollars worth of rock cocaine. "Yeah. Plenty time, mister Chief of Police."

"Watch your language, my low-life friend, and get ready. I'm going to be at Eighth Street, just a block from you, by ten to six. Be there to pick me up."

"What's a matter? You don't like the Hospital lot?" Sanchez wondered why the top man was coming so close to the roach-infested apartment building.

"They saw me there last night. I can't take a chance of going there again. Just be on Eighth near Union, ten before six." The commander was getting equally frustrated with his own man now.

"Okay. You the boss."

CHAPTER THIRTY-FOUR

It was the longest, most complicated arrest report that she had written since joining the Police Department. Nina Kaplan felt it was important to include every scrap of information, so these dope fiends could stay where they belong: behind bars. She was not only conscientious, she was an idealist. It was common in Southern California for criminals to serve around half the term they were sentenced to. The Los Angeles County Jail was rumored to have fitted revolving doors to the back of the building.

The South Bureau Narcotic Team had busted a trio of dealers when they served a search warrant late on Friday night. Nina was the case agent and she bore the responsibility of tying together all of the loose ends and making sense of the reports. Other team members booked the suspects and the lengthy list of evidence too. Jim Young stayed with her until three in the morning before feeling she could comfortably finish the report by herself.

She put the finishing touches to it and made the required number of copies by four fifteen. It had been almost twelve hours since she ate and the prospect of breakfast before heading home was most agreeable.

Leaving Southwest station with her driver's window down, she cruised east on King Boulevard letting the cool air toss her long black hair behind her. Now that she was off duty she allowed the silken tresses to fall past her shoulders. When she reached Figueroa Street her six-year-old Ford Thunderbird made a northbound turn without any particular destination in mind. After less than a mile, the bright lights from an all-night coffee shop drew her attention. This would be as good as any place for a light breakfast and lots of strong coffee.

A girl much younger than Kaplan showed her to a small booth. As they passed the register at the end of the counter, Nina thought she recognized the back of a man waiting to pay. The idea was dismissed as a result of her fatigue. When she sat in the comfortable, high-backed, leather seat a menu was handed to her and coffee was requested. The items on the list failed to come into focus as she felt compelled to look back at the man she had passed. Now that he and his companion were receiving Styrofoam cups and a small white bag each, they were turned a little in her direction.

"Franco!" She whispered it to herself with a short gasp for air.

Nina had not spoken with Franco Perez for a week and she had not seen him for almost two. He looked terribly old and weary, with a gaunt look about his features. It almost seemed as if he was bent over a little. She wanted to rush to him and tell him that everything would work out. It was common knowledge, at least among her squad, that the FBI was eagerly seeking Franco. The man with him looked familiar to. In fact, she was sure he had interviewed her the night of Franco's latest shooting. He had given her comfort and seemed genuinely disturbed by the attempts of Internal Affairs Division to railroad Franco. But what were they doing here at this time of the morning? What were they doing together?

The coffee arrived just as the two detectives started to leave. Much to the consternation of her waitress, Nina handed her two dollars and apologized as she left the coffee shop.

For their brief visit, Jeff parked on the east side and they now crossed the street to return to the Cougar. Nina stood in the shadows next to the entrance and watched as what appeared to be a typical surveillance vehicle headed towards downtown. Her car was in the lot and a rapid stride had her mobile in ten seconds. There had been little requirement for her to follow drug suspects before, given the nature of the investigations she took part in. Fortunately, the driver of her target was taking things quite carefully.

The Cougar continued all the way downtown until turning right on Sixth Street. There was a little traffic but not enough for her to lose the car, and they both made several green lights then headed north on Wall Street. She could not figure out why they then turned into Central Station. Perhaps, she reflected, Franco was about to turn himself in. It was a question that must be answered to her satisfaction, so she flashed her badge at the entrance to the multi-story lot, and headed up the ramps.

It was now five fifteen and there would be nothing unusual about other cars arriving at this time. Day watch roll call started at seven, so some early risers might be expected to be pulling in to get dressed for work. The Cougar went all the way to the roof section and Nina parked on the last ramp. After creeping stealthily to the wall, she could not see them from her vantage point, but snatches of the conversation drifted her way.

"Damn, it's got a flat." Franco cursed the front passenger wheel of the van.

"It has a spare but we don't have the time to waste on that right now." Jeff looked at the deflated tire and then at his Cougar. "We can't get everything in the Mercury. I don't think we can get even one bundle past the front seat." As with most cars provided for surveillance, it was a two-door model.

"How about the trunk?" Franco scratched his head then gently rubbed his ribs.

"What else is there? Let's try it."

Jeff popped the trunk and Franco unlocked the back doors of the van. Together they slid one of the remaining four bundles of cash to the edge of the cargo compartment. It sent a painful reminder of the fracas in the ally to Franco's brain when he helped lift the currency into the trunk. It slipped into the space available but the lid would not even come down more than a couple of inches. It looked so obvious to them.

"Well, if we get stopped for having an unsafe load, maybe we can pay the fine right away." Jeff was almost in a light-hearted mood.

"I thought that kind of thing only happened in New York." Franco followed suit.

"Actually, if you look at all we've done recently, it makes New York PD look like a bunch of angels." Jeff made a move to the driver's seat.

At the sound of the engine starting, Nina returned to her Thunderbird and lay down across the front seat. When the car with the strange load passed, she proceeded to follow it again. During the trip across town to Rampart Division, she was never quite close enough to make out what was protruding from the trunk. It did look familiar, but she could not be sure. The load was certainly too bulky for that car to be transporting it.

After passing the Central Receiving Hospital on the right, the Cougar made a northbound turn onto Loma Drive. Since daylight had not fully taken over, she felt safe in making the same turn herself. It was a surprise when the next turn came almost immediately, as the car pulled into the rear lot of the hospital. She was staggered to see almost a dozen large sedans in the lot. There were as many well-groomed, dark-suited young men standing around in a huddle. Although she should have tried to be discreet, it was tough not to stare at the sight of what she accurately speculated was a squad of federal agents. They paid no attention to her nondescript car as it passed then made a u-turn a short distance away. The group was evidently waiting for the arrival of Franco and the other detective. Some considerable excitement was generated by the spectacle of the cargo in the Mercury Cougar. Nina wished she had her binoculars with her at this moment, but they were in her locker at work.

"Goddamn! Must be millions of dollars. Look at it." One of the agents could not hold back his remarks.

"So, this is what it's all about, huh?" Martinet was somewhat more reserved but equally amazed.

"We had nothing to cover it with." Jeff was almost apologetic. "At least we got here without anyone noticing."

"Lucky it's a Saturday morning." Martinet was now examining the bills and noticed there were no small denominations. The only cash this cartel cared about was twenties, fifties and hundreds. He nodded in approval.

The senior federal agent announced to the gathering that everything was on schedule. There were fine details to cover, but he had every confidence in the capabilities of the assembly before him.

Jeff looked around and saw that not one person from his Police Department was present; not even George Franklin. "Shouldn't we have somebody from LAPD?"

Martinet gave Jeff a lop-sided grin. "Oh, boy. Detective Shackleford, you are so naïve. **We** are the law. Your pathetic department only plays their little games with stuff they show on TV. Don't worry about it, my friend."

Under any other circumstances Jeff would detest this slick agent calling him 'my friend.' However, with the tight spot he and Franco were in, it felt comforting to be on the same side. "What about Franklin?"

"I gave him the rare opportunity to see real cops in action, but he declined. I can't say I blame him. He probably feels he overstepped his authority tonight."

Nina looked on with amazement. Was this a conspiracy of sorts? If the Feds wanted Franco, how come they were so friendly? After five minutes she saw each of the agents go to the trunk of their respective cars. Each one removed their stereotypical, dark suit jacket and replaced it with a bulletproof vest. Additional guns were strapped on, around waists and using shoulder holsters.

There was to be a serious operation going down soon. The part that worried Nina most was that Franco and his friend were not dressing in protective gear. In fact, it did not appear that they had any weapons either.

CHAPTER THIRTY-FIVE

Just a few blocks away there was a new Ford Crown Victoria sitting in a most unfriendly neighborhood. Commander Montgomery was early and impatiently awaiting the arrival of his henchman, Sanchez. Although he did arrive right on time, there was a harsh reprimand for Federico Sanchez. He was severely hung over from his reveling with others who also should have known better. His brain forced many of Montgomery's words to evaporate and thus have a lessened effect.

"Get me inside the building before those two cops get there." The order was barked out abrasively, without due respect for the years of service from the beleaguered Sanchez. The unappreciated lackey was losing both reverence and commitment for the commander's cause.

It was a multi-story apartment building situated at 729 South Union Street. Montgomery and Sanchez hustled up the stairs to the third floor room where Jessica, Teresa and the boys had been held since early Thursday morning. There was a disgusting odor that came from the unwashed goons who guarded the hostages. Even the police families were now a little ripe as a result of the unsanitary conditions.

In spite of the early hour, everyone was wide awake. An air of anticipation clung to the stench that permeated the tiny accommodation.

"Let me see, you must be Shackleford's wife and you are Mrs. Perez, I presume." The commander correctly picked out each wife and smiled broadly as he bowed to the twins. Both Anthony and Daniel cowered from his unwanted attention.

"So you are the spineless leader they refer to." Teresa sneered at him as she spoke. "You don't look like you fit in with this gang."

"No. I suppose I don't, but somebody has to lead these ragged souls. It might as well be me." He then turned to Sanchez and set the wheels in motion. "I'll take care of these boys and girls as soon as you finish off the foolish detectives. Take those pathetic wretches to help. Together with your other two men, five should be enough." He referred to the hostage guardians and the other two crooks staying in the next room with Sanchez.

"Three of you should get in the van from Arizona and two in your own car. I see they are parked apart from each other. That should give you good angles to take out the cops." He was looking down from the third floor window to the parking lot immediately north of the building. On the far side of the lot was the swap meet. Franco and Jeff could never have guessed their loved ones were so close to the meet location.

As soon as the others left Montgomery alone with his hostages he removed a nine-millimeter handgun from his shoulder holster. After checking the safety was off and a round was in the chamber, he replaced it carefully and snapped it in place. His position at the window was between Teresa and Anthony. All of them were cuffed to the pipe that ran the length of the room, past the window. The women were one side and the boys on the other.

Teresa spoke in Spanish. "This pig does not deserve to be a public servant." She waited for his response.

To make doubly certain that he understood no Spanish she made another comment. "He is a filthy pig and his mother is a bitch too."

The words startled her sons but she had to find out if the commander knew what she was saying. His only response this time was to tell her to be quiet. This was done in a passing manner and he obviously knew none of her second language.

"He has ordered his men to kill your father. If this happens, he must die too." She was deadly serious and both boys nodded agreement, though they had no idea how this could be accomplished.

"Third times a charm, bitch." He had heard enough of her rambling on in Spanish. Montgomery found the tape that had been used earlier to keep all four quiet, and applied a generous amount to Teresa's mouth. His attention was next drawn to the activities in the lot below. Two crooks climbed into the Nissan Sentra. Sanchez and the other two men entered the Ford Econoline that had made the arduous trip from Tucson.

It was now precisely 6:00 am, Saturday, September 7th, 2002.

"Here they come. Suckers!" Montgomery leaned closer to the window to gain the most advantageous view of the proceedings. "Yes. Come on into the lot my boys. I guess I'll need two replacements in Narcotics after today." He laughed wildly and compulsively.

Automatic gunfire shattered the relatively peaceful Saturday morning. Teresa flinched with every crack of the rounds being discharged. They seemed to go on for an eternity, and Jessica screamed out painfully. She cried unashamedly with a convulsive shaking of her body.

Anthony looked into his mother's eyes with dismay over the dreadful loss. Tears instantly welled up and made it difficult to see clearly. What he did see, however, was his mother gesturing with her right leg raised up. The message was distinct and he in turn lifted his left leg.

Following the slightest nod from Teresa, they both swung a leg in a wide arc. They put all they had into this final defiant act and connected with Montgomery in the small of his back. Such is the strength of two people with severe limitations under dire circumstances; Montgomery was flung violently through the windowpane, his legs flipping up behind him. There was no chance for him to recover from the surprise attack. His body left the room for the parking lot three floors below.

Seconds later there was a silence, broken only by Jessica's crying. Then came voices from the lot below. Many voices were shouting over one another, making the words indistinguishable. A baby in a nearby apartment began to cry also. Anthony and Daniel added their sobbing to that of Jeff Shackleford's beloved wife. Teresa fought hers back with a misguided feeling that she should continue to be strong for the boys. By now, even the telltale smell from the barrage of gunfire was filtering up and through the broken window.

CHAPTER THIRTY-SIX

Nina continued her surveillance as the agents drove from the hospital lot in single file. They left the two detectives standing next to their vehicle. Jeff held his right hand out and Franco grasped it firmly.

"I feel like we're brothers." Jeff felt disconsolate, as if there had been too little time for them to be this close.

"More than that. Whatever it takes to be closer than real brothers, we've experienced it." Franco covered their handshake with his left hand. "We sure had a hell of a time while it lasted."

"I'll second that."

They climbed into the car and Jeff drove south on Loma Drive, following the same route as the federal agents. Nina wanted to know more and suspected she might never understand what was happening. She drove her Ford until she was directly behind the Cougar, which was waiting for the red signal before turning right onto Sixth Street.

There was plenty of light now; it was barely a minute before six o'clock. What were they doing with a huge package of money? It looked like more cash than she would ever see in her lifetime. It could not be some payoff from the feds because Franco had arrived there with it. She assumed, based upon her observations, that Franco and the other detective were being used as some kind of bait. Whatever it involved must be dangerous, otherwise the agents would not need their bulletproof vests.

They were westbound on Sixth now and setting up for a south onto Union. Nina wanted to warn them; of what, she was not sure. She only knew she must stop this madness. The light was green at Wilshire Boulevard as Jeff continued south. Nina got caught on a red and a moderate build up of cross traffic prevented her from running the light. She pressed her hand on the horn. She must stop them somehow. The cycle of the signal was interminably slow. Women's intuition told her that the threat lay close by.

Jeff looked in his rearview mirror at the sound of the horn. He saw an older model Thunderbird stopped at the last light and wondered what he had done to anger the driver. The distance between the cars was too great for him to ever recognize the driver. He also made the light at Seventh Street and now had the swap meet building on his right. There were no feds in sight but he knew they must be very close. He hoped they were close enough.

An extremely slow speed seemed prudent as he made his turn into the parking lot. It was walled in on the north by the swap meet and on the south by an apartment building. There was no access to the alley at the rear, just another high wall. The driveway he used was one of two, and a length of eight-foot high chain link fence stretched between them. About a dozen cars were scattered about the lot and none of these were government owned vehicles. After they were well into the lot and headed to the far end of it, Franco pointed out what he believed was the Econoline van they bought in Arizona. It was parked close to the fence.

"If you're right, then they may already be here." Jeff was looking in all directions for signs of danger. He had slowed almost to a stop.

Nina Kaplan was frantic. She burned rubber when the light changed and she raced to get through Seventh. The Cougar was a block ahead and turning into what might be an alley or a parking lot. The final traffic signal was against her when she sped through, causing several early Saturday commuters to brake sharply.

When she skidded into the lot, there were three men leaping from the rear of a van. Each of them carried an automatic rifle and none looked like law enforcement officers. They stood in a line and carefully took aim towards the rear of the lot. Her mind registered the sight as resembling a firing squad. When she saw the target of their intentions, she realized that was exactly what these three men represented.

Her Ford skidded to a halt as the weapons all burst into life. With the window down it was a deafening sound. She braked hard to avoid coming into the line of fire. The man closest to her stopped shooting and held his rifle up with the right hand. His left waved vigorously for her to back away. His last word was "*Vamanos*." Nina leveled her nine-millimeter at him and expended three rounds, each striking the chest area. When he fell backwards it was with such force that his head split open on the hard surface of the lot.

The fourth and fifth crooks had joined in the shooting spree after climbing from the Nissan. They were parked near the second driveway, putting them just south of the van.

Jeff and Franco ducked down towards each other across the front seat the moment the first rounds were heard. Bullets tore into the back light fixture, and into the bale of money. Shreds of US currency flew in all directions. Both rear tires were destroyed.

Half a dozen federal agents were screaming up to the two entrances, but more than a hundred rounds were discharged before any of them could get their car doors open.

An event took place that would, under other circumstances, stop any person from continuing their everyday business. Perhaps without any sound, the flailing form of a man fell from a broken third floor window. His crumpled form lay still for a moment after it hit the ground. Then miraculously there was movement from the distorted body of Commander Montgomery. He had sustained many broken bones but they were not serious enough to prevent him from standing, then leaning back against the wall of the apartment building.

Sanchez stood in the middle of the three that alighted from the van. In retaliation for the killing of his *compadre*, he turned his weapon towards the Thunderbird. He sprayed it with rounds but just one projectile struck Nina. There was no pain; the round entered her brain through the temple. As her trim yet lifeless frame fell forward onto the steering wheel, her foot slipped from the brake pedal. This led to the Ford running freely towards the south side of the lot, across the still continuous bombardment of bullets.

The situation was having the opposite effect on the Cougar. With both rear wheels having little rubber left on them, the car dragged slowly to a halt. Jeff could care less about the speed or direction of his vehicle, as shards of glass from the rear window flew on top of his head. However, there was every indication that the three-foot cube of cash was bearing the brunt of the fusillade.

Several agents were engaging the enemy who were caught off guard by the rear assault. In fact, Sanchez and his nearby partner were so engrossed with filling the Cougar with lead, they knew nothing of the weapons pointing in their direction. Nina's Thunderbird was raked once again as it passed in front of them. Picking up a little speed it headed directly at the already broken body of the cartel's head man in Los Angeles. With only a second to put his arms out in front of him, Commander Neaville Montgomery was crushed against the wall. Many vital organs were torn apart, but he took several agonizing minutes to die.

As if a movie director had said 'cut,' the shooting stopped altogether. A dozen men walked carefully forward into the lot and checked the bodies for movement. One federal agent had a steady stream of blood down his neck from beneath the jawbone. A fragment of glass hit him when his windshield was shattered. Not another government man was injured.

High above the devastation there was an eerie sound of a woman sobbing. A baby joined in with its own persistent crying. Smoke filled the whole parking lot from the powder that had been ignited over the last minute and a half. There would be no suspects to question. Not a single man from the cartel was left alive.

While others closely inspected the gory remains of Sanchez and company, Martinet walked slowly towards the Cougar. He genuinely dreaded the sight he was anticipating, so he called out to them. "Shackleford, Perez. You okay?"

"Up here. We're okay." It was a high-pitched scream from a woman. The sound came from high above him.

Jeff and Franco heard it too, since there was not a single window left in the car. Now that they heard Martinet's voice, it was as good as an 'all clear.' The delightful sound of Jessica coming from close by was music to their ears. Ears that had been almost deafened from the barrage of shots.

"That was Jessica, Franco. Let's go find them." They scrambled out of the Cougar as carefully as possible, to avoid serious cuts from the broken glass.

"My God, I can't believe it." Martinet's relief was far from hidden. "Looks like the cash saved your butts."

They saw that the money was riddled with bullet holes. Pieces of bills were scattered around the back of the car mike confetti. The cause of their downfall had indeed saved their lives.

"Did you hear where Jessica's voice was coming from?" Jeff was more concerned with the whereabouts of his wife.

"Up there, as far as I can tell." Martinet pointed at the smashed window.

Franco and Jeff started to head to the front of the apartment building, but the federal agent caught one arm of each detective. "Wait a second. It might still be dangerous if they are being guarded." He then raised his voice for the benefit of Jessica. "Mrs. Shackleford, are you alone up there?"

Her voice was clearer and more excited. "Just Teresa and her sons. Is Jeff alright?"

Jeff answered the burning question that both women and boys wanted answered. "Honey, I'm fine, and so is Franco."

While these exchanges were going on, Jeff noticed Montgomery pressed against the wall by a Thunderbird. He was obviously dead, and Jeff had no regrets about his elation over this matter. There was a woman in the Ford that he could not see well, but the car looked strangely familiar.

"That's the car that honked at me, Franco. Looks like some innocent passer-by got killed."

Franco diverted his attention momentarily and was horrified to see a car that he knew to be Nina Kaplan's. "Oh, no! How could this have happened?"

When all three approached the driver's door, it was too much for Franco to look at. Jeff confirmed it was Nina from his lengthy interview of her the night of the Manhattan Place shooting.

"Nina Kaplan. That's your only witness, Perez. I remember reading the statements. Doesn't look good for you now." Martinet almost sounded sorry for Franco.

"I don't care any more. I know I shot that kid in self-defense. If the DA proves differently, so be it." Franco looked up at the third floor. "I'm going to hold my wife and kids for a long time."

As Jeff and Franco went inside, there came the distant sounds of sirens wailing. Martinet turned to his men to give directions. Two agents were dispatched to the apartment, primarily to preserve any evidence of the kidnapping that might be found inside. To the remaining men he proclaimed: "Let's make sure we protect the whole crime scene, boys. The locals are on their way."

CHAPTER THIRTY-SEVEN

The reunion was emotional and no recriminations were even considered at this moment. Teresa and her boys loved Franco dearly and would forgive him anything. Jessica Shackleford cursed her husband more from the release of passion that stemmed from her adoration of him.

They would never fully understand how Nina Kaplan ended up in the middle of the shoot out. Forensic evidence would show that she was responsible for the death of one of the crooks, in addition to the crushing blow laid upon the commander. Her presence would remain a mystery in spite of a thorough investigation.

Homicide detectives were frustrated with their work at the parking lot because of the arrogance of the federal agents. In fairness, the FBI had a greater insight into the occurrence because of their prior knowledge and personal involvement. There was, of course, the tragedy of the commander's culpability in the affair. This proved very embarrassing for the department and resulted in the suggestion from the Chief himself that the DA consider dismissing the state charges against Perez.

Surprisingly, Martinet appeared in court for Franco's preliminary hearing and added his weight to the same argument. He believed that Franco Perez had been railroaded by his late boss, and deep down he began to see the possibility that there was a case for self-defense. Franco's whole family was in court three weeks later when the case was dismissed 'in the furtherance of justice.'

Jeff Shackleford was also there and took his turn in hugging Franco after each family member had done so. "Here. You owe me half of these bills." Jeff handed some documents to Franco who sat down in the hallway to inspect them closely. Both of them had already quit their jobs as per the deal with Martinet, and the financial future looked bleak for the Perez family.

There was a small bill for a few dollars that covered a tire repair. The second was much steeper. It was three weeks rental on a van. Franco looked at Jeff suspiciously.

Jeff clarified the issue. "It's still there, Franco. I fixed the tire and even took it out for a wash. Nobody followed me. Nobody knows about it. Do you realize what I'm saying?"

Franco leaned close to Jeff's ear, whispering his response. "That we're a couple of lucky, rich sons-of-bitches."

When they hugged again, everyone thought it was due to Franco's freedom. They were right, of course, but there was more; much, much more.

"How about breakfast at Nick's tomorrow?" Jeff suggested the place where the true beginning of their conspiracy was born.

"I got nothing else to do. See you at nine." There was a gleam in Franco's eye again. It had been missing for too long.

The same waitress was still serving, and still working hard at that hour of the morning. Jeff Shackleford ordered a hearty breakfast and Franco told her to bring the same for him.

"If it's good enough for my partner, it's good enough for me." Franco and Jeff high-fived each other and for the first time in a month, Franco did not flinch. His hand was virtually healed, as were his bruised ribs. "I feel like a new man."

"Don't let Teresa hear you say that." Jeff teased him.

They both laughed heartily and later ate with appetites they lost almost a month earlier.

"How we going to do this?" Franco was sure Jeff had a scheme plotted out.

Two more weeks passed before the great day of shuffling vehicles around. They first drove their cars to the location where they rented the van and left Franco's old Buick there. The perilous trip came next: it involved driving to Central Station and picking up the money van. Jeff passed the parking lot entrance several times before he gathered enough courage to drive in. He displayed his Auto Club card as if it was his police ID. It worked but only after his blood pressure shot sky high.

Franco drove the money to a used car lot in Glendale where they bought a motor home that would comfortably accommodate six. In a secluded park they transferred the cash to the motor home and hid it in the sleeping compartment over the cab.

After the van was returned and fully paid up to date, they drove to Valencia and parked the motor home at Jeff's house. Another long journey back to Los Angeles was required to pick up Franco's car.

Both families placed their homes in the hands of capable realtors, with instructions to accept offers that would insure quick turnkey sales. Jessica closed up her salon with hopes that she might one day get back into the business.

Three more weeks later and they were ready to embark upon a journey that might be a one-way ticket. Both families had packed their valuables and a moderate amount of clothing. Franco asked Jeff if he had told Jessica of their plans.

"I had to. It took a few days for it to sink in. Then she realized it was the only way to have any future." Jeff was relieved he had his wife on board with the scheme. "How about Teresa?"

"Same. She is fed up with the way the City and the Department have treated me. We don't know what to tell the boys right now, but it'll work out, I'm sure."

"Pick you up in a couple hours or so." Jeff ended the telephone conversation.

EPILOGUE

After taking their time to get to Green Valley, they pulled the motor home off at Esperanza Boulevard and headed for the Best Western.

"Looks quite nice, honey. Is this where you guys stayed?" Jessica was interested in finding out just enough to satisfy her imagination. There would be details that would happily remain a secret.

"Yep. It's really nice but they roll up the sidewalks early." Jeff grinned at Franco as their lives were close to a new beginning.

They spent a leisurely day at the hotel, with the twins having a ball at the pool. One last dinner at the hotel restaurant was on their itinerary, and then it was southbound to the border the following day.

When they arrived in Nogales it was time for lunch and the twins jumped at the chance of eating at Burger King. Jeff nudged Franco and suggested they had some business that must be taken care of. When they were driving away from the fast food spot, Franco expressed concern for leaving his family alone.

"I know what you mean, but this should be done." Jeff dug a slip of paper out of his wallet and handed it to Franco. It had the address of Juan Maldonado's family written on one side and a crude map on the back.

"Are we going to do the **right** thing for his family?" Franco understood what was happening as they took highway 89 out of town to highway 82. After a few wrong turns, Jeff was finally able to find his way to Mercedes Street. The house was on the corner with Durango Street and looked, to all intents and purposes, like the home of a decent family.

“I’ll do it if you feel uncomfortable with it.” Jeff gave Franco an out.

“We’ve been through everything else together. Let’s do this the same way.” The bond between the two ex-detectives was as strong as ever.

Jeff knocked on the door. It was a neatly kept residence and seemed as far from the cartel operation as one could get. A short and homely woman answered the door and Franco asked if she was the wife of Juan Maldonado. Tentatively, she acknowledged that she was his widow.

Jeff told her they were from the government and that Juan had been working on a top secret matter when he was killed. There was nothing for the family to be ashamed of and she should accept a payment that Juan was due for his services. At this, Jeff handed over a large envelope that contained fifty thousand dollars in hundreds. There was an awkward moment when she stated she could not accept it, but Jeff insisted. He explained that they would face a severe reprimand if it was not properly delivered.

She relented and kissed them both on the cheek as her tears flowed freely. This caused tears to flow freely down the faces of Jeff and Franco too.

When they left the Maldonado home there was the relief that comes when a great weight is taken from the shoulders. They tried their best to dry their eyes before rejoining the women and children.

After loading up in the motor home again, they headed south across the border into Nogales, Sonora.

“Goodbye, US of A. I loved you once upon a time.” Franco had his mind set on a future in Mexico.

Jeff glanced in the rearview mirror and almost whispered his own farewell. “America, you’ve been very, very good to me.”

Less than fifteen minutes later they made the stop at the Mexican immigration office. Paperwork was routine for ‘visitors’ and they were on the road again in short order. As the motor home headed south, a Mexican border official looked long and hard at the forms. He smiled and then picked up the phone to make a call.

Printed in the United States
28053LVS00003B/1-51

9 781420 832532